The
Whisperwicks

VOLUME 1

The
Labyrinth
of
Lost
and
Found

JORDAN LEES
Illustrated by VIVIENNE TO

SIMON & SCHUSTER BOOKS FOR YOUNG READERS
New York   London   Toronto   Sydney   New Delhi

SIMON & SCHUSTER BOOKS FOR YOUNG READERS
An imprint of Simon & Schuster Children's Publishing Division
1230 Avenue of the Americas, New York, New York 10020
This book is a work of fiction. Any references to historical events,
real people, or real places are used fictitiously. Other names, characters,
places, and events are products of the author's imagination, and any resemblance
to actual events or places or persons, living or dead, is entirely coincidental.
Text © 2024 by Jordan Lees
Originally published in Great Britain in 2024 by Penguin Random House UK
Cover illustration © 2024 by Isobelle Ouzman
Cover design by Lizzy Bromley
Interior illustration © 2024 by Vivienne To
All rights reserved, including the right of reproduction in whole or in part in any form.
SIMON & SCHUSTER BOOKS FOR YOUNG READERS
and related marks are trademarks of Simon & Schuster, LLC.
Simon & Schuster: Celebrating 100 Years of Publishing in 2024
For information about special discounts for bulk purchases,
please contact Simon & Schuster Special Sales at 1-866-506-1949
or business@simonandschuster.com.
The Simon & Schuster Speakers Bureau can bring authors to your live event. For more
information or to book an event, contact the Simon & Schuster Speakers Bureau
at 1-866-248-3049 or visit our website at www.simonspeakers.com.
Also available in a Simon & Schuster Books for Young Readers hardcover edition
Interior design by Lizzy Bromley
The text for this book was set in Adobe Garamond.
The illustrations for this book were rendered digitally.
Manufactured in the United States of America
0424 OFF
First Simon & Schuster Books for Young Readers paperback edition May 2024
2 4 6 8 10 9 7 5 3 1
CIP data for this book is available from the Library of Congress.
ISBN 9781665950138 (hc)
ISBN 9781665950121 (pbk)
ISBN 9781665950145 (ebook)

For Caroline and Violet

ONE

WITH THE CRACK IN THE WALL

The dollmaker will come when a baby is born. Into a room she will take the newborn; nobody else, not even a parent, is permitted to be present. Candles will be lit, which smell sweet and wild and otherworldly. Listening at the door, one will hear the dollmaker whisper her strange, trembling words. It is said, in making the doll, that the dollmaker is fashioning the child's soul.

—*A Brief History of Wreathenwold*,
Archscholar Collum Wolfsdaughter

IT BEGAN with the crack in the wall.

Edwid Cotton found it one morning on his bedroom wall. It was around twelve inches long, a thin black smile in the pale stone. It must have happened sometime in the night, though exactly how was a mystery to Edwid.

There was something instantly sinister about this crack in the wall. Peering in, Edwid saw only darkness, as though the wall were hollow. Cold air threaded out, smelling of dust. Stranger still, he was sure he could hear the faintest whispering from within. A shivering Edwid dismissed this as a figment of his imagination.

Certain Hansel would blame him, Edwid decided to cover it up—he was already in his father's bad books and didn't want to make things worse. Parchment sketches of famous Mapmakers covered the walls, so it was straight-forward enough to move one over and hide the crack. The moment it was covered, the room felt warmer, Edwid's mood lifted, and any thought of whispering from within the wall was put down to childish fancy.

Nothing much happened that day or during the night that followed. Edwid slept serenely, dreaming of the adventures he hoped to have in the future.

When he woke the next morning, the crack in the wall had returned.

The covering sketch was torn across the middle, and through it the crack could be seen again. Whorls and curls of parchment had fallen to the floor. And Edwid heard that same whispering once more, faint and menacing, joined by a trickle of wispy laughter. He leaned in and listened.

"What did you say?" he hissed, bringing his ear to the crack. But all he heard was a tangle of whispers, a snake pit of hushed voices.

"*What?*" he whispered.

"Who are you talking to?" demanded another voice.

Edwid reeled. Elizabella, his twin sister, stood in the doorway, hands on hips and eyes narrowed. Each was mirrored in the other: the pale hair, the round face, the sharp nose spattered with freckles. They were the same height, with the same wiry build. They even moved in the same way, darting here and there like foxes up to no good.

"Nobody," said Edwid, crossing his arms.

He leaned against the wall, covering the crack. Elizabella's stare grew flintier.

Not long ago, he would have told his sister about the crack in the wall. They would have investigated it together, worked up theories, laughed and bickered and created a shared story with the mysterious crack at its center. That was how they had always been—like a child and its reflection, down to the last freckle.

Things were different now. A distance had grown between them. And Edwid was to blame.

Pain flickered across Elizabella's face. Edwid felt it too, but neither voiced it. Elizabella shrugged, then strutted off. Moments later, her bedroom door slammed.

Flooded with a familiar sadness, Edwid returned to the crack in the wall.

"Now look what you've done," he said quietly. "She already hates me."

Whispers chattered like crickets in long grass.

"One at a time," said Edwid.

Remarkably, one voice did rise above the others.

"It's your own fault," it said.

Edwid flinched, recoiling from the wall. His heart galloped. Gradually he found the courage to lean forward again.

"Who are you?" he asked.

"Nobody," said the whisper.

"Everybody is somebody," replied Edwid.

"I was somebody," said the voice. "Then I was trapped here, forced to live forever in the walls of Wreathenwold. Never sleeping, never eating. Unable to die, but unable to escape. That makes me nobody."

"You don't sound like a nobody," said Edwid.

"You're very kind."

"It must be terrible," whispered Edwid. "Is there anything I can do?"

"I knew you were a good boy, Edwid," said the voice. "That's why I like being here, in your bedroom wall. There might be a way to get me out. But I wouldn't want you to put yourself in danger for an old nobody like me. No, better to leave me here."

"I want to help," said Edwid.

"You would really do that for me?" said the whisper.

"Why not?"

"I couldn't possibly let you."

A minute or two passed in which Edwid argued with the crack in the wall, until finally it was persuaded to accept his help. A tiny sob marked the end of the debate.

"You're a good boy, Edwid Cotton," said the voice. "Do you know of Olfred Wicker?"

Edwid did. Olfred Wicker was a children's author who wrote the Jamima Cleaves books. Jamima was a twelve-year-old detective who solved magical mysteries with the help of her poppet doll, and the books were some of the most popular in Wreathenwold. Elizabella loved them. Edwid once did too—it was another thing he and Elizabella used to share that now seemed lost.

"Well, it was Olfred Wicker who put me here," said the voice.

Edwid was stunned. He asked why.

"It saddens me to tell you this," said the crack in the wall, "but Olfred Wicker is the most miserable fraud. He stole every one of his plots for the Jamima Cleaves books from somebody else. And, after he steals somebody's ideas, he throws that somebody inside the walls of Wreathenwold so they never expose him. From me, would you believe, he stole the ideas for *Jamima Cleaves and the Circus of Hidden Souls* and *Jamima Cleaves and the Killer Effigy*. Then he locked me in here so nobody would ever know."

"But that's ridiculous," said Edwid.

"I knew you wouldn't believe it," said the crack in the

wall, sounding morose. "Nobody would. That's what I said to the rogue as he bundled me into this wretched prison, but he didn't listen."

It was a wild story, but Edwid thought the voice in the wall sounded very honest. Why would it lie about a thing like this, in any case?

"How can I help?" he asked.

"Well, you'd need to go to Olfred Wicker's house."

"What am I looking for?" said Edwid.

"The key to release me," said the whisper. "I'll meet you there and together we can find it."

Unsure precisely how a crack in the wall could travel, let alone meet anybody anywhere, Edwid prepared his things. Into his satchel went a small, cracked spyglass, his battered notebook of erroneous maps, the last of his pocket money. He also packed a change of clothes; his favorite moth-eaten flat cap; and a spinning top, a Midsommer gift from Elizabella—to remind him of home; of his father, Hansel; and particularly Elizabella, his best friend.

Getting away was going to be the biggest challenge. Hansel was keeping a very close eye on Edwid. Fortunately, Hansel also had a soft spot for drinking poppysyrup in the snug, a cozy room with a log fire and threadbare armchairs, after Edwid and Elizabella were in bed. Poppysyrup, strictly for adults, was a clear liquid that smoked when poured and had scorched the twins' nostrils when they once took a sniff. By the third glass, Hansel tended to fall asleep by the fire, which would be Edwid's best chance.

The real problem was Elizabella. She was more vigilant and considerably smarter than both Hansel and Edwid. Elizabella watched Edwid from a distance, out of the corner of her eye, mistrustful and hawkish, tracking him while busying herself with other things. However careful Edwid had to be with Hansel, he'd need to be twice as wary around Elizabella.

Night came, and Edwid pretended to go to bed. Soon after, he heard Elizabella blow out her oil lamp through the adjoining wall. An hour later, Hansel ambled along the hallway and creaked Edwid's door open. Satisfied his son was asleep, Hansel likewise checked on Elizabella before shuffling back along the hall, gathering his poppysyrup and tumbler and settling in the snug.

Edwid waited patiently. The house was silent. Finally, after what felt like an age, the signal came: Hansel's first snore. Quietly Edwid dressed, grabbed his satchel, tied his doll to his hip, and snuck through the house. He made it all the way to the front door.

"Where do you think you're going?"

Edwid spun. Elizabella was standing there, hands balled and eyes glaring from the shadows.

"Go back to bed," said Edwid.

"Where are you going?" demanded Elizabella.

"There's something I need to do," said Edwid. "Go back to bed. I'll be home soon, I promise."

"I'm coming with you."

"No."

"I'm calling Hansel, then."

"We never tell on each other," said Edwid. "That's the deal."

"I made that deal with the old Edwid," said Elizabella.

Her words struck Edwid in the stomach. He turned to leave.

"Why do you hate me now?" said Elizabella, her voice as small as he'd ever heard it. "What have I done?"

"You haven't done anything," said Edwid, feeling an ache in his chest.

"Then why are you keeping secrets from me? We've never kept secrets."

"I'll tell you everything when I get back," said Edwid. "I promise." And he meant it.

"I won't let you go," said Elizabella.

She took a step forward, her hand drifting to her hip where her doll hung. A threat. Instinctively, Edwid's hand moved to his own poppet. The twins stood this way for a moment, like statues in the shadows, on the verge of a battle with their dolls that would almost certainly wake Hansel and that Edwid would most likely lose.

Keeping his eyes on Elizabella, Edwid took a step backward. And another. Then, never lifting his gaze from her, he opened the front door and backed out. Elizabella only moved at the very last moment—not to pluck her doll from her hip, but to brush something from her eye.

Olfred Wicker lived in a little cottage at the end of a lane of other squat stone cottages. Smoke twisted from their chimneys, lamps glowing warmly behind the curtains. Wraithlike flowers of white and black bloomed from the flower beds.

Olfred's cottage was different: dilapidated and lopsided. A great bonewood tree rose from the overgrown garden, its ghostly white branches sprawled across the thatch. No warm lights smoldered within, no smoke twining dreamily from the chimney. All was darkness, every window boarded up.

Nervously Edwid navigated the wilderness of Olfred's front garden and knocked on the door. No one came—nor was there the slightest sound from within. It seemed that nobody lived here. Had Edwid been tricked?

Then there was a cracking sound. A tiny fissure streaked across the stone wall of the cottage until it was a foot long, suspended in a black smile. The crack looked the same as it had on Edwid's bedroom wall.

"He's inside," whispered the familiar voice.

"Doesn't seem like it," said Edwid.

"He is," said the voice. "He wants to be left alone. Wants to make sure nobody ever finds the key to release his prisoners, who will expose him as a fraud."

Edwid didn't like how this was beginning to feel. Something tugged in his stomach, a doubt or suspicion that all was not as it seemed. Dark and cold, Olfred's cottage gave him the shivers. He should have stayed home with Elizabella. If he'd told her about the crack in the wall, she'd have made him see sense.

"We can't even get inside," he said.

At that, the crack in the wall grew, spearing across the stone in a trail of puffing dust until it reached the front door. There it spread, a spiderweb of ruptures, throwing out splinters of wood until an entire panel fell away. It was just large enough for Edwid to crawl through.

He took a deep, thoughtful breath. Behind him was home, Hansel, Elizabella; in front was this creepy cottage, uncertainty, the possibility of danger.

Another deep breath and Edwid clambered through.

Inside it was deathly quiet, the air stale. A tap dripped in the nearby kitchen. Books were crammed, stacked, and piled everywhere. On the wall were paintings of scenes from the Jamima Cleaves books, many of which Edwid recognized: Jamima chasing down the culprit at the end of *Jamima Cleaves and the Tongue Thief*, Jamima and her poppet fighting the villain in *Jamima Cleaves and the Moonlit Killer*. Had Olfred really stolen all his ideas from other people?

Edwid crept onward, and the crack in the wall joined him, snaking along the cottage wall, spouting flakes of stone and timber as it went.

"Where is the key?" Edwid whispered.

"Through there," said the crack in the wall.

It must have meant straight ahead, where weak candlelight splashed upon the length of the doorframe.

"If Olfred's in there, he'll catch us!" said Edwid.

"Who's that?" came a sudden shout from beyond the door.

Edwid froze, heart thundering in his ears.

"Stay away from me!" cried Olfred Wicker. "Leave at once!"

"He knows we're onto him," said the crack in the wall. "Go on, Edwid—the key!"

Compelled by some terrible curiosity, Edwid edged forward and pushed the door open. Beyond was a cramped study, a ceiling lined with bonewood timbers, and teetering towers of books in every direction.

In a rickety chair in the corner was a very old man, tiny and hunchbacked and filmed with candlelight. Upon seeing Edwid, his eyes stretched with terror. He scrambled backward in his chair, crouching like a frightened child. One of his liver-spotted hands flew up and clamped over his mouth.

"Who are you?" said Olfred, through his fingers.

His voice was a cobweb, his face a maze of wrinkles. Wisps of white hair were gathered round his ears—otherwise he was bald. On the desk beside him was a typewriter and a stack of paper. He trembled as though Edwid were the most terrifying thing he'd ever seen.

"I'm sorry," mumbled Edwid. "I just . . ."

"Please," said Olfred. "You have to leave, young fellow. Nobody can be here!"

The crack in the wall lashed across the ceiling like a tail of black lightning, sending down a cascade of dust and wood. Olfred saw it with horror, shrinking farther into his chair.

"No . . . ," he muttered. "No, no . . ."

"Get it," ordered the crack in the ceiling. "Now's our chance!"

"But where *is* it?" called Edwid, not seeing a key anywhere.

"Boy, don't you know what that thing is?" groaned Olfred, eyes fixed on the crack. "Don't you know what it wants . . . ?"

Edwid shook his head, mind swirling. What he would give to be back at home.

"Go to him, Edwid," said the crack in the ceiling. "He will tell you where the key is."

Terrified, Edwid approached. Olfred trembled and cowered until their eyes met. The old man's were watery and bloodshot, awash with terror. Then another expression overtook his face. Now he just looked immensely sad, resigned to defeat.

"I'm so sorry, young fellow," he croaked.

Then he leaned forward and whispered into Edwid's ear. The moment he finished, the old man leaned back, shut his eyes, and died right there in his chair.

Edwid fell backward. His ear throbbed with the horror of what Olfred had whispered to him. The crack in the ceiling *had* fooled him. And it was something very different from what it had told Edwid.

Edwid groaned, head spinning, as he looked up at the crack in the ceiling.

"What did he say, Edwid?"

The voice had grown fiercer, as sharp and deadly as a knife. A nasty splitting sound rang out as the crack shot across the ceiling and struck a lightning-shaped fissure down the length of the wall. Cold air spilled out, and Edwid stumbled backward.

"Tell me what he said, Edwid."

Just then, something silvery appeared in the crack, bewitching Edwid. It was a tiny curl, like a new moon suspended in the night sky. Edwid stared and stared, frozen in place. When it momentarily vanished, only to quickly return, he understood what he was seeing.

It was an eye.

"Tell me what he said, Edwid. And then it will all be over."

Edwid shook his head, staggering backward. Again the eye blinked.

Then came a tremendous cracking sound, and the wall ruptured, fissures striking outward like an earthquake. Dust and stone plumed, icy air flooding out. Amid the fog was a dark, terrible shape, hurtling out and descending upon Edwid in a storm of shadow and smoke.

Edwid's final thought was of Elizabella, of how sorry he was not to have told her everything. Then he ran.

TWO

WITH THE BOY IN THE BOOKSHOP

Folklore has long held of another world woven throughout our own. Between our world and this other one—according to the folklore—have traveled poets, scholars, adventurers, fugitives, and even, on occasion, unlikely heroes.

—*A Brief History of Wreathenwold,*
Archscholar Collum Wolfsdaughter

NOTHING REMARKABLE or stirring ever visited the sleepy village of Wyvern-on-the-Water. Excitement would instead visit the nearby town of Bramleigh or the cobbled, mossy village of Hatchet, which boasted a history of notorious pirates and famous sieges. As for Wyvern-on-the-Water, only its name was interesting, derived from the legend of an Arthurian dragon said to sleep beneath one of the heathery hills overlooking the river. It had never bothered to wake.

Picture a steepled church with primly tolling bells. Picture Sunday fetes with coconut shies and bake sales. Picture sailing boats, children mudlarking at low tide, an underwhelmed heron picking through the shallows. That was Wyvern-on-the-Water. It was all stout, orderly cottages and narrow lanes that speared and twisted according to no real logic. Hawthorns and cherry blossoms would paper the streets with white and pink petals in the spring. Summer would see blackberries fatten on the trails along the river. There were three tearooms, two pubs, a drugstore, a hairdresser's, a library, two bric-a-brac stores, a pottery studio, and a bookshop called Once Upon A Time.

Once Upon A Time was an unassuming establishment, a converted house hugged by two neat Georgian cottages, spidery letters spelling out its name upon a weathered green frontage. There was a striped red-and-white awning to shelter the tables out front. Arranged in the window were rare and special editions, sealed off from the busy fingers of book buyers—it was well known that dirt and grease could spoil a book quicker than a lazy plot twist.

Step inside Once Upon A Time and the door will shudder. A bell chimes. Needless to say, the original architect did not have a bookshop in mind. You find yourself instantly crowded by books in what was once a porch, surrounded by displays in what was once a sitting room, confronted by stalagmites of novels in a former dining room. Down a veiny staircase is a cellar full of yet more thousands of books.

The place was altogether labyrinthine, illogical, swimming in dust, its rafters strung with cobwebs.

The signs identifying the various sections of the bookshop had become obsolete, so that it was not uncommon to chance upon *Alice's Adventures in Wonderland* in the Cookery section or *Debrett's A–Z of Modern Manners* in Crime and Thrillers. This was irksome to the students and professors of the nearby university, whose reading was altogether more serious. Other readers found it charming. Once Upon A Time smelled how bookshops should smell—like pages and binding and ideas. Columns of light fell from the occasional windows, where dust played in dreamy patterns. Otherwise it was quite dark.

Finding the counter was far from straightforward—it was nestled at the base of the staircase behind a partition of leather-bound classics. Often you would find an eleven-year-old boy sitting there, hunched over a book. His name was Benjamiah Creek, and he had a lot in common with his surroundings. Unassuming and untidy, he might easily have been mistaken for another quaint but uninteresting detail of a quaint but uninteresting village. But nothing could have been further from the truth—like any good

bookshop, Benjamiah Creek was full of mysteries not yet known and surprises not yet sprung.

On the first morning of the summer holidays, Mrs. Foxglove went into Once Upon A Time and did indeed find Benjamiah behind the counter. He had his nose in a book of chess theory, something of which Mrs. Foxglove thoroughly disapproved. She considered chess a waste of time, along with comic books, video games, and playing the guitar. Mrs. Foxglove tended to disapprove of anything she didn't understand.

She was a wrinkled, webbed, long-necked busybody who lived in one of the riverside town houses. Benjamiah was certain she never read any of the books she bought— she only left home to inflict misery.

"You have a *customer*," said Mrs. Foxglove. "Perhaps you should put your book down, boy."

Benjamiah flinched and stood, his book sliding to the floor. Redness bloomed in his cheeks. Mrs. Foxglove regarded him with eyes like a snakebite. Standing up hadn't added much meaningful height to Benjamiah. He was short and thin for his age, and pale from rarely playing outside. He had tufts of mousy-brown hair that no brush could tame, and eyes of chestnut brown. From his mum, he had inherited an unlikely nose, jabbing out of the middle of his face and bending inexplicably to the left.

"What nonsense are you reading today?" said Mrs. Foxglove.

Benjamiah opened his mouth, but Mrs. Foxglove gave a dismissive wave of the hand.

"Shouldn't you be doing some *homework*, boy? Or tidying up this messy shop? Let me tell you, in my day . . ."

Benjamiah listened carefully while Mrs. Foxglove ranted about the virtues of her day, whenever that was. She continued until her mouth went dry.

"Where are your parents?" she snapped when she could think of nothing else to complain about.

"They're . . . away," said Benjamiah.

"Away?" said Mrs. Foxglove, licking her lips. "Oh yes. I heard all about their little—ah—*problems.*"

Benjamiah blushed deeper, hot enough to catch fire. It only delighted Mrs. Foxglove.

"Margie from the pottery studio told me they had a big row at the Tom o' Bedlam on quiz night," she continued, her slimy tongue playing over her lips. "Getting divorced, are they?"

Benjamiah's throat had closed up—unable to swallow, unable to speak.

"I never thought they'd last," said Mrs. Foxglove. She wetted her lips again. "And where's your grandmother?"

"She's upstairs. Resting."

"Well, don't just *stand* there. Help me find my book. I can't make out a thing in this mess. It's a lovely story set on an old country estate. A love story, but also a mystery novel. It begins with the ghostly sighting of a woman. I read it as a young girl. A *real* book—not like the guff they publish these days."

"What's the title?" said Benjamiah, which was a mistake.

"How should I know!"

"Sorry," he said. "What about the author?"

"Oh, a man," said Mrs. Foxglove. "Definitely a man. Isn't that enough information? Are you going to just stand there? In my day, customers were treated with . . ."

And so began another rant. It sounded to Benjamiah like *The Woman in White*, but the suggestion was immediately dismissed. Benjamiah spent the next twenty-five minutes offering books to Mrs. Foxglove, only for each to be routinely sniffed at and cast aside.

"Oh, this is ridiculous," she snapped eventually. "I'll just take this one."

It was *The Woman in White*, of course. Back at the till, Benjamiah took Mrs. Foxglove's money and handed back her book in a striped paper bag.

"Have a lovely day," he said.

"Are you trying to be clever?" said Mrs. Foxglove, before stalking out of the shop as if Benjamiah were a bad smell.

The bell chimed and Benjamiah was left in peace. He set about addressing the chaos left in Mrs. Foxglove's wake, dismantling towers of rejected books and returning them to their shelves.

Benjamiah had been feeling sick for months, and Mrs. Foxglove's comments about Mum and Dad had only made things worse. It was one thing Benjamiah having to know about their marital problems, but did the whole village have to as well? Why did Mum and Dad have to take their battle to the Tom o' Bedlam when home was already a war zone?

For months, their flat above the bookshop had been a place of slamming doors, the back and forth of bitter accusations, or otherwise soft, sorrowful voices through thin walls, late at night, when his parents thought Benjamiah was sleeping. Life had become a patchwork of resentful silences and explosive arguments, every day ornamented with sighs and puffy eyes, croaky voices and muted sobs. Benjamiah was sick to his back teeth of Mum's forced cheer, of his dad—before always smiling, always laughing—now glum and stony-faced.

Now they had gone to a cottage in the Purbecks in one final attempt to save their marriage. Like Mrs. Foxglove, Benjamiah suspected their differences were the problem. Mum was a professor of astrophysics at the local university, while Dad ran the bookshop. Jim Woodyard came from a family of fanatical readers, mediocre writers, zealous collectors and curators of books and stories, while Zoe Creek favored interstellar and extrasolar mysteries, preferring facts and proof over Dad's fanciful worlds of dragons and warriors and warlocks.

Benjamiah had only two allies while he awaited the outcome of his parents' trip—Grandma and his books. Grandma was the bedrock, secure and immovable: kind, patient, formidably loving. She was his dad's mum and the only extended family Benjamiah had.

Books were Benjamiah's siblings, cousins, and friends. Only *real* books, though, about *real* things. Benjamiah took firmly after his mum in this regard. For Benjamiah, books were for the accumulation of knowledge. He wanted facts, truths, practical information. Right now, he was reading his book about the Sicilian Defense. Before that, he'd read a tome on Henry VII, and next he had a very exciting book about bridge engineering.

That was meaningful reading for Benjamiah—quests to melt rings in distant mountains or slay dragons were a waste of time as far as he was concerned. Benjamiah could tell you the atomic weight of phosphorus or list lots of Jupiter's moons; he had no interest in green eggs served with ham or the adventures of the Famous Five.

Benjamiah's books proved Mum and Dad had no excuse. Everything has an answer, every problem a solution.

History celebrated those who never gave up, from Darwin to Marie Curie, from Newton to Dorothy Hodgkin. Did the idea of absolute space and time get in Einstein's way? No, he threw them out. Did bad weather stop Drake's campaign against the Spanish in 1577? Of course not. He waited it out, fixed up the galleons and set off again for the Americas.

Every problem could be solved if people tried hard enough. His parents would do well to remember that.

He was still tidying up when the bell chimed again.

"Just coming!" he called out, but there was no reply. Only silence.

"Hello?" said Benjamiah.

He peeked round the corner of a bookshelf, but saw nobody, so he threaded his way from room to room. Every section was empty, as was the cellar. Had he imagined the chiming of the bell? Or had a summer breeze pushed the door far enough to set it off? Then he heard a book fall to the ground somewhere in the shop. His heart climbed up his throat.

"Is somebody there?" he said, in a thin voice.

Nothing. Perhaps Mrs. Foxglove had crept back in to frighten him. It seemed the kind of twisted thing she'd do. Not for the first time, he wished the lighting were a little brighter. Still, with his parents away and Grandma resting, Benjamiah had to take charge of the situation. Trembling with the force of his own heartbeat, he inspected every section again, expecting at any moment some terrible rogue to lunge out and ambush him. He found the book that had fallen—a thick copy of the Bible that had wriggled right off the Sci-Fi and Fantasy shelf. Hands shaking, he put it back.

The bell chimed again, and Benjamiah jumped out of his skin.

"Grandma?" he called.

Yet again, there was no reply. Silence hung heavy in every direction. He crept back to the door, looked out on to the street, then returned to the till, feeling thoroughly spooked.

There he found a parcel on the counter, addressed to him. It must have been the postwoman all along. Why was she sneaking around like that? He'd always thought she was an oddball. But fear was giving way to reluctant excitement. Nobody ever sent him anything. It could only have been from his parents, though it would take more than a gift to bring him onside. He wanted his family to remain whole. *That* was the present he most wanted.

It was an oddly shaped parcel, clumsily wrapped and lighter than he'd hoped. Strangely, Benjamiah could find neither an address nor a stamp on the shabby packaging. Surely Mum and Dad could wrap a gift better than this?

"What have you got there?" said a voice.

For the third time in quick succession, Benjamiah

flinched. But it was only Grandma this time, shuffling down the stairs. She was short and squat with curly gray hair and magnificent tortoiseshell glasses, lending her hazel eyes a bulbous and wobbly quality. Forever cold, she was a matryoshka doll of cardigans—one each in mauve, blue, and mustard today.

"A package," said Benjamiah, showing her. "For me."

"Ah, must be from Mum and Dad," said Grandma, frowning. "Well, let's see it."

Benjamiah tore through the thick brown paper. The candle of excitement was snuffed out the instant he saw what was inside. It was a floppy doll of red leatherlike fabric, with a tuft of black string for hair and two big white buttons for eyes. It had no other facial features, no hands, no feet—just little leathery arms and legs ending in nubs. He held it up and watched its head loll miserably to one side.

"How odd," said Grandma.

"A *doll*," said Benjamiah. "Why would they send me a *doll*?"

"It isn't just a doll," said Grandma. "It looks like a poppet. A doll used for witchcraft. Is there a note with it?"

Benjamiah explored the torn packaging, but found nothing. Witchcraft? This had Dad's fingerprints all over it. It was just the kind of thing he'd find interesting.

"Well, I think it's fascinating," said Grandma.

"You have it, then," said Benjamiah, his fury spilling over.

He slapped the poppet down on the counter and stormed past Grandma, up the stairs, and into his room. To drive home his point, he slammed the door.

THREE

WITH BENJAMIAH'S SULK

Much as I have tried, I have never found proof of this other world. If such a place exists, only a chosen few have ever traveled between the two. For the people of Wreathenwold, our entire world is this labyrinth, sprawling forever—where straying too far from home can mean never finding it again.
—*A Brief History of Wreathenwold*,
Archscholar Collum Wolfsdaughter

A *DOLL*. A doll! He would expect it of Dad, but why had Mum allowed it? She knew him better than that. They could have sent him a book, a puzzle, a model ship or airplane—none of which would have made him forget about their collapsing marriage, but at least he wouldn't feel insulted. Needless to say, Benjamiah had no appreciation for creepy, unsmiling dolls that had something to do with magic—which he knew very well didn't exist. Magic was what people in the past called physical phenomena they didn't understand. He threw himself down on his bed, stewing and sulking with his arms crossed.

His room was testament to the character his parents had offended, evidence of the enlightened world that had left magic behind. Benjamiah had certainly inherited his mother's fascination with science. Star charts were plastered on the walls, and by the window was a secondhand telescope. Grandad's old globe, a crack across South America, dominated the bedside table. On his desk were the odds and ends of various projects—an orrery he hoped to repair, bought from the bric-a-brac shop nearby, a half-built model pirate ship surrounded by blobs of glue and tangles of excess rigging. Imposing books were crammed and stacked on every shelf, on his bedside cabinet, piled up in his wardrobe. Books on biology, history, mathematical problems. The room was L-shaped with a sloping ceiling and a narrow bed with dark blue bedding, scattered with stars.

There was a knock on the door. To further express his dissatisfaction, he punched air out of his nose like a snorting bull—something he'd learned from Mum.

Grandma opened the door and poked her head round it.

"There's no need for that," she said, eyes narrowing.

In she sidled. She'd brought the doll with her. Benjamiah snorted again, then rolled onto his side, showing Grandma his back. The mattress sank as she perched on the bed.

"Ben," said Grandma. "Look at me."

"No."

Grandma sighed. She patted him on the arm.

"I've never known you to be ungrateful," she said.

"I don't want a doll," said Benjamiah.

Grandma, after a careful pause, said, "What do you want?"

Benjamiah was silent, stubborn.

"It's okay to talk," she said.

Silence.

"Talking isn't a weakness," continued Grandma.

Silence.

"And nor is being scared," she added.

A tiny fidget was Benjamiah's only response. Grandma put a hand on his arm.

"Would you like to talk?"

"No."

"Well, you know where I am if you change your mind," she said. "I'm worried about you, Ben."

"Worry about *them*."

"I'm worried about Mum and Dad, too, but they're grown-ups."

"Tell them to act like it," replied Benjamiah.

Without siblings, Benjamiah's world was a small and fragile arrangement, like the orrery on his desk. His life was Mum, Dad, Grandma, his books, his models, the bookshop.

Now it was threatening to collapse, and—unlike the orrery—it was beyond his power to repair. It was up to Mum and Dad. Why couldn't they try harder?

Maybe some friends might have provided a distraction, but Benjamiah had none. He used to spot birds and bugs with Samuel Peters on the woodland trails until Samuel discovered he was good at football—at which point, he was absorbed into a more popular group, and Benjamiah was cast aside.

At Mum's insistence, Benjamiah had invited Hassaan from school round for something that she had appallingly christened "a playdate." At first, there was hope because Hassaan liked to read as much as Benjamiah. But Hassaan wanted to play Huckleberry Finn or Prince Caspian, whereas Benjamiah was keen they played something with a little more substance—like acting out the discovery of penicillin or the Yalta Conference.

Benjamiah didn't understand most of the kids at school. When teachers asked questions, his hand would rocket upward. He was always excited to give the right answer, but it seemed to irk the other children, which Benjamiah could never comprehend. Wasn't that what school was all about? Questions being answered, problems being solved.

Lucy Thompson hadn't liked it when Benjamiah loudly talked her through the different kinds of triangle after she'd become muddled in math. Pointing out to a group of classmates all the procedural errors of their "cops and robbers" game last year had left them staring at Benjamiah like *he* was the weird one. Benjamiah found it all very confusing. Didn't people want to get things right?

"We all love you tremendously, Ben," said Grandma. "Hold on to that, if nothing else."

In reply, he snorted again.

"I bet there's more to this doll than you think," she said. "Let's call Mum and Dad tomorrow and ask them. I bet it's something fascinating."

"I'm not speaking to them."

"Are you sure? It might just make things worse. It always helps to talk, even when we're afraid of what we might say. Or hear."

"I don't care about any of that," said Benjamiah, underlining his point with another emphatic snort.

Grandma went quiet. She leaned over and set the poppet down on Benjamiah's desk, propped up against a pile of books on the anatomy of mammals and reptiles. Its head flopped onto its shoulders and its button eyes stared. Benjamiah glanced at it and shivered.

"I thought about making something special for dinner," said Grandma. "Your favorite, if you're interested."

Of course he was interested in toad-in-the-hole, but he couldn't very well admit it without giving up on his sulk.

"Whatever you like," he grunted.

"I'll take that as a yes . . . ," said Grandma. "Now, are you going to mind the shop, or stay here and sulk? I'll need to pop to the shops."

"Fine," he said, giving in. "But I'm still cross with Mum and Dad."

"Of course."

"And I'm going to stay cross at them."

"Absolutely."

"And I won't ever forgive them if they don't fix it."

"Well, you feel that way now, but . . ."

"I'll feel this way tomorrow and the day after, and every day until I'm dead."

Grandma's only reply was to give him another pat on the arm. The mattress squeaked in relief as she pulled herself up, groaning beneath her breath—her knee was giving her trouble again. She shuffled out, leaving the door ajar.

Benjamiah stared at the poppet and the poppet stared back. Finally he crept back down to the bookshop, fished out his book on chess theory, and minded the place while Grandma went shopping.

FOUR
WITH THE BIRD IN THE NIGHT

There is no greater gift than a poppet. Our dolls represent
the best of us: imagination, knowledge, friendship. They are
our companions and protectors. None of our kind are without a doll; if they perish, so do we. As they are our weapons
and defenders, so they are our greatest vulnerability.
—*A Brief History of Wreathenwold,*
Archscholar Collum Wolfsdaughter

SOMETHING STRANGE happened in the night.

Benjamiah had gone to bed feeling a little better
about life. Grandma's toad-in-the-hole was the best
ever, and there was a surprise to follow—apple crumble
with custard. Feeling guilty about taking out his frustra-
tions on her earlier, Benjamiah washed up and cleaned
the kitchen afterward. Then they'd read books on the
sofa until Benjamiah nodded off, head lolling onto

Grandma's shoulder, before she sent him to bed.

Some might say an eleven-year-old should have no need of a night-light, but it wasn't really any of their business. Benjamiah had never slept without one. Plugged into the socket, it sprayed glorious stars up the wall and across the ceiling—Benjamiah fell asleep as though he were a rock drifting through the great silent cosmos.

The strange thing happened deep in the night—that soft, shadowy, quiet span where everything seems half-real and half-dreamed. A bizarre noise hauled Benjamiah suddenly from his sleep.

It was the sound of a bird in his bedroom, intense and vivid—a quick thrum of wings, a chirp, then a scratching sound as though it had perched on the curtain rail above his bed. Silence followed.

Benjamiah lay perfectly still, his duvet over his face, heart throbbing. Logic said the bird must have belonged to his dreams. He liked logic. Logic was reliable. Logic was an anchor, holding you in place amid the treacherous waters of life. He supposed a bird *could* have found a way into his room, perhaps hopping through the open window earlier that day.

Seconds crawled by, and Benjamiah heard nothing more. No wings flapped, nor did the phantom bird give another chirrup. Finally he mustered the confidence to peek out from beneath his duvet. No sign of a bird. All was entirely still, everything as it should be.

The last thing he saw before sinking back to sleep was the poppet on the desk, watching with its white button eyes. Sitting there like butter wouldn't melt in the mouth it didn't have.

By the morning, Benjamiah was convinced the bird had been a dream. It had been creepy nonetheless, the memory bringing a prickle to his neck hairs. He ate toast and drank orange juice while Grandma busied herself with bills and a calculator, sighing, squinting through her tremendous glasses.

"I was thinking of calling Mum and Dad this afternoon," she said, not looking up. "We could ask them about the doll. . . ."

"You do that."

"You're welcome to join," said Grandma.

"No, thanks."

"Have it your way. . . ."

Benjamiah had a busy morning in the shop. A steady trickle of customers came, none as mean and difficult as Mrs. Foxglove, but each challenging in their own way. There was the studious young man with the bowl haircut and tiny mouth, who wanted a very specific book about butterflies. There was the old man who couldn't remember the books he'd read and the books he hadn't. There were the twin girls who knocked over a display of Agatha Christie books while playing tag. Grandma helped when she could, but for the most part Benjamiah was alone, selling books and tidying up and dispensing advice.

By lunchtime, he was famished. Grandma had left a sandwich in the fridge, and he shoveled it down, then sloped off to his bedroom. He thought he'd do a little work on his model pirate ship while Grandma minded the shop. When he saw his room, he gasped.

It had been trashed. Pages had been ripped from books and scattered all over the floor. His pirate ship was a shipwreck on the desk. Paper clips, staples, and pencils littered the carpet, while one of the star charts had been ripped from the wall. His underwear had been pulled out of the drawer and thrown all over the place. A pair of blue pants hung from the lampshade on the ceiling.

In fact, only one thing remained where it was. The poppet sat precisely where Grandma had left it yesterday, reclined against the pile of books. Did it look smug? No, dolls couldn't look smug. What was he thinking?

Grandma appeared behind him.

"Goodness me, Ben! What on earth have you been up to?"

"I didn't do this!" he protested.

"Who was it, then? A ghost?"

"Obviously not, but . . ."

"I know you're upset," said Grandma, "but really this is no way to behave. This is your own room, and these are your own things. You're only punishing yourself. And you're the one who's going to tidy it all up."

"It wasn't me!"

"I'm disappointed, Ben," said Grandma before shuffling off.

This was outrageous. Not only had his room been ransacked, he was being blamed for it! It was a miserable injustice. How had this happened? The wind, perhaps? The bird from last night, hiding somewhere, popping out unseen to terrorize him? Benjamiah spent the rest of his lunch break tidying up his room, saving what could be saved, moodily throwing out what was beyond repair.

He returned to the bookshop exhausted. Thankfully, the afternoon was quieter. Rain swarmed upon the door and the windows. Wyvern-on-the-Water had a certain charm when the sun shone and the boats swanned along the river. On gloomier days, it felt like the drabbest place on earth. Benjamiah spent most of the afternoon with his nose in his chess book, committing variations to memory for when he someday had a friend to play against.

Concentrating proved difficult. Chess required careful thought and calculation. Instead, his mind, like an aimless fly, flitted back to the mess in his room, to the bird in the night, to the stupid doll his parents had sent him. To what it would be like if they no longer loved each other, lived together, walked along the estuary holding hands while he ticked off birds and insects on his checklists. A real family, together, indestructible . . .

At closing time, he flipped the sign on the door, and swept up and turned off all the lights, then traipsed upstairs. From the kitchen, he heard Grandma talking.

". . . feeling a bit lonely," he heard her say.

Careful to avoid the creakiest floorboards, he crept across the hall and hovered by the gap in the door.

"Tell him . . . miss him . . . make it . . . to him—" came Mum's voice.

It was a video call and the connection was shaky, lending their voices a fractured quality. Some words were cut out completely.

"Can . . . speak to . . . ," said Dad.

"He's still upset," said Grandma. "God knows, I've tried. He'll come round. Give him some time. He had a bit of a tantrum earlier, actually. Made a big mess in his room."

"That's not like—" said Mum.

"We'll . . . home soon," said Dad.

"Well, nice try with the gift, anyway," said Grandma. "I'm sure he'll like it if we give him a bit of time. Where did you get it?"

"Gift?" said Mum.

"The doll," said Grandma.

There was a crackling sound. Grandma tutted. Dad was trying to say something, but the words came through garbled and tangled.

"Say that again," said Grandma.

"Didn't . . . doll . . . ," said his mum.

Then the connection died. Grandma sighed and muttered something about "good old telephones," while Benjamiah crept off to his room.

He was relieved to find it as he'd left it. Grandma was wrong—he wouldn't come round soon. Adults always made children out to be unreasonable, he thought. Though Grandma was right about one thing. He *was* lonely. Had Mum and Dad thought the doll would be some kind of company? If so, he hated it even more. The idea was humiliating.

He picked it up, the hairs on his neck prickling suddenly. There was a heaviness to the poppet that defied its delicate material. It had a skin of thin cloth and was lightly stuffed, yet there was a dim, intangible weight that Benjamiah found unsettling. Like the emptiness itself was in some way substantial. The hairs on his arms, just like his neck, shivered and became barbed, all of him suddenly quilled like a porcupine. He set the doll down, shuddering.

He read until dinner, which proved a quiet and tense meal. Grandma tried to draw Benjamiah into conversation, but he felt deflated, adrift from his family. He stabbed at his pasta and chased it round his plate, grunting in reply to Grandma's questions. Eventually she gave up, and he was excused.

After a bath, he did what he could to salvage the model pirate ship. It was hopeless—the mast broken, the rigging an impossible knot, all of which meant he went to bed in a pretty foul mood.

FIVE

WITH THE MONKEY IN THE NIGHT

Dollcasting allows the casting of poppets into the form of animals, if the spells are learned correctly. Scholars of long ago write of greater, stranger magic possible with our dolls. If these spells ever existed, they are lost to us now.

—*A Brief History of Wreathenwold*,
Archscholar Collum Wolfsdaughter

BENJAMIAH WASN'T WOKEN by a bird that night. He was woken by a monkey.

He recalled the high-pitched, squeaky chatter from the zoo. This felt too clear and vivid to be a dream. Tonight the sound continued after he woke, his eyes open and his mind lucid. Heart thumping, he slid the duvet from his face and looked up.

Hanging from the lampshade was a capuchin, draped in the revolving stars of the night-light. His fur was a deep black, tinged with reddish stripes. A long black tail extended out, the tip burnished with red. Most terrible and disturbing were his completely impossible eyes—big, empty white buttons. Just like the poppet. *The poppet*...

The poppet had become a monkey.

The capuchin rocked playfully on the lampshade, tail snaked round the flex. Benjamiah stared, paralyzed by the absurdity of this, the violent impossibility. Then the monkey smiled, baring his teeth beneath those nightmarish button eyes.

Benjamiah couldn't contain himself any longer. He shouted out, scrabbling for the lamp on his bedside table, howling for Grandma. Two things happened at once—his bedroom door flew open, and his fingers finally found the switch. The room was bathed in light, snuffing out the stars.

"What on earth's the matter?" said Grandma.

"A monkey!" said Benjamiah hysterically. "There's a monkey... It was a monkey!"

The capuchin had vanished from the lampshade. Benjamiah leaped up and spun round, peering behind the curtains, lifting up cushions, checking the wardrobe. Grandma watched, bewildered.

"It was just a dream, dear," she tried to say.

"No, it wasn't! He must have escaped through the door. Quick, Grandma. There's a monkey in the house!"

A search was conducted, led by a frantic Benjamiah,

attended by a drowsy but patient Grandma. They checked the kitchen and Grandma's room, Mum and Dad's room, the living room. They even did a brief sweep of the bookshop below. Eventually Benjamiah gave up, out of breath, exhausted, and confused. Grandma wrapped an arm round his shoulder and led him back to his room.

"It wasn't a dream," said Benjamiah. "It *wasn't*. It was . . ."

He was about to mention the poppet, but couldn't bring himself to say it aloud. Any suggestion the doll had transformed into a living, dangling monkey was ridiculous. And yet Benjamiah had seen its eyes, the lifeless white buttons, just like the doll's.

"Where's the poppet?" he said.

It wasn't on the desk where Grandma had sat it.

"Well, I'm sure it's somewhere," said Grandma. "It'll turn up."

She helped Benjamiah back into bed. His heart had steadied, but his mind reeled. His eyes roamed the bedroom as Grandma flicked the light off, checking every dark pocket for movement. Stars from the night-light once again freckled the room.

"You've been working too hard," said Grandma. "My fault. It's too much for a young boy. Tomorrow you'll take the day off."

"I don't need a day off," said Benjamiah. "I want to help.

This was . . . Grandma, I'm telling the truth. There was a monkey here."

A tired smile tugged at Grandma's mouth. She stroked his forehead, perched on the edge of his bed. Something caught her eye.

"Well, look," she said, reaching down.

It was the poppet. Benjamiah flinched, eyeing it warily. The doll flopped lifelessly in Grandma's hand.

"Maybe you saw this before you fell asleep," said Grandma, returning the poppet to its position on the desk. "And it gave you a nightmare."

"Grandma, it *wasn't* a nightmare . . . ," said Benjamiah.

It was hopeless. Nobody listened to him. Just like with Mum and Dad's problems, it was *Benjamiah*—not the grown-ups—who had to try, who had to *learn* and *understand*, Benjamiah who was being difficult or obstructive. He was fed up with it.

"Get some sleep," said Grandma. "Day off tomorrow. Something to look forward to."

It felt like hours before Benjamiah fell asleep. Every so often, he cranked his head round to check on the doll. It sat completely still, completely innocent. Eventually he crossed the room and stuffed it inside the desk drawer for peace of mind.

He woke late. Sparkly raindrops speckled the window. Brushing sleep dust from his eyes, Benjamiah saw that the poppet was back on the desk. Hadn't he put it in the drawer last night? He dragged himself out of bed and picked up the doll, sensing again that almost imperceptible weight, feeling the hairs on his arms and neck bristle.

In the cold light of day, Benjamiah realized how stupid he'd been for even momentarily thinking the poppet had become a monkey. What nonsense. Still, it had seemed so *real*. But what else could it have been but a dream? An unnaturally vivid dream—for the second night in a row—was the only rational explanation, and they'd started after this doll arrived. Was it somehow causing them? Clearly, the poppet was unnerving Benjamiah, so he would do what he always did in response to uncertainty. He would turn to the only source he could count on for answers: the bookshop.

"I told you to take the day off," said Grandma, padded out in multiple cardigans, doing a crossword at the till.

"I am," said Benjamiah. "Just came for some books."

Slowly he gathered a pile that looked promising. Ignoring Grandma's suspicious glare, he lugged the stack upstairs, spread them out on the kitchen table, and set to work. Over the next two hours, he read passages about voodoo dolls and Japanese hōko, corn-husk dolls, effigies and corn dollies, and the ushabti of Ancient Egypt. The only specific mention of poppets he could find was in an old tea-stained book about witchcraft, which said poppets could be used to cast spells. There were even pictures and instructions on how to make one out of sticks, cloth, wax, and herbs. It looked nothing like the doll on his desk.

Benjamiah went to his bedroom and picked up the poppet. It didn't smell like it was stuffed with herbs or dried fruit—just padded with cotton. Examining closer, he could find no stitching, no label. He stared into its white button eyes, remembering with such intensity how they'd adorned the capuchin.

He thought back to last night. What had his mum been trying to say on the call with Grandma? *Didn't . . . doll . . .* Was she saying that they didn't send it? But if they didn't, then who did?

Benjamiah spent the afternoon chewing over this question, trying to make a breakthrough. He certainly wouldn't ask Mum and Dad. Nothing was important enough to abandon his campaign of silence. All day, the poppet never strayed from his thoughts, always propped on the edge of his mind, watching him. It lingered as he practiced his card tricks and as he finished his chess book. Even as he ate dinner with Grandma, he wondered about the strange doll and its origins and its power to make his dreams so wild.

Benjamiah went to bed without answers, the mystery of the doll like a splinter he couldn't excavate.

Please, he thought, *let it be a quiet, unbroken night.*

Off went the light. On went the night-light. There he lay, wide awake, guarding against impossible sounds, hoping to scare them off.

Around midnight, he heard a clatter. Something on his desk had been knocked over. Then he heard a little hoot, a rush of little limbs, the patter of small paws. Trying to steady his heart, Benjamiah looked up.

The monkey was on the lampshade again, studying him. Black and red, white buttons for eyes, the poppet nowhere to be seen.

Obviously, it had to be a dream, even though Benjamiah was certain he hadn't yet fallen asleep. The problem was it didn't *feel* like a dream. Every one of his senses was keen and functional, everything around him as detailed and ordinary as it would be during the day. Were it not for the button-eyed monkey on the lampshade, Benjamiah would have bet his books he was absolutely wide awake.

This time, he didn't call out for help.

"Hello," he said, and the monkey smiled.

What do you say to an impossible monkey hanging from your lampshade? Benjamiah was at a loss.

"Can you talk?" he asked.

Which was a stupid question. Not his finest moment.

Of course monkeys couldn't talk. But what about dream monkeys? No reason *they* couldn't talk, he supposed. The capuchin rocked back and forth on the lampshade, tilting his head from side to side.

"What do you want?" said Benjamiah.

The monkey dangled from his tail and pointed toward the bedroom door.

"I don't understand," whispered Benjamiah.

A scrabble, a squall, and a leap, and the capuchin landed on his bedside table, revolving playfully on Grandad's old globe, sending Benjamiah's alarm clock clattering to the floor.

"*Shh!*" Benjamiah hissed.

The monkey obeyed. Benjamiah sat with bated breath, listening for Grandma. Next to him the monkey did the same, still and silent as a coconspirator. When Benjamiah was satisfied Grandma hadn't woken, he turned back to the monkey.

"What do you want?" he repeated.

Again the monkey jabbed his finger toward the door.

"You want to go out there?"

The capuchin slapped a paw against his own forehead, then pointed at Benjamiah, then again at the door.

"You want *me* to go out there?" said Benjamiah.

Delighted, the capuchin emitted a gleeful squawk. Benjamiah waved for quiet, tensing again. No sound from Grandma's room.

"Where are we going?" he said.

The night got a little stranger still. The capuchin stiffened, then toppled off the edge of the bedside cabinet. In midair, the monkey transformed. As quick as a click of the fingers, his head shrank and his legs thinned and his arms shriveled and flattened. Feathers sprouted, a beak poked out where his nose had been, and his tail reeled itself in and spread into a fan. Now the capuchin was a tiny bird, black-feathered and mottled with red. He still had the white buttons for eyes—only much smaller.

Benjamiah recognized the bird's shape—it was a nightjar. With a thrum of his wings, the nightjar landed on the handle of Benjamiah's door. Then, with a chirp, he fluttered through the gap onto the landing beyond.

Reminding himself it was only a dream, Benjamiah decided to follow the impossible bird.

SIX

WITH THE IMPOSSIBLE DOOR

All the magic of our world draws upon the aether. The aether is the substance beneath all substance. Some characterize it as dusty nothingness, others as living emptiness. We each have some small part of aether at our command, in the form of our poppets. When we cast our poppet, we are manipulating the aether.

—A Brief History of Wreathenwold,
Archscholar Collum Wolfsdaughter

BENJAMIAH HAULED on the clothes he'd worn earlier and stole out on to the shadowy landing where the button-eyed nightjar perched on the frame of Grandma's door. He fluttered downstairs, toward the bookshop. Benjamiah crept in pursuit. All the creaks and grumbles of the rickety house were amplified tenfold, as though determined to betray him.

Curiosity tugged him one way, caution the other. But it was only a dream, after all. What was the worst that could happen? Curiosity won out.

Benjamiah and the nightjar entered the bookshop, the shadows lending it an eerie quality. He was led round the corner to the cellar staircase.

"You want me to go down there?" whispered Benjamiah, not finding much to like about the idea.

The nightjar, perched on a Douglas Adams hardback, gave a jubilant trill.

Benjamiah made a move for the light switch. The bird pecked his fingers.

"Ow!" whined Benjamiah. "What's the matter with you?"

Again he went for the switch—again the bird denied him. Benjamiah glared, nursing his hand. He'd never known dreams this sore.

"You want me to go down in the dark?"

From the nightjar's beak came another happy cry, which he assumed meant yes.

Caution made him wary. The dark harbored dangers. Curiosity saw things differently. The whole world would be one vast darkness if it weren't for curiosity, after all.

A deep breath and down he went. The stairs groaned, the nightjar fluttering about like a wraith. Benjamiah fumbled into the cellar, feeling familiar towers of books and boxes at the tips of his fingers.

Just as panic threatened to take over, his eyes adjusted. The nightjar was perched atop a stack of boxes on the far wall, twittering and crooning, bouncing around as though he'd located treasure. Benjamiah was baffled. Had they come for a book?

"In the box?" he said.

Losing patience, the nightjar transformed back into a capuchin. The monkey howled, stamping his feet, slapping the tower of boxes with his palm. It took Benjamiah a moment to interpret the gestures.

"*Behind* the boxes?"

The capuchin danced around delightedly. Benjamiah found the celebrations a little sarcastic, but he hauled down boxes while the capuchin watched, sometimes squeaking encouragement, at other times stamping impatiently. When enough had been removed, the monkey leaped forward and slapped his palms happily against the wall. Except it wasn't a wall—Benjamiah could tell by the sound. Not stone but wood. It was a door.

"There's no door here . . . ," said Benjamiah, feeling the cold wooden frame carefully. It seemed so *real*. He supposed that doors could pop up anywhere in a dream.

The capuchin became a nightjar again. He landed on the doorknob, hopping, chirping.

"This must lead into Tom and Harry's cellar," said Benjamiah.

Once Upon A Time was built flush against the neighbors' cottage.

"I can't just walk into somebody else's house," he said. "I'm not like you."

At this, the nightjar cheeped indignantly, flapped his wings in irritation, his chirrup rising to a screaming din.

"*Shhhh!*" begged Benjamiah. "Please. Just give me a second to think. . . ."

He ran his hands along the edges of the door. In that moment, he perceived the same intangible feeling he'd had when he lifted the doll earlier—there was some trembling, secret density to the wood, to the dark strips between the door and its jamb, some sorcerous intensity that made the hairs on his arms and neck prickle. He knew then, as he turned the doorknob with a shaking hand, that he wouldn't find himself in Tom and Harry's cellar.

The door opened outward. Benjamiah took a deep breath, then through he went, accompanied by the elated nightjar.

This cellar was not so different from the one he'd just left—full of books, crates of more books, some upturned wooden chairs coated in dust, a pretzel-shaped musical instrument a little like a fiddle. It was smaller and squarer than the Once Upon A Time cellar. The stairwell was directly in front of Benjamiah. Coming from above was the most unsettling feature of all—it was *daylight* up there.

A quick appraisal of the nearest books brought more confusion. *The Book of Barely Believable Stories* by Mildred Fogge. *Well-Lurkers of Wreathenwold* by Odelia Summersly. *Great Dollcasters and Their Poppets, Vol. IV* by Scholar Thomis Loops. What was all this nonsense? Benjamiah didn't recognize a single one of them, which made no sense whatsoever. He lived in a bookshop, after all.

"Where are we?" he demanded of the nightjar.

In response, the little bird flapped across the room and landed on the banister of the staircase. He wanted Benjamiah to go *up*, into more strangeness and mystery, into the impossible midnight daylight.

"I'm not going up there," said Benjamiah, shaking his head. It was all too much. "I've had enough. I'm going back to bed. To sleep. Or to wake up, I suppose. You do what you like."

He turned, but what he found struck a deep, cold blow.

The door was gone. It had simply vanished. Where there'd been a door, now there was smooth stone. Benjamiah laid his hands desperately upon the wall, fumbling for evidence his eyes were playing tricks. He did the same all over the walls, on every side of the cellar, before finally conceding that the door had dissolved.

While flailing around, Benjamiah stubbed his toe. Pain soared through his body, his eyes watering. No dream could hurt this much. But if it wasn't a dream . . .

Panic bottlenecked in his throat. For a moment, his head spun, dizzy with fear. The nightjar's happy chatter reached him.

"Where are we?" hissed Benjamiah. "Why have you brought me here? What are you?"

The nightjar cocked his head, twittered some more.

"Will you take me home again?"

Another excited chorus came in reply. Did that mean yes? Benjamiah breathed through his panic, then joined the nightjar at the foot of the staircase. What choice did he have? The only way out was upward.

They climbed the stairs together, emerging in a bookshop. It had all the gloominess of Once Upon A Time, but none of its charm. Oil lamps flickered on the walls. The shelves were loaded with leather volumes of dark or pale hue, everything severe and serious and without character. The floor was rough flagstone. Even the air tasted different, as though there had been some shift in its chemistry—a tang of iron, alien and disturbing.

The bookshop was quiet, apparently empty. Benjamiah peered round a partition of books, bringing into view the only window. Through it, he saw that it was daylight outside—a gloomy day, misty at the edges. How could it be daytime outside the bookshop when it was nighttime in Wyvern-on-the-Water? Exactly where had the door led him? This was utterly impossible.

Outside was a bewildering scene. People crisscrossed in Victorian-esque garb, frock coats and bonnets, top hats, canes and cravats, a throng of pinstripes and petticoats, flat caps and breeches. And every single person had a poppet doll hanging at their waist, held there by a neat string loop. Poppets of different colors, with different details—much like the doll Benjamiah had been sent, though no two were exactly alike.

He stubbed his toe again, deliberately this time. Again pain flared. Still, his toe had to be wrong—this *couldn't* be real.

A noise made Benjamiah start. Somebody was nearby, among the shelves. Where was he to go? Back down into the doorless cellar, hoping the door returned? Should he ask the person for help? What exactly would he say? The nightjar landed on Benjamiah's shoulder, now tranquil. It seemed Benjamiah was on his own from here.

"Thanks a lot," he whispered.

At a loss, he crept forward.

"What the devil are you doing here, boy?" bellowed a voice behind him. "No children!"

Benjamiah swirled round. Looming over him was a skinny man in an apron, pincering Benjamiah with mean, bloodshot eyes. Before Benjamiah could say a word, the man clamped his fingers round Benjamiah's ear and dragged him toward the door.

"Out of here!" he yelled, casting Benjamiah onto the street. "Next time you won't be so lucky."

With that, the bookseller slammed the bookshop door and gestured for Benjamiah to get out of his sight. But where was he to go? How was he ever going to get home? The nightjar hopped happily on Benjamiah's shoulder.

"This is your fault," he moaned, shrugging him off. "You brought me here. Take me home!"

But the nightjar simply fluttered out of reach, landing on the sign of Horis & Hoggish Books, waiting for Benjamiah to make a move. Around him roamed adults and children in their Victorian-style clothing, poppets swaying limply at their hips. It was a tight, cobbled street, revealing only a slither of gray sky. In either direction, the street speared into an enclosed, chaotic marketplace, like a bazaar. There was music, smoke, nonsense everywhere.

"Out of the way, boy!" shouted a woman.

Benjamiah spun. Looming over him was a magnificent black horse, except it wasn't *real*. It was mechanical, a complex and fabulous clockwork creation—Benjamiah could see, up through its nostrils, an elaborate brain of wheels and barrels, cogs and pistons. Its eyes were marbled and without spirit. Otherwise everything about it was lifelike, from its hooves to its mane ruffling in the breeze.

Everything was impossible. His head was spinning. The clothes, the smells, the dolls . . . Benjamiah found

he couldn't think straight. It was too much to take in, too much at which to marvel. This wasn't Wyvern-on-the-Water. This wasn't *anywhere*.

Nearby was a scruffy boy, a little younger than Benjamiah and dressed in rags. Like everybody else, he had a poppet—pale purple cloth with two rusty coins for eyes. Benjamiah watched the boy pull the doll from where it hung and throw it. In midair, the doll transformed: the limbs growing, the torso reshaping, the cloth spreading into a coat of purplish fur. As quick as a click of the fingers, the inanimate doll was a living creature.

Now it was a tabby cat with blinking coins for eyes. It scampered up the scruffy boy's back and sat smugly on his shoulder.

Benjamiah wobbled, thinking he might faint. How could these dolls possibly become living creatures? Some kind of elaborate mechanical trick? The wonder, the impossible strangeness, engulfed him. He thought his knees might buckle. He missed Mum so intensely. She was a scientist—she would have made sense of what was happening somehow.

One last time, Benjamiah stubbed his toe. It still hurt. Still absolutely awake, apparently.

He took a breath, feeling the cold air thread into his chest. This was happening. He was really here. But where *was* here? Was this an alternate universe? The laws of physics didn't strictly forbid them, though wormholes required moving quicker than the speed of light. And he typically came last on school sports days, so couldn't have run that fast. Psychosis? A hallucinogen? What had Grandma put in last night's dinner? Or was it all a very creative concussion? He felt fine. . . .

Buffeted by the traffic, Benjamiah was swept into the bazaar. A cloth canopy cut off the sky. Within was a tremendous din, merchants howling from the cramped stalls on either side. There were stalls for hats, stalls for masks with magical properties, stalls for jewelry and dice and stoppered vials of something called drowsipowder, stalls of unrecognizable fruits and vegetables. One table had vials of a dark liquid called quickshadow, which swam and twisted and climbed within the glass like black mercury. Merchants accosted Benjamiah with wares that were wild and impossible.

"Memories, get your memories. Two bits each, three for five bits and five pieces . . ."

"Finest poppysyrup in Wreathenwold, Company-sealed, aged for . . ."

"A bunch of flowers for your sweetheart, sir? Will-o'-wisps, ne'er-do-wells, broken bells, only seven pieces a bunch . . ."

"Some dreams for you, my friend?" said a tall, greasy man with two front teeth missing.

Lining the inside of the man's coat were rows of trinkets—they looked like white metallic spiders, no bigger than a fingernail. They didn't *look* like dreams.

"Finest dreams in all of Wreathenwold," said the man, offering his gap-toothed smile. "Dream of your favorite food. Dream of your love. Dream you can fly, or swim, or find your way at will . . ."

"I don't understand," mumbled Benjamiah. "Those aren't dreams. Those are . . ."

But he trailed off. What were they? The man stared at Benjamiah like *he* was crazy.

A broad-shouldered woman descended upon the dream-seller. She was a merchant from a nearby stall selling bottles with impossible contents. One bottle was full of mist and flurrying water—a rainstorm for sale, according to the label. Another bottle apparently contained the hoot of a barn owl. Others contained yet more absurdities: a fiddle solo, moonlight, patience . . .

"Away with you, you rogue!" she shouted.

The gap-toothed man disappeared into the chaos of the bazaar with a bow and an unpleasant leer. Benjamiah noticed the woman had gripped her poppet—apparently, some kind of threat.

The woman looked at Benjamiah. She had a flat nose, reddened with flared capillaries, and small, round spectacles.

"You weren't going to buy any, were you?" she demanded.

Benjamiah shook his head.

"Good. They're fake. Only buy from a licensed dream-seller. Even then, I wouldn't recommend it. . . ."

A dream-seller? Selling dreams that looked like white metal spiders?

Now the woman examined Benjamiah's clothes, frowning. He did look very out of place, he supposed, but only because he was dressed normally, in jeans and a thin gray sweater. She opened her mouth to speak, but the sound of smashing interrupted her.

Benjamiah's heart sank. The nightjar had transformed back into the capuchin. And now the little monkey was jumping round the woman's stall, smashing bottles with his hands and tail. Out of one erupted the whinny of a horse; out of another rose a scatter of beautiful embers.

The woman grabbed Benjamiah. "Stop it!" she cried, wide-eyed with shock. "Why are you doing that?"

What did she mean? Benjamiah wasn't doing it—the stupid poppet was!

While Benjamiah stood there, stunned, the woman threw her poppet. In midair, the gray doll transformed into a lynx with black buttons for eyes, its coat the same color the poppet had been. The lynx, lithe and swift, chased the capuchin round the stall, snapping its jaws while the troublemaking monkey squeaked with laughter. With every smashed bottle came more nonsense—an eerie laugh, a swirl of smoke making faces, a handful of snowflakes momentarily blinding the lynx.

"Why are you doing this?" the woman shouted again, shaking Benjamiah by the shoulders. Then, to the crowd that had gathered, she shrieked, "Somebody get the Hanged Men!"

"There's one coming now," said a voice.

Merchants and customers laughed as the chase continued, the monkey leaping and hooting, every shelf now a bed of shattered glass.

"What's going on here?" said a voice from behind Benjamiah.

Everything fell deathly quiet. The crowd hushed, with many dispersing. Even the despairing merchant fell silent. Her lynx poppet abandoned the chase, padding over and eyeing Benjamiah menacingly. He turned.

The Hanged Man wore a tunic and trousers of deep blue, a line of silver buttons between the collar and his black belt, from which hung an obsidian baton. Around his shoulders was a dark cape fastened with a silver clip in the shape of a glaring bull. Shining black boots and a black broad-brimmed hat that would look at home in one of Dad's Westerns. He also wore silvery gloves coated in fine prickles, like the leaves of stinging nettles.

But it was his face that invoked such terror in Benjamiah. Or rather his complete lack of one. The Hanged Man wore a hood of sackcloth that outlined his jaw, nose, and chin, the hat perched neatly on top. There were no holes for eyes, no gaps to breathe through. How quickly the dream had become a nightmare. Benjamiah nipped himself, desperate to wake up.

Trailing in the Hanged Man's wake was a poppet in the form of a great and terrible tiger. Its fur was ashy gray, patterned with sackcloth stripes. It was all muscle and violence, each paw a wrecking ball studded with claws. It kept its head low, rocking from side to side, giving Benjamiah a glimpse of its cavernous mouth. A deep rumbling rose from the tiger's breast, vibrating every nerve in Benjamiah's body. He thought he might be sick.

"Good morning," said the Hanged Man.

His voice was soft and clear, commanding and disarming. He took another step forward. His boots squeaked. The tiger followed. The sackcloth hood turned from side to side, taking in the scene. Finally, his gaze settled on the despairing merchant.

"What's all this about, Winfrid?"

"Look at what he's done!" said Winfrid—pointing not at the monkey but at Benjamiah—before gesturing to the carnage around her. "Look at the wreckage! He just attacked my stall. Make him pay for all this damage!"

The Hanged Man turned his attention to Benjamiah.

The tiger growled, drawing closer. Benjamiah wished he were like the treacherous doll that had led him into this mess. Then he could transform into a bird and soar away.

"Well, let the boy speak for himself," said the Hanged Man, in that soft and silken voice.

He lowered himself into a crouch. Now the sack was level with Benjamiah's face.

"Look at me," he said.

Benjamiah did so, his heart hammering, head spinning.

"Is this your doll?" The Hanged Man gestured to the monkey.

"No."

"The little liar!" said Winfrid.

A single look from the Hanged Man and she fell silent.

"Is this your doll?" he repeated.

"No. He isn't mine. I . . . I didn't mean to be here. You see, he was sent to me in the post. Then he came to life in the night, and led me down into our cellar, and there was a door that led into another cellar—the cellar of Horis and Hoggish Books. And then . . . and then . . ."

The silence was like a solid weight on Benjamiah's chest. He was telling the truth. Why did grown-ups never listen?

"And then?" said the Hanged Man quietly.

"And then the bookseller caught me," said Benjamiah, "and threw me out, and I ended up here. And this . . . the doll, it just does whatever it likes. It isn't mine. I don't have a . . . Where I come from people don't have . . . Do you know how I can get back to Wyvern-on-the-Water?"

He was losing his thread. There was too much to explain.

"He's off his rocker," said Winfrid. "Mad as a whooper."

"Are you mad?" asked the Hanged Man.

"*No.*"

"Are you playing a game with me?"

"No! I just want to go home."

"To where?" said the Hanged Man.

"Wyvern-on-the-Water," said Benjamiah.

"He's completely mad," said Winfrid, dismayed. "Who's going to pay for the damage? I want one of his eyes for this. I bet he has nothing else."

One of his eyes? Did she mean . . . Was she going to *cut out* one of his eyes? Benjamiah swayed, thinking he might faint. Winfrid was right that he had no money. All he had in his pocket was a fifty-pence piece and the pack of playing cards he used to practice his tricks.

Just when Benjamiah thought it couldn't get any worse, the capuchin returned to deliver his coup de grâce. Out of the corner of his eye, Benjamiah saw the monkey bare his teeth in a mischievous grin. Then he snuck onto the stall behind the crouching Hanged Man.

The capuchin swung a paw and knocked the Hanged Man's hat right off his head.

Everybody froze. Nobody spoke. Benjamiah didn't know quite what was happening, but he knew enough to understand that this was very grave, and somehow his fault. Gradually the silence was broken by the gathering growl of the tiger—a dreadful stormy crescendo.

"You'd better come with me, boy," said the Hanged Man, setting the hat back on his head with menacing deliberation.

SEVEN
WITH THE HOUSE OF HANGED MEN

Having learned of an impending revolution, the magi—dark sorcerers who had ruled Wreathenwold for thousands of years—commanded that a man from every household be hanged as a warning against rebellion. Standing at the gallows, their families pleaded for mercy. The magi gave the men a choice: be hanged or spend eternity policing Wreathenwold. Most chose to serve and became the Hanged Men, condemned to forever keep the peace of our world.
—*A Brief History of Wreathenwold*,
Archscholar Collum Wolfsdaughter

BENJAMIAH WAS ESCORTED from the bazaar like a common criminal, the gloved hand of the Hanged Man on his back, the prowling tiger carving a path through the crowd.

They emerged on a cobbled road. Skinny, crooked houses loomed on either side. The street was long and straight, with the buildings pressed so tightly together that they formed great stone enclosures.

Every passing stranger had a doll at their hip. A pigtailed girl was playing fetch with a poppet dog. Adorning the city were creepy stone gargoyles, crouched on ledges, walls, and plinths. They had skinny legs and arms and pointed wings—and they had the heads of bulls. Stone tongues protruded from gaping mouths, their eyes bulbous, horns spearing from their skulls.

The street ended in a fork. A stone archway marked the entrance to both streets, each topped with another bull-headed gargoyle. The Hanged Man led Benjamiah through the left-hand archway, and they stepped into sudden rain, great drops bludgeoning them from a sky of seamless gray. Just the other side of the archway, the sky had been cloudless and brilliantly blue. Apparently, the weather changed with every street whenever they passed through an archway. Rain became mist, mist became snow, snow became sunlight again.

Benjamiah buried his face in his hands. It was all completely impossible. Surrounding them now were more shabby, forbidding houses and shops—an apothecary and an alchemist's, a barber's and a tavern, something called a color-broker's, another tavern boasting of its range of rose-waters and poppysyrups. They passed beneath the branches of a magnificent tree, its bark snowy white, its leaves white and webbed with strands of black.

Benjamiah was thoroughly miserable. Rain had slicked his hair to his skull. From every direction, quick, unfamiliar eyes watched him. He wanted to go home where, for all its difficulties, it was dull and familiar and *logical*.

"Here we are," said the Hanged Man.

It was a tall, slightly warped building of dour lime-stone, with a flight of steps and grandiose pillars like the British Museum. Ranked above the entrance were more of the bull-headed gargoyles. Two Hanged Men stood guard, indistinguishable from the one who had arrested Benjamiah. Their poppets hung from their hips, also identical—simple gray dolls with tiny sacks over their heads. The doors were paneled with white wood, much like the tree Benjamiah had passed beneath. Carved into the stone were the words: EIGHTY-EIGHTH HOUSE OF HANGED MEN.

It looked a terrifying place. The kind of place people entered and never left.

"Please," said Benjamiah, dragging his feet, "I don't want to go in there. I just want to go home. This is all a mistake. Please . . ."

"You should have thought of that earlier," said the Hanged Man, dragging him forward.

While struggling, they clattered into two people on the steps. A man was weeping on the shoulder of a woman.

"My son . . . ," he sobbed. "My poor son . . ."

This was brought to an abrupt end when Benjamiah and the Hanged Man collided with them.

"What's going on here?" demanded the woman, parting from the man.

She was tall and broad, with light brown skin and a long dark ponytail. Through her spectacles, Benjamiah saw one of her eyes was a sparkling hazel, the other an empty, colorless gray. Her outfit was similar to those of the Hanged Men, deep blue with a black cape and a bull clasp. At her hip was a violet doll, a big smile sewed on with white thread.

"A criminal, Inspector Halfpenny," said the Hanged Man. "For the dungeon."

The dungeon? Could this day get any worse?

The man who'd been sobbing was tiny and wizened with crazy white hair. He reminded Benjamiah of Albert Einstein. Wrinkles webbed his forehead like cracked glass. He was dressed shabbily, in limp gray clothes that looked decades old. In his hands was a bedraggled flat cap. His eyes were colorless and bloodshot from crying. He looked more lost than Benjamiah.

"A criminal, eh?" said Inspector Halfpenny. "What did the rogue do?"

In his soft, deathly voice, the Hanged Man described the poppet trashing the stall and knocking off his hat. Halfpenny hid a smile with her hand.

"A beastly crime," she declared. "The boy must never see the light of day again."

Benjamiah's stomach plunged until he spied a twinkle in Halfpenny's one colorful eye. She didn't mean it—in fact, she looked like she wanted to laugh.

"It wasn't me," he said. "It was that . . . *doll*. It's nothing to do with me!"

The troublesome doll hung limply in the Hanged Man's glove. The wizened man who'd been crying was studying the poppet with a curious, wide-eyed gaze.

"Well, that doesn't make a lot of sense, does it?" said Halfpenny, not unkindly. "In Wreathenwold, there are no people without poppets, or poppets without people. If he isn't yours, then whose is he? And where's yours?"

"But I'm not *from* Wreathenwold," said Benjamiah. "I'm from Wyvern-on-the-Water."

Halfpenny paused. "How did you end up at the bazaar?" she said gently.

Benjamiah described the arrival of the doll, the door in the cellar, finding himself in Horis & Hoggish Books. When he finished, the Inspector looked solemn.

"What's your name, young man?" she said.

"Benjamiah Creek."

"Benjamiah, did you have a bump on the head perhaps?"

"No!"

"Tell me about where you live."

So Benjamiah told Halfpenny about Wyvern-on-the-Water, about his street, his school. He rambled on about his teachers, Mum's job at the university, about Grandma and the bookshop. By the end, he was breathless and Halfpenny grave.

"Well, I suppose you'd better take him inside," said Halfpenny. "Perhaps Dr. Sallow can help. . . ."

Benjamiah felt helpless. Nobody was *listening*. Who was Dr. Sallow? And how was he ever going to get home? The Hanged Man grabbed Benjamiah's shoulder, ready to escort him inside.

At that moment, the wizened man met Benjamiah's eyes, narrowing his own and studying Benjamiah fearfully—or was it something else?

"Is that you, Wilfrid?" he said suddenly.

Benjamiah froze. Then he shook his head. "My name is Benjamiah Creek."

"It *is* you!" said the wizened man, laughing.

"You know this lad, Hansel?" said Halfpenny, amazed.

"Absolutely," said Hansel, bobbing his head. "His name is Wilfrid. He's the youngest of Ewart Shiren, a few doors down from us. What the devil are you doing here, Wilfrid?"

While Halfpenny struggled with this turn of events, Hansel stared at Benjamiah and gave the tiniest wink. He was only pretending to recognize Benjamiah. But why?

"Hansel, are you sure?" said Halfpenny.

"Oh, he's just a troublemaker," said Hansel, waving his hand. "Always telling tales. Wilfrid, enough of this. Tell the Inspector who you are."

"Is this true?" said Halfpenny, cocking her one bright eye toward Benjamiah. "Are you Wilfrid Shiren? Do you know this man?"

Benjamiah's mind was whirling. Who should he trust? The man was a complete stranger, but could it be worse than the dungeon?

"I'd better send for Ewart Shiren," said Halfpenny.

"Inspector, if I may," said Hansel, lowering his voice and taking Halfpenny's elbow in his hand. "Ewart can be a little . . . quick to anger. Might I suggest instead that we perhaps leave him out of this?"

"I understand," said Halfpenny, "but the lad doesn't seem to know you. I can't very well let him wander off with a stranger."

Hansel again winked at Benjamiah, tightening his lips in a prompting smile. The Hanged Man still held Benjamiah's arm in a pincerlike grip. He wanted him punished.

A commotion broke out nearby. Two other Hanged Men were dragging a howling man up the steps toward the ghoulish building. The man was hysterical, writhing like an animal caught in a trap.

"Please . . . ," screamed the prisoner, tears hurrying

down his cheeks. "Don't take me to the Viper. Please, please . . ."

The Hanged Men, losing their grip, cast their poppets. Two tigers sprang from the spinning dolls. A warning snap of their jaws and the man fell limp, defeated. He was duly dragged through the doors and out of sight.

Who—or what—was the Viper? Would that be Benjamiah's fate too? Was a giant snake going to eat him? That would be the cherry on top of his day.

"I am Wilfrid," he decided. "Everything Hansel says is true. I'm nothing but a troublemaker and a tale-teller, and I'm very sorry, and I won't ever do it again. Just *please* don't tell my father. He'll . . ."

Letting the sentence trail into silence did the trick. Halfpenny was moved by Benjamiah's speech, disturbed by the implied ferocity of Ewart Shiren's temper.

"Will you take him home?" she asked Hansel.

"Of course," he said. "Thank you, Inspector. Come on, Wilfrid. Let's get you out of here before Ewart wonders where you are. . . ."

"This child is a criminal," said the Hanged Man, digging his fingers even tighter into Benjamiah's arm. "He isn't going anywhere."

"Oh, get over it," said Halfpenny. "I wouldn't mind knocking your hat off myself. We have bigger problems."

"Like finding my son," said Hansel, his voice cracking.

"Halfpenny, if there's any news, please send word immediately. I just want him home. . . ."

She gave a grave nod, looking troubled. Finally the Hanged Man unclamped Benjamiah's arm and handed back the poppet that had caused all the problems.

Benjamiah scuttled off with Hansel before the Hanged Man changed his mind.

EIGHT
WITH THE OTHER BOOKSHOP

A doll must be named. A doll without a name is prone to
misbehaving, is more difficult to cast, and will be poorly
bonded to its owner. A name gives life to the connection
between a person and their doll—a connection that could
mean life or death in moments of danger.

—*A Brief History of Wreathenwold*,
Archscholar Collum Wolfsdaughter

BENJAMIAH AND HANSEL walked together through
the rain. Benjamiah missed home and Grandma enormously. He even missed Mum and Dad, despite how bad
things were between them—even their problems made
more sense than this place. Still, at least he wasn't in the
Hanged Men's dungeon.

Benjamiah glanced up at the man called Hansel. A new
anxiety tightened in his chest. As far as he could tell, he'd

passed from the custody of one stranger to another.

"You know I'm not Wilfrid Shiren," he said.

"I do," said Hansel. "You said your name was Benjamiah Creek? Well, it's a pleasure to meet you, Benjamiah. My name is Hansel Cotton."

Though colorless, his eyes mustered a sparkle. He walked with a slight limp, the flat cap now on his head, pinning down the turbulent white hair.

A cart rumbled by, smashing through puddles, heaved by eerie clockwork oxen and laden with odd pale vegetables. They passed beneath another of the great white trees, mighty and snowy-leafed.

"Why did you help me?" said Benjamiah.

"You seemed to need it," replied Hansel. "Your prospects were bleak otherwise."

"So?" said Benjamiah. "You didn't have to."

"Being lost is unpleasant. I wanted to help."

Benjamiah was skeptical. There was something else, something he couldn't put his finger on.

"Why?"

"People are always getting lost in Wreathenwold," said Hansel. "Children in particular. It's been that way a long time."

"I'm not lost," said Benjamiah. "Well, I am. But I mean I'm not from Wreathenwold at all. In fact, I don't even *believe* in Wreathenwold because Wreathenwold doesn't make any sense. I need to get back to Horis and Hoggish Books. Maybe the door to my world has come back, and I can forget any of this ever happened."

"Well, that might prove difficult," said Hansel.

"Why?"

"Do you really not know?" he said, eyeing Benjamiah carefully.

"I don't know anything about this place," said Benjamiah, feeling hopeless.

Not knowing things was an unusual experience for him. And lonely, too. Was this how he made the other children feel at school?

"Well, let me tell you, then. Every street of Wreathenwold is the branch of a vast labyrinth. Nobody knows where the edges are, if indeed there are edges. Nobody can find the center, and nobody in their right mind would try. The city is impossible to map. None exist—certainly not *real* ones. So I'm afraid it isn't clear how we'd even find our way back to Horis and Hoggish Books. And, if that weren't enough, the city has a way of making you forgetful."

"What do you mean?" said Benjamiah.

"Well, tell me the way back to where you began," said Hansel gently.

"I . . ."

How odd. Benjamiah had always been proud of his neat, orderly memory. Mum, Dad, and Grandma had

often marveled at his feats of recollection, his ability to recite long lists of numbers, facts, properties of various scientific phenomena and structures. But now—as he tried to summon the series of streets he'd traveled down since arriving—he was at a loss. Competing pictures clamored, and became confused, and overlapped, each invading the last. There had been a misty street, a sunny street . . . Where had the bazaar been, and through how many different streets had the Hanged Man escorted him?

"I can't," he said, panic budding in his chest.

"It's all right," said Hansel, perching a thin hand on his shoulder. "Just stay calm. We'll work it out."

Staying calm was easier said than done. Not only did Benjamiah find himself in this impossible world—he might be stuck here forever.

"Everybody was blaming *me* for what this stupid doll did," he said. "Why?"

"Like Halfpenny said, every person has a poppet, every poppet a person. The people of Wreathenwold are dollcasters. As babies, dolls are made for us. We are never without them. If we die, so do our dolls. Likewise, if our doll dies in battle, we die with it. A needle through the heart of our dolls would kill us, too."

"But what *is* a poppet?" said Benjamiah. "Is it mechanical, like the clockwork animals? Or . . . or . . ."

But he had no other sensible explanations. And he knew

full well the dolls were not mechanical. The one in his hand was made of cloth and stuffing, string and buttons, lighter than a bag of sugar.

"No, not clockwork," said Hansel. "They are a friend. And a means to perform magic. Like so . . ."

He unhitched his poppet from the loop of string at his waist. Hansel's doll was snowy white, with a little red tie around his throat and black boots. He threw the doll upward. In midair, it turned into an owl, white-feathered with a mottle of red. It looped in the air and became a bat, then landed as a dog, then a mongoose, then a baboon. . . .

Benjamiah inspected his own skull, searching for a sign he had indeed banged his head.

"That's impossible," he said, not finding any lumps. "Magic isn't real."

As if determined to contradict Benjamiah, the doll in his hand burst into life. The nightjar soared toward Hansel's poppet, then transformed into the capuchin. He played and wrestled with Hansel's doll, who was now a spider monkey.

"You aren't controlling him?" said Hansel, astonished.

Benjamiah shook his head. When would this end?

"What do you mean, controlling him?" he said.

"Ah, you really don't know," said Hansel. "It's rather difficult to explain. It's like another limb, controlled by impulses in your mind. It's like having two minds at once."

"I just want to go home," said Benjamiah. For all the

tension there, he'd give anything to smell the bookshop and hug Grandma. "I just wish somebody would believe me."

"I believe you, Benjamiah."

Benjamiah cranked his head upward, astonished. "You do?"

"Of course."

"Why?" Benjamiah was suspicious.

"I've heard stranger things," said Hansel, wiping rain from his spectacles, "that turned out to be all too true."

Benjamiah wasn't convinced. There was something Hansel wasn't telling him—something connected to the way Hansel eyed Benjamiah's poppet, as though it were somehow familiar to him. But how? They walked in silence for a couple of minutes, the two poppets chasing and playing round them.

"I heard you say," began Benjamiah, "something about your son . . . ?"

Hansel nodded, looking suddenly haunted and old.

"Edwid," he said. "He was . . . *taken* . . . two weeks ago. Halfpenny is doing her best to find him. She's one of the good ones. But in a city like this . . ."

"I'm sorry," said Benjamiah.

"Thank you," said Hansel, and fell silent.

The street ended in another fork, with archways covered in moss and bull-headed gargoyles atop them, mouths split in silent, stony screams. Benjamiah stopped. Rain rattled upon the umbrellas of frock-coated figures hurrying past.

"Where are you taking me?" he asked.

"Home," said Hansel. "My home, that is. So you can get some rest, and have something to eat. Then we can see about finding *your* home."

"But you're a stranger," said Benjamiah. "I can't do that."

"Very wise," said Hansel. "Very wise indeed. But may I ask you a question?"

Benjamiah nodded.

"Is there anybody in Wreathenwold who *isn't* a stranger?"

Benjamiah shook his head.

"As I thought," said Hansel. "So you must, I think, choose somebody to trust."

Benjamiah stood, looking one way and the other. He had never felt so tired. Cold, too, his clothes clammy upon his skin.

"Let me give you something," said Hansel. "To reassure you."

From an inner pocket of his jacket, he withdrew a slate-colored coin. It was slightly warped and the size of a fifty-pence piece. Engraved on either side was the same barely discernible insignia—three crescent moons, arranged to form a spiral.

"Money?" said Benjamiah.

Hansel laughed, then frowned. "No, it isn't money," he

said, examining Benjamiah closely. "Do you have coins in your world?"

"Yes. Coins are money."

He retrieved the fifty-pence coin from his pocket and showed Hansel. Hansel took it, examined it with wonder, then returned it.

"Fascinating," he said, apparently struggling to grasp the concept. "Well, in Wreathenwold, a coin is a promise."

"A promise?"

"You have promises in your world, don't you?"

"Yes . . . ," said Benjamiah. "They're just things people say. But they always break them. Especially parents."

"Not here," said Hansel. "Here a promise can't be broken. I give you this coin, and I tell you I will keep you safe, and do everything in my power to get you home. You keep that coin until my promise is satisfied."

"And if you break your promise?" asked Benjamiah.

"Then the coin will break," said Hansel. "I will have no promise to give anybody ever again. Nobody will ever trust me. I'll be ruined, a pariah. Do you know what a pariah is?"

With a nod, Benjamiah said, "An outcast."

"Precisely."

Benjamiah couldn't help but smile. It seemed like nonsense, but then the entire day had been nonsense from start to finish. He pocketed the coin and followed Hansel through the right-hand archway.

The next street was cold and overcast. Shopkeepers were reeling in the awnings of their stores. A pair of shabbily dressed women were lighting streetlamps with their poppets, the dolls aflame in their hands.

"Are dollcasters immune to fire?" said Benjamiah, feeling stupid.

"Ah, only the flame of our own poppets," said Hansel.

Apparently at Hansel's command, his doll soared into his outstretched hand. The poppet returned to its doll form, then burst into flame. Hansel's hand was encased in fire, but he seemed to feel nothing.

Benjamiah racked his brains. Spontaneous combustion? It wasn't exactly spontaneous, though. Some kind of elaborate incendiary device? Surely everything had a sensible explanation, even if it *looked* like magic? Mum would have an explanation, he was sure of it.

"I have a daughter about your age," said Hansel, extinguishing the doll and fastening it to his hip. "Elizabella."

"What's she like?" asked Benjamiah.

"She's . . . well, strong-willed," said Hansel. "Spirited. A good heart, certainly."

If anything, this made Benjamiah more nervous. They emerged on to a street where snow fluttered, and Benjamiah was almost trampled by an enormous clockwork elephant hauling a train of wagons. They passed a factory, its chimneys smoking, and a man who tried to sell them more dreams arranged on the inside of his coat. A Hanged Man lingered beneath a tree, his gray tiger lounging regally in the snow.

"Are the Hanged Men the police?" said Benjamiah.

Hansel nodded, solemn. "They enforce the law. The Inspectors do the investigating."

Benjamiah shivered at the sight of the Hanged Man. They hurried on.

"This is our street," said Hansel, leading Benjamiah left beneath another archway.

The sky was mostly clear, save for a few clouds tinged with the auburn and violet light of a stunning sunset. A hard wind gusted the length of the street, which itself was cobbled and charming, dipping and weaving out of sight and lined with scruffy but characterful houses. Blackish vines clung to the stone. A row of small trees ran along the center, their bark and leaves as white as snow. Hansel told Benjamiah they were called bonewood trees.

Two small children chased pale butterflies nearby. An old couple were playing chess in their front garden. Benjamiah felt another pang of homesickness. He played chess with Grandma sometimes, and he'd been planning to try out some tricks from the book he'd been reading.

"You said nobody could find their way," said Benjamiah. "But you knew the way home. The Hanged Man knew the way from the bazaar to his headquarters, too."

"Ah, well observed," said Hansel. "Certainly the Hanged Men, who are no longer really human, can navigate the city. As for the rest of us, it's possible to remember journeys of three or four streets in one direction or another. It takes years of familiarity, though. Any more than that, and you risk never finding your way home. That's a fate all too common in Wreathenwold. Sadly our world seems intent on luring us astray with tricks and deceptions."

It gave Benjamiah the shivers. Hansel led him down the pleasant street, waving and calling out greetings to neighbors. There were more smiles here than Benjamiah had seen anywhere in Wreathenwold, the air fresh and clean, the smell of delicious but mysterious cooking unfurling from open windows.

"Here we are," said Hansel.

"Really?" said Benjamiah, his heart lifting unexpectedly, like a bird taking flight. "You live here?"

"Absolutely."

It was a bookshop called Follynook—a tall, narrow building of pale stone, topped with a slate roof, dark vines hanging beneath the windows and the eaves. Houses were pressed tight on either side. Out the front was a small courtyard, a bonewood standing sentinel with its white branches splayed, in its shade a few tumbledown tables and chairs. Lanterns were tied to the branches of the bonewood, hanging above the seats.

"Not much, I'm afraid," said Hansel.

"It's wonderful," said Benjamiah.

"You think so?" Hansel looked pleased. "Come on."

Benjamiah felt instantly relieved upon stepping into the bookshop. He was like a ship that had spent months at sea—long, perilous months, characterized by fear and doubt, horizons without end—coming into port. It didn't matter that the harbor was a strange and foreign one. It was enough to leave the dark, sorcerous depths of the ocean behind. Here was a place he knew, even if it was a place he had never been before. There was familiarity in the smell of pages and binding. The quiet magic of books lived in the air, as soft and rich as incense.

Like Once Upon A Time, it was shadowy and confined, with bookshelves looming and overflowing in every direction. Follynook was lit by oil lamps, their flames gently trembling. Dust lay upon everything, swirling in the air. The layout was altogether less labyrinthine than his family bookshop, with various orderly sections to one side or another, so that Benjamiah could see the counter from where he stood in the doorway.

Sitting behind it was a girl.

Girls around Benjamiah's own age tended to set his cheeks aflame—today was no exception. The girl had light hair pinned up neatly under a straw hat. Freckles covered her nose and cheeks, haphazard and uneven as though spattered by a paintbrush. Her teeth were crooked, a big gap between the front two. She wore a frock of a drab color and condition, and button-up boots that might once have been a smart brown, but were now scuffed and faded.

Hanging at her side was a poppet, midnight blue with white strings for hair. It had small, smoky marbles for eyes, sunk into the fabric.

"This is my daughter, Elizabella," said Hansel, nervously turning his cap in his hands. "Elizabella, this is Benjamiah. He . . . Well, he needed some help."

Elizabella maneuvered round the counter and stood with her hands fastened to her hips. Her eyes were deep green, like brilliant, glittering stones.

"Some help?" she said.

"Yes, he's . . . Well, he's a little lost, you see. So I offered to help him, you know . . ."

"Let me get this straight," said Elizabella, in a voice as thin and sharp as fishing twine. "You went out to find my brother. You failed, yet again. And instead you bring a different boy home. Is that about right?"

"Elizabella, darling . . . ," began Hansel.

But Elizabella gave Hansel a withering look, prompting him to fall silent. She had a stare that could leave blisters. Both Benjamiah and Hansel felt its scald. The stare dared them to say a word. When neither did, she turned and stalked away. A door slammed, a puff of dust issuing from the rafters above.

"She's very upset about Edwid, of course," said Hansel, looking a hundred years old, and as slight and flimsy as a poppet. "Why don't you have a look around?"

He gave as bright a smile as he could muster, then drifted behind the counter. The weight of the world seemed loaded upon his shoulders.

Benjamiah wandered the bookshop. All the books were bound in leather, the colors universally dull and muted, grays and browns and worn blacks. He leafed through *The Life and Death of Henree Trafalgar: Trickster, Color-Poacher, and Murderer*, and a book listing species of impossible flowers, and a battered volume of a book called *A Brief History of Wreathenwold* by Archscholar Collum Wolfsdaughter.

"None of this can be real," said Benjamiah, frustrated.

Hansel had closed the bookshop and was shuffling papers at the counter. Darkness had fallen outside.

"None of what?" he asked.

"This," said Benjamiah, running his finger along the books. "This place. These books. Am I really here? It's . . . There's no such thing as magic! Or dolls that come to life, or worlds that are endless labyrinths. Nothing is endless, even the universe itself!"

"There's no magic in your world?" asked Hansel.

"Of course not," said Benjamiah.

"I'm sure that can't be true," said Hansel. "Magic comes in all shapes and sizes."

The poppet that had led Benjamiah to Wreathenwold had been lying on a shelf of children's books. At that moment, to Benjamiah's dismay, he came to life. A capuchin again, he hooted and scampered along the shelves, and finally landed on the counter in front of Hansel. Hansel's eyes shone and his lips trembled faintly, finally finding a smile. He held out a single finger, and the monkey held it.

"Hello there," said Hansel, soft as a candle flame.

The capuchin hooted, scrambling off, and Benjamiah feared more carnage was about to unfold. Hansel only laughed as the capuchin ran up the bookshelves and sprang about the rafters.

"Don't be embarrassed," said Hansel, looking delighted. "Have you thought about naming him? Poppets always behave better when they've been named."

"He isn't mine," said Benjamiah.

"Tell him that," said Hansel. "He certainly seems attached to you."

So Benjamiah named him Nuisance.

With the door locked and the oil lamps extinguished, Hansel led Benjamiah up a rickety staircase and into the

Cotton home. He gave Benjamiah a brief tour. Here was a bathroom, and here was a study, and here was Hansel's snug. On the top floor were three bedrooms, one each for Hansel, Elizabella, and the missing Edwid. Elizabella's bedroom door was firmly shut. Her brooding cast a pall over the entire house.

Benjamiah sat at the kitchen table while Hansel made dinner. Elizabella had left a book there, *Jamima Cleaves and the Light-Eater* by Olfred Wicker. Jamima was a child detective who solved mysteries with her poppet. Even by Wreathenwold standards, it didn't seem like Benjamiah's kind of book.

"Olfred Wicker died recently," said Hansel, stirring a big pot on the hob. "Very sad. A talented man. Elizabella loves the Jamima books."

The kitchen was poky, low-ceilinged, and cluttered. The worktops looked hewn from hundred-year-old bonewood. Lined on the windowsill were herbs and spices of unfamiliar shapes and textures. A flower of smoky white drooped from a chipped pot on the table. Hansel said it was called a ne'er-do-well, though he didn't know why.

"You must be hungry," he said. "Do you like soup? It's plumpkin, with sweetdough and . . ."

He trailed off, seeming to forget. The soup boiled over, and smoked and hissed. He rushed one way and another, setting the table, cutting bread, sprinkling spices in the strange-smelling broth. Nuisance was in the form of a nightjar again, hopping round the larder.

The kitchen door opened. Hansel and Benjamiah flinched.

"Oh, hello, darling," said Hansel, a bag of nerves. "Good timing."

Elizabella sat opposite Benjamiah, eyes smoldering. Benjamiah, blushing, screwed his nose into the Jamima Cleaves book, practically camped among its pages.

"Is that my book?" she said.

Benjamiah promptly put it down. A tense Hansel dropped his ladle.

Elizabella looked up at Nuisance chirping and fluttering back and forth.

"That's a little rude," she said. "In somebody else's house. Assuming you don't live here now, of course. We *do* have a spare room, thanks to Hansel. But perhaps you could put the bird away?"

"Ah, the poppet isn't Benjamiah's," said Hansel. "He's . . . Well, perhaps you could explain, Benjamiah?"

Benjamiah gave his most garbled version of events yet. When he was finished, he glanced at Elizabella, cheeks burning. Beneath her freckles was a wide, dangerous smile.

"Great," she said. "You're absolutely crackers. No wonder Hansel felt sorry for you."

"Enough, Elizabella," said Hansel over his shoulder. "Benjamiah is a guest."

She stared intensely at Benjamiah, a glare hot enough to blow glass.

Hansel delivered the steaming pot of plumpkin soup to the table, and bowls, and a board of pale, crusty bread. There was a bowl of something called phantom leaf, too— large, crisp leaves, like lettuce, only juicier. The soup was cream-colored and smelled decidedly pumpkin-y.

"It's not much, I'm afraid," said Hansel. "But enjoy!"

Beneath Elizabella's stare, Benjamiah spooned himself a bowlful of steaming soup. Elizabella went next, then Hansel. Benjamiah tasted the soup—it was delicious, sweet and spicy and fruity all at once. He told Hansel so, at which Hansel looked pleased.

"Would you pass me the bread, new person?" Elizabella said to Benjamiah, and he froze.

Hansel sighed. "Please, Elizabella . . . ," he said.

"Are you shy?" asked Elizabella.

Benjamiah blushed.

"Don't they have girls where you're from?" she said.

Benjamiah blushed deeper.

"Or have you just never spoken to one?"

Benjamiah blushed so deep he thought he might melt.

"I know you're upset about Edwid, Elizabella," said Hansel. He reached for his daughter's hand, but she pulled it away. "I am too. I'm terrified and hurt. But please. Benjamiah is a guest."

Elizabella snapped her stare on to Hansel.

"Is he your new son?" she said.

Benjamiah could hear the pain in her voice, could see how the fear for her missing brother made her wild and furious at the world.

"That isn't fair," said Hansel.

"Where will he sleep?"

Quiet fell, broken only by the chirruping of Nuisance the nightjar. Benjamiah didn't know where to look. Elizabella glared at Hansel. Hansel stared down into the soup he'd barely touched.

"I thought he could sleep in Edwid's room," he said eventually.

Elizabella nodded. A tiny smile lit up on her mouth, but Benjamiah only saw pain. Then she threw down her spoon, making everybody jump, and stormed off. Again her bedroom door slammed.

"I'm sorry," said Benjamiah.

"Not your fault at all," said Hansel, looking old and frail.

They finished their soup quietly. Benjamiah didn't know what to say, and Hansel seemed lost within the maze of his many worries. Even Nuisance was quiet, perched sleepily on top of a cabinet.

"You must be exhausted," said Hansel when Benjamiah had finished.

"I am, but I don't need to sleep in Edwid's room. I can sleep anywhere."

"No, you must," said Hansel. "He would have wanted you to. Elizabella knows that too. She's just upset."

He made them both a pot of something called treacle tea, which was hot and sweet and possibly the best drink Benjamiah had ever tasted. After a few sips, his eyelids became too heavy to hold up. Seeing this, Hansel led a sleepy Benjamiah out of the kitchen and upstairs, into the bedroom next to Elizabella's.

Benjamiah hardly saw the room. He was too exhausted. He climbed into bed, sank into its softness, and was out like a blown candle.

NINE

WITH THE BOY WHO WAS TAKEN

No two dolls are precisely alike. Most poppets have at least some features: eyes or noses of stones, coins, marbles, or buttons; a mouth of thread, matchsticks, twigs, or wire; hats, cravats, coats, boots, or gloves. More outlandish poppet designs are said, without much evidence, to signify a more outlandish personality.

—*A Brief History of Wreathenwold*,
Archscholar Collum Wolfsdaughter

WHEN BENJAMIAH WOKE the following morning, he hoped desperately to find himself back in Wyvern-on-the-Water. Was that Grandma he could hear shuffling up the stairs? A bell chimed somewhere below. Could it be the door to Once Upon A Time? Please let it all be over—he couldn't face another day of impossible nonsense.

He opened his eyes and his heart sank.

Edwid's room was boxy and low-ceilinged. The narrow feather bed was in one corner, a tallboy smelling of beeswax in another. Beneath the window was a bureau, books and oddities piled upon it. Covering the walls were sketches of what looked like famous adventurers, their poppets cast as fearsome creatures battling other poppets. One dollcaster—apparently Edwid's favorite, considering the number of times he'd drawn her—actually rode her poppet: it was cast as a magnificent wyrm, a great wingless dragon spouting a torrent of flame at her enemies.

Benjamiah also noticed a crack in Edwid's wall—long and thin, like a jagged smile. For some reason, it made him shiver.

He drifted over to Edwid's bureau, finding cuttings of wood—some kind of puzzle that Edwid had yet to finish. What had happened to Edwid? Who had taken him, and why?

Between the bureau and the wall was a satchel. Benjamiah slipped it out. Inside was a small, cracked spyglass and something like a jewelry box made of pale wood. Carved into its lid was a simple labyrinth. The box had a little silver latch, but was also tied with red thread. There was nothing inside. Benjamiah also found a notebook of yellow, well-thumbed pages, apparently filled with attempts at maps of the labyrinth.

He closed the notebook. Also in the satchel were

two pairs of spectacles, though Benjamiah quickly found neither had any magnifying quality. There was one other item—a long silver spoke like a knitting needle, wrapped in fine threads spiraling to its tip. Benjamiah had no idea what it was.

"What do you think you're doing?"

Startled, Benjamiah shoved everything back in the satchel and spun round. Standing in the doorway was Elizabella, looking typically incensed.

"I was just . . ."

"How dare you touch my brother's things!" she said.

"I'm sorry, I . . ."

"Keep your nose out and your hands off, or you'll regret it."

With that, she strode in and snatched Edwid's satchel, then stomped back to the doorway. There she paused to deliver one final blow.

"And put some clothes on, for all our sakes."

Benjamiah didn't immediately understand. He looked down to find he was standing in his underwear, all pale and knobbly. The shame threatened to melt him on the spot.

Elizabella left, cackling.

Why did she have to be so cruel? It wasn't *his* fault Edwid had gone missing and, as far as Benjamiah could tell, it wasn't Hansel's, either.

Hansel had left out some of Edwid's clothes for him,

something that caused Benjamiah yet more mortification. Wearing them would only enrage Elizabella further. And that was before he even considered how silly he'd look in a tunic, shorts, and button-up boots, even if it was the fashion in Wreathenwold.

Once he'd dressed, Benjamiah wandered over to the mirror. He looked as ridiculous as expected. Once more, he carefully examined his head for any bumps or injuries. Still he found nothing—still he was expected to believe in magical dolls and endless labyrinths.

As a reminder of home, Benjamiah took the pack of playing cards and the fifty-pence piece out of his jeans and put them in the shorts' pocket. Objects from the real world whose weight he found reassuring.

He had breakfast alone—sweetdough bread with opple spread, which tasted like spicy apple. Hansel was rushed off his feet, minding the shop, forever up and down the stairs. Elizabella was nowhere to be seen. Somehow her absence was as ominous as her presence. Nuisance was making a nuisance of himself, sometimes as a dormouse, other times a capuchin.

With nowhere else to be, Benjamiah passed the morning in the bookshop, browsing the shelves. From *A Brief History of Wreathenwold*, he learned that color was the most valuable commodity in Wreathenwold. Color was bought, traded, stolen. Color could be lifted from any surface, except for poppets, with the use of a special serum and an instrument called a spectractor, which explained why everything about the poorer streets, like Hansel and Elizabella's, was dreary and colorless—the buildings, the books, the clothes. Even the flowers were black, white, or ashy gray. The most valuable colors were red, yellow, and blue—nothing could be distilled back into these primary colors, making them particularly precious.

The colors of people's eyes could be extracted, too. This was less to do with the actual color than with the rare and unique beauty of all eyes, which made every eye color extracted a singular prize of exceptional worth. Poorer people often sold their eye colors to pay debts. With both horror and sadness, Benjamiah thought of Hansel's gray eyes, and Inspector Halfpenny's colorless one. They must have had to sell them.

"Isn't that a little dry?" said Hansel, noticing the book Benjamiah was reading. "What about a Jamima Cleaves instead? A bit more fun for a young boy."

"Reading isn't about fun," said Benjamiah, at which Hansel nodded gravely.

"There's a great Jamima story about monkeys-of-the-inkpot," he said. "A problem we have at Follynook, you might have noticed."

Hansel explained that the inkwells around the house were plagued with tiny monkeys—no bigger than a fingernail—

who feasted on the ink when nobody was looking. Benjamiah spent ten minutes casting wary looks at the unattended inkwell on Hansel's counter, wondering if he'd been joking.

In quieter moments, Hansel would ask Benjamiah about Wyvern-on-the-Water, the bookshop, his family, his journey to the House of Hanged Men, dissecting the story for revealing details. Hansel said he would consult books and ask friends—it was clear he had no clue how to get Benjamiah home.

"A door in is a door out," said Hansel, not convincing anybody.

Any mention of home sent a pang through Benjamiah's chest, mostly because of Grandma. She'd be worried sick, beside herself. Mum and Dad would likely be hurtling back from the Purbecks too. Was their marriage still intact?

A customer bustled in who reminded Benjamiah of Mrs. Foxglove, drawing Hansel away. This gave Benjamiah time to explore another section of the bookshop: Spellbooks. He approached it with deep skepticism. Only yesterday he'd known magic wasn't real. The books he found there were slender and simply titled: *Boa Constrictor*, or *Common Magpie*, or *Mountain Gorilla*. Benjamiah presumed each related to a transformation a poppet could make, but there were no instructions inside—only in-depth descriptions of each animal's biology, behavior, and habitat, accompanied by black-and-white sketches.

Hansel and Benjamiah had lunch together—sweetdough sandwiches and milk punch to follow—and speculated further on how Benjamiah might get home. It appeared a couple of ideas were forming in Hansel's mind, though he kept them to himself.

"Tell me," he said, "do you look more like your mum or your dad?"

"Mum, mostly," said Benjamiah, thinking it was an odd question. "Especially the nose."

Hansel seemed to find that very interesting.

"I have to see Halfpenny again," he declared when lunch was over.

"Again?" said Benjamiah.

"Yes," said Hansel. "Every day. I mustn't let her forget about Edwid. Elizabella is minding the shop. Perhaps you'd like to help her out? I think you'd like each other, if she'll give you a chance. . . ."

Hansel grabbed his jacket and hat and dashed off. Benjamiah stole down the staircase and into the bookshop.

Elizabella smirked from behind the counter.

"I didn't recognize you," she said, "with clothes on."

While Benjamiah reddened, Elizabella took a closer look at the tunic Benjamiah wore. Amusement fell quickly from her face. He knew what was coming.

"Are those my brother's?" she said, dangerously quiet.

"Hansel told me I could. . . ."

Her eyes reduced to fine, deadly points. Besides the two of them, the bookshop was empty—there would be no witnesses to his gruesome murder. What if she cast her poppet as some terrible beast? Then, unexpectedly, Elizabella gave a big and painfully false smile.

"Well, that's wonderful," she said. "I'm so pleased the two of you have found each other. Hansel has a son again, and you aren't in the Hanged Men's dungeon. Nobody needs to worry about Edwid anymore."

"I don't think that's fair . . . ," began Benjamiah, before faltering.

"Oh, *really*?" said Elizabella.

Benjamiah backed off, Nuisance the button-eyed dormouse roosted on his shoulder.

Terrified of Elizabella, he went outside and sat in one of the courtyard chairs. Sunlight fell through the branches of the bonewood tree, a tortoiseshell of light and warmth, in which Benjamiah read *A Brief History of Wreathenwold*.

Benjamiah was still sitting there when Hansel returned.

"Enjoying it?" he said. He looked downcast as he patted Benjamiah on the shoulder, doing his best to smile.

"Was there any news about Edwid?" asked Benjamiah.

Hansel shook his head. "I'm afraid not," he said. "Halfpenny is doing her best. We can only hope."

"What happened?" asked Benjamiah.

With a heavy sigh, Hansel lowered himself into the chair beside Benjamiah. He looked tiny between its arms, shrunken by pain and fear.

"Edwid was always trouble," he said. "A good heart, but a born troublemaker. Elizabella isn't so different, really. They're twins, you know. But Edwid was always the more mischievous. Always getting into bother with his school-masters. This street was never big enough for him. He wanted more. He wanted to travel Wreathenwold and have adventures, which of course is impossible. You saw the sketches on his wall? They are famous Mapmakers— which means famous fools. Wreathenwold does not want to be mapped. The practice of mapmaking is illegal, in fact, given the dangers involved.

"Not that Edwid would listen, of course. His head was always in the clouds. He got that from his mother. She passed away shortly after the twins were born, so neither Edwid nor Elizabella ever knew her. Must be in their blood, though. I'm the opposite. I get all the adventures I need from my books."

Benjamiah nodded. This he could very much understand.

"One morning," continued Hansel, "Elizabella and I woke to find Edwid had run away. This was around three months ago. He left no note. Elizabella was heartbroken—

they'd always been so close. She had no idea where he could have gone, and neither did I. And where can a child go in Wreathenwold, Benjamiah? A street or two one way or another. But any farther and you will never find your way home. After several long days had passed, Elizabella and I were confronted with the very real possibility that Edwid was not coming back.

"I had never known such fear, such horror. Where had he gone, and why, and what could I do about it? Absolutely nothing. I would lie awake all night, worrying. Elizabella, too. She doesn't like to show she's scared, but she was. Every minute, I feared he was lost in the city, unable to find his way home. Wreathenwold is full of lost people, forced to give up on ever finding home. Some accept it and begin a new life elsewhere. Some go mad trying to find their way back.

"And then, two weeks later, he suddenly came back," said Hansel. "Such enormous joy and relief! But something was different about Edwid."

Benjamiah could see the toll it was taking on Hansel just to tell the story. He couldn't imagine what it had been like to live through.

"His eyes were colorless, like mine," said Hansel. "When he left, they had been green and beautiful, like Elizabella's. He had sold his eye colors. Or somebody had taken them by force. Edwid never told us what happened.

Nor where he had been for two weeks, nor how he had found his way back. Either way, I was furious. I had done everything to protect their eyes. We're not wealthy, as you can probably tell, but I would have given up anything else before that. Part of our character lives in our eyes. And we give it up forever when we let their color go."

Benjamiah looked into Hansel's bleached, faded eyes.

"Edwid told me nothing. I said some things to him that I regret. I was so *angry*. So hurt. One night, he left again and was gone for days and days. I'd been watching him so closely. He'd been different since he ran away the first time. Moody, removed, troubled. Even with Elizabella. They'd been inseparable before. Elizabella actually caught him at the front door when he left the second time. Edwid told her there was something he had to do and that he'd be back soon. But he never said what, or where he was going, or how he was going to get there. Those days were just as long and terrible as the first time he left."

Hansel took a deep, rattling breath.

"He came back after a few days, terribly unwell. Babbling about a magus of all things. Have you read about the magi in your book yet? Well, they were terrible sorcerers who ruled Wreathenwold for most of its history. Long gone now. And good riddance. Yet Edwid kept rambling about a magus, and some crack in his bedroom wall. He was feverish, confused, and in terrible pain. Dr. Moonwater couldn't diagnose it. It certainly wasn't ouroboros flu. And Edwid wouldn't tell us, of course. Even when his life was in such peril. So stubborn, that boy! He was mixed up in something very serious, Benjamiah. It seemed his condition would never improve. And then . . ."

At that moment, Hansel was interrupted by Nuisance, the nightjar releasing a tremendous squall from the branches above, which drew dismayed looks from neighbors. Hansel only smiled, removing his spectacles to dab at his eyes.

"A couple of weeks ago, somebody broke in and took Edwid. Just . . . *took* him and ran out of the house, and before I could make sense of what had happened the rogue was away, clattering down the street in a black coach."

"Who was he?" said Benjamiah.

"Nobody I know," said Hansel. "A shadowy figure. We didn't see his face. He burst in and just *took* . . ."

Benjamiah didn't know what to say. Hansel lapsed into contemplation, eyes glassy. After a big sniff, he gave Benjamiah a fragile smile.

"Is a magus like a dollcaster?" asked Benjamiah.

Hansel shook his head. "Legend says the magi created the universe," he said. "Folding the skies and the water and the earth out of the aether itself with a flourish of their canes. A magus does not have a doll, you see. For us, a poppet is all the aether we can command. But for a magus, all the aether of the world is theirs to manipulate. That made them incredibly powerful, dangerous and unhinged—driven mad by living so close to the aether, of which everything is made.

"There were only a dozen or so left by the end. It was they who made Wreathenwold into a labyrinth. They twisted all the world into a maze and lived at its center. That way, they were safe from the people. So they said. Absurd, really. It was the magi who tormented and subjugated the dollcasters for centuries. The last few wanted to live forever, ruling all of Wreathenwold from its heart.

"But like I said," continued Hansel, "they're all gone now. More than a hundred years ago now, every magus was murdered."

"What happened to them?"

"A terrible, violent end," said Hansel. "And, I think, a story for another day. I wouldn't want you thinking Wreathenwold was all lost children and warring sorcerers."

Something in the way he said that made Benjamiah uneasy. If the magi were so powerful and terrible, who had murdered them all?

"Do you wonder if Nuisance led you here for a reason?" said Hansel, changing the subject.

Nuisance was singing noisily in a branch above.

"To get me into as much trouble as possible, probably," said Benjamiah moodily.

Hansel laughed. "Maybe," he said. "You know now that

everybody in Wreathenwold has a poppet. Not the Root Folk, but everyone else. There are no stray poppets. Doesn't that make you wonder?"

"There must be stray poppets," said Benjamiah. "Nuisance isn't mine. I can't make him become anything else. And I can't make him behave."

"Not yet," said Hansel. "But he's certainly yours now. And I wonder if he led you here for a specific purpose. But maybe I'm just an old man, rambling away. . . ."

Not *yet*? What did that mean? Did Hansel think that one day Benjamiah might be able to cast spells with Nuisance? Something shivered through Benjamiah's midriff. It felt like excitement, which couldn't be right. Benjamiah Creek had absolutely no interest in magic, thank you very much.

Hansel left with another pat on Benjamiah's back.

Dinner that night was toadstool broth and sweetdough bread. There were sweet, sticky biscuits for dessert, and a delicious cup of treacle tea afterward. Hansel had a glass of poppysyrup, the clear liquid giving off a cloud of dreamy smoke as it was poured.

Throughout the meal, Benjamiah got the impression that Elizabella was planning something. The anger from last night had faded—now she seemed focused, lost in private preparation. Benjamiah only hoped it had nothing to do with him. . . .

"I'm glad you're in a better mood today," said Hansel.

"I'm sorry for yesterday." Elizabella said it to both Benjamiah and Hansel.

"No need to apologize, darling," said Hansel. "You've been through so much recently."

She smiled—a small, distracted smile. Hansel didn't seem to suspect a thing, but Benjamiah felt *sure* she was up to something.

After dinner, Hansel retired to the snug. Before bed, Benjamiah went in to wish him good night.

"Come in," said Hansel, misty-eyed. "Sit for a moment. Enjoy the fire."

The second glass of poppysyrup had quickly become a third or fourth for Hansel, now drowsy and meditative. Above the mantelpiece was a portrait of Hansel, Elizabella, and Edwid. The painting was done in dark tones, blacks and whites and grays—color paintings were too expensive. Edwid was practically identical to Elizabella.

Rising from a vase on the mantelpiece was a flower of astonishing beauty. It looked like a large tulip, a sublime shade of purple that was the brightest and most colorful thing Benjamiah had seen in Wreathenwold. It topped a stem of thin dark glass, surrounded in the vase by other flowers of black and white. Benjamiah could scarcely draw his eyes from the tulip; its color was so vibrant, the purple shimmering and flickering within the petals like fireflies.

"What is that?" he asked, pointing at the flower.

Hansel smiled. "We call them soulblooms," he said. "When a dollcaster dies, they merge with the aether of their doll and live on as a flower."

Benjamiah's eyes went back to the portrait. Somebody was missing.

"So it's . . . ," he began.

"Ada," said Hansel. "Elizabella and Edwid's mother. My wife. My best friend, too. I miss her very much."

Benjamiah didn't know what to say, gazing instead at the soulbloom. Its color swam, the air around it curling and shivering like invisible smoke. Ada's vase was to the left of the mantelpiece—on the other side was another vase, this one filled with a bunch of the same white and black flowers but no soulbloom. The door opened behind them. It was Elizabella, come to say good night.

She gave Benjamiah a sad smile, Hansel a hug, then drifted off. Benjamiah turned and caught her eye as she was leaving. The smile was gone—what remained was the same glazed, distant determination. What was she up to?

Not long afterward, Hansel began to snooze in his chair. He snored and mumbled in his sleep, and Benjamiah thought it best to leave him alone. Before creeping into

Edwid's room, he listened at Elizabella's bedroom door. Nothing.

Benjamiah tried to sleep. Nuisance was on the bedside table, back in doll form. After an hour, he heard Hansel lumber out of the snug and into his own bedroom. Snoring resumed quickly through the wall. From Elizabella's room across the landing, Benjamiah heard nothing. He was certain that would change. He had never been surer of anything.

Hours later, he was proved correct. The tiniest creak of a door opening. Another creak—a foot on the landing. Benjamiah tensed. Onward the creaks carried, across the landing, on to the stairs, downward. Benjamiah hurried out of bed, scrabbling back into Edwid's shorts, the tunic back to front. Barefooted, he crept down the stairs and into the darkness of the bookshop.

Up ahead, Elizabella was unlocking the door. She had a bag over her shoulder and wore her straw hat and a coat. She was leaving.

"Where are you going?" whispered Benjamiah.

Elizabella whirled round, eyes flaring in the darkness.

"Are you *following* me?" she hissed, drawing closer.

"You woke me."

Elizabella took another step toward him, into the

moonlight pouring through the window. Her fury made her eerie and intense, eyes afire, hair tucked neatly into her hat.

"Haven't you done enough?" she fumed. "Taking advantage of my father. Sleeping in my brother's bed. Wearing my brother's clothes. Why don't you go home to your *own* family, and stay out of *mine*?"

"You can't leave," said Benjamiah. "Hansel's already heartbroken about Edwid."

"And what is he doing about Edwid? Absolutely nothing! Well, if he won't, then I must."

"So that's where you're going?"

"What if I am?" hissed Elizabella. "What's it got to do with you?"

Briefly, Benjamiah wilted beneath Elizabella's fury. She was right—it had nothing to do with him. He should trail off back to bed and stay out of it. Then he recalled the pain on Hansel's face earlier.

"You can't," he said. "I won't let you. It isn't fair on Hansel."

"You won't *let* me?" said Elizabella. "And how exactly are you planning to stop me?"

Nuisance appeared—not as anything magnificent or imposing, but as a dormouse. He scampered between Benjamiah's feet, rose onto his back legs, and squeaked. Elizabella responded by unhitching her own poppet, tightening her fingers round the doll.

"Just try something," she whispered. "See how it works out for you."

Benjamiah didn't want to try anything, but he couldn't be sure about Nuisance. For the moment, he remained a dormouse, squeaking and scampering back and forth in the most unthreatening of attack patterns.

"You'll get lost," said Benjamiah. "Hansel told me. People get lost and never find their way back."

"So what?" said Elizabella. Briefly Benjamiah saw a flash of fear before the anger returned. "It's still no business of yours."

"Please, just stay," said Benjamiah. "I'm sure Halfpenny will find Edwid soon."

Elizabella gave a humorless smile. "Halfpenny might as well be called Halfwit," she said. "Now go back to bed, or you'll regret it."

"How will you get around?"

"None of your business."

"Where will you sleep? What will you eat? You have to plan things properly!"

"Get back to bed."

"What about money?" said Benjamiah, feeling increasingly desperate.

Elizabella drew something from her pocket, brandishing it triumphantly.

"I have enough," she said.

It took a few seconds for Benjamiah to process what he was seeing. In Elizabella's hand were neither coins nor notes. She was holding up six or seven playing cards. On the top was a six of clubs, overlaying a three of diamonds.

"But that isn't money," said Benjamiah. "They're playing cards."

"You are so *weird*," said Elizabella, pocketing them. "Playing cards *are* money. You're completely crackers, do you know that?"

Benjamiah said nothing. Instead, he reached into his pocket and withdrew the complete deck of playing cards, the only thing—along with the fifty-pence piece—he'd brought from home.

"So how much money is this?" he said.

Elizabella was stunned. She reached out tentatively, but Benjamiah drew the cards away. Her features snapped back into coolness.

"Not much," she said.

"One of every card," said Benjamiah. "Must be a lot more than you have."

"Give them to me," she said, dangerously quiet. She was gripping her poppet tighter in her hand.

"If you try anything," said Benjamiah, "I'll scream. Loud enough to wake Hansel."

For a moment, Elizabella considered this. Then her grip slackened.

"So what do you want?" she said. "Me to just get back into bed like a good little girl? I never will. You can scream tonight, but you can't watch me every second. And I don't care what Hansel does to keep me here, anyway. My brother is out there, and I'm bringing him home."

"You can have the cards," said Benjamiah.

Elizabella froze. Her eyes contracted suspiciously.

"Just like that?"

"Yes," said Benjamiah. "If I can come with you."

It took Elizabella a beat to process what Benjamiah had said.

"Not in a thousand years."

"I'll come, anyway," he said. "I'll follow you. You'll never get rid of me."

It was like she had swallowed something very unpleasant—Elizabella's face wrinkled, shaken by the dilemma she'd been presented with.

"But if you let me come," said Benjamiah, "you can have these. Think how much easier it will be to find Edwid."

He held the deck of playing cards out—only halfway toward her.

"Why are you doing this?" said Elizabella.

He thought of Mum and Dad and their inadequate attempts to save their marriage. Grandma, beside herself with worry, and nobody to help her with the bookshop.

He thought of his own bed, his night-light, his star charts.

"I need to find a way home," he said. "Hansel doesn't know where to begin."

"So?"

"I saw Edwid's notebook. I know what he was up to. He was working on maps. If we find him, maybe he'll know how I can get home."

Elizabella shook her head. "He won't," she said, her voice a little lower.

"He might."

"He *won't*."

"I'm coming," said Benjamiah, voice cracking as he tried to sound tough, and Elizabella seethed.

"Get everything you need, then," she said through gritted teeth. "A jacket and a hat. Some spare clothes. Use Edwid's things. Hurry."

Her expression was inscrutable, her change of heart concerning. Benjamiah kept the cards with him as he darted upstairs—as quickly and quietly as he could—and hastily gathered together everything he'd need. First he changed into something warmer, breeches and a shirt and a waist-coat. He found a flat cap, a warm tweed jacket that was too big for him, grubby socks, and the button-up boots. Into a scruffy bag, he threw some extra clothes.

All the while, he fretted that Elizabella would be gone when he returned downstairs.

There was one last thing Benjamiah had to do. He found a scrap of paper on Edwid's desk and wrote:

Hansel—
I promise I'll bring Elizabella
and Edwid home safely.
From Benjamiah Creek

Then he set the note on Edwid's bed, placing his fifty-pence piece on top. A promise, and one he didn't plan to break.

Elizabella hadn't left without him. She was waiting by the door, shrouded in darkness. Nuisance the dormouse ran up Benjamiah's leg and onto his back, positioning himself on his shoulder.

"I'm ready," said Benjamiah.

"The cards," said Elizabella, holding out her hand.

"Not yet," said Benjamiah, trying to sound tougher than he felt.

Elizabella studied him for a moment. Then she turned and led the way. They left the bookshop together, out into the vast labyrinth, in search of Edwid Cotton.

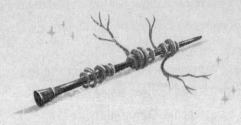

WITH THE SMOKING ORCHARD

This land was once a vast wilderness, populated by those we know today as Root Folk and numberless species of remarkable animals—many of them now extinct. To this day, the Root Folk are symbiotic with the natural world. They are born from the soil, become trees, flowers, and shrubs at the end of their lives, and preserve what is left of the original wilderness with a passionate and—at times— violent determination.

—*A Brief History of Wreathenwold*,
Archscholar Collum Wolfsdaughter

"WHAT DO YOU call your street if it has no name?" asked Benjamiah.

"Where We Live," said Elizabella. "Now be *quiet*."

That seemed like a flawed system to Benjamiah. Wouldn't everybody call their street the same thing?

Where We Live was eerie at night. Wind shook the

bonewood trees, their branches spread wide and spectral across the dark air. Smoke unfurled from chimneys. A moth—big and dark, freckled with silver—rose from a picket fence as Benjamiah and Elizabella passed.

"Where do we start?" he said. "Looking for Edwid, I mean."

"We start with the ground rules," said Elizabella. "You haven't been invited. You have forced your presence upon me. If you jeopardize the search, or embarrass me, or irritate me, I'll ditch you. I don't need your help. I don't *want* your help. You do as I say at all times. We aren't friends. And if you get lost I'll leave you behind."

"Rude," muttered Benjamiah.

"What was that?" said Elizabella, glaring. When Benjamiah remained silent, she added, "Another rule: no muttering under your breath."

The road twisted, dipped, narrowing and widening and narrowing again. Nuisance was a nightjar now, fluttering between bonewoods, hopping between chimneys. His big button eyes looked ghostly in the darkness. Elizabella's poppet hung neatly and obediently at her waist, held by a string loop around her throat. He'd learned from *A Brief History of Wreathenwold* that this was called a noose.

"Does your poppet have a name?"

"Emba."

"Did you choose it?"

"Another new rule," said Elizabella. "No stupid questions."

How was Benjamiah supposed to know what was a stupid question? He muttered under his breath again, at which Elizabella threw him another withering glance. They passed a big smoke-colored house behind a bed of white flowers, and a shop called Shakestone's CuriOddities, and a long, flat building of dark stone that looked like a schoolhouse. The street seemed to go on forever, twisting this way and that, no end in sight.

"Have you ever left your street?" said Benjamiah.

"Yes."

"What's the farthest you've been?"

"One street this way," said Elizabella, "and one street the other way."

"That's all right, then," said Benjamiah. "As long as Edwid's just hanging around on one of those two."

"Is that supposed to be funny?" said Elizabella.

"Just an observation."

"No observing," said Elizabella. "New rule."

There seemed to be a lot of rules.

"How much money do I have?" said Benjamiah.

"Will you keep your voice down?" said Elizabella. "I've lived every day of my life on this street. People will recognize me."

"Sorry," whispered Benjamiah. "How much money do I have?"

"You really have one of every card?" said Elizabella, and Benjamiah nodded.

"Then it's one hundred and sixty-three bits and eight pieces," said Elizabella, shaking her head in disbelief.

"That means nothing to me. How many pieces in a bit?"

"Ten."

"How much is a bag of sweets?"

"One piece," said Elizabella. "Sometimes two."

Benjamiah did some quick math, then gasped. If his calculations were correct, the deck of playing cards in his pocket was the equivalent of more than a thousand pounds back home. He'd paid ninety-nine pence for it in a Wyvern-on-the-Water bric-a-brac shop.

He opened his mouth to tell Elizabella, but was promptly hushed. Up ahead was a fork, the two mossy archways crested with bull-headed gargoyles. They were really doing this, it seemed, despite the dire warnings Hansel had given about getting lost. Two or three streets on, they'd begin to forget the way home—they might never see it again. Benjamiah was already lost, Edwid, too, but what about Elizabella?

"Are you sure about this?" he asked her.

In response, she gave him another dangerous look, then strode confidently right. Benjamiah hurried after her. He joined her on the next street, where rain spattered and swirled. They walked on, bordered on either side by more dark, skinny town houses, and strange shops, and the bull-headed gargoyles with their swollen, predatory eyes. They were called grotesques, according to his book.

Farther along was a tavern, a group of men and women smoking pipes and drinking outside. Their swaying and slurring suggested they'd been there for hours.

"Keep your head down," said Elizabella. "Don't let them see your eyes."

"Why?"

"Don't you realize how much money each of your eyes is worth? A lot more than you have in your pocket, that's for sure. There are color-poachers everywhere. Or people willing to sell you out to color-poachers."

The thought made Benjamiah queasy. He kept his eyes on his feet as they passed the tavern, feeling the drinkers tense and grow quiet. Mercifully, nothing happened.

"What are we going to do during the day?" said Benjamiah.

"Hide them."

"How can we hide our eyes all day?"

She said nothing more. The street arrowed endlessly onward, just like Where We Live. Moths of various sizes and patterns milled around above their heads.

"Where are we going?" asked Benjamiah.

"No questions," said Elizabella. "Remember?"

He was quiet for half a minute, then said again: "Where are we going?"

"You are so irritating!" snapped Elizabella. "We're going to the Smoking Orchard. To ask about *this*."

She drew something out of her bag and handed it to Benjamiah. He recognized it from earlier—the metal spoke wrapped in delicate threads from Edwid's satchel.

"What is this?" said Benjamiah, turning it over in his hands.

"A key," said Elizabella. "It might have something to do with what Edwid was up to. If I can find out, perhaps I can learn why he was taken. Now give it back."

"Doesn't look like a key to me," said Benjamiah, returning it. "How do you know it's from the Smoking Orchard?"

"The threads around it," said Elizabella. "They're roots. It's a Root Folk key. So we need to go to a Root Folk street, like the Smoking Orchard. Omelia from school told me it's at the other end of this street. Any more questions?"

Elizabella said it like she had answered every possible inquiry, but Benjamiah had so many more. It didn't *look* like a key. What if the Smoking Orchard wasn't at the other end of this street? And why was it called the Smoking Orchard? And what did a weird key have to do with Edwid being taken? Still, he was relieved to know there was at least some kind of plan. Benjamiah always planned carefully, whether it was homework or chores or his reading list.

As he opened his mouth to ask more questions, Elizabella handed him something else. It was one of the pairs of spectacles from Edwid's satchel. To his surprise, she perched the other pair on the bridge of her nose.

"I don't wear glasses," said Benjamiah.

"You do now."

She turned to face him. Through the lenses, her green eyes were entirely dulled, every speck of color evaporated. Now they were gray and unremarkable. Some trick of the glass, Benjamiah supposed, refracting the light to hide the colors. Although Elizabella would no doubt say it was more *magic*.

"Despectacles," she told him. "We can't have color-poachers after us. I can't afford any distractions."

"Where did Edwid get them?"

"No idea."

"We should make a list of all our avenues of investigation," said Benjamiah.

"Excuse me?"

"We need to think about who would take Edwid and why," said Benjamiah. "If we consider everything logically, we'll solve the problem."

Elizabella snorted. He had the impression her approach to things was going to be very different from his own. More a chaotic, unthinking hurtle through the labyrinth than a rational, considered investigation.

It was another hour before they reached the end of the street. Before them was only a left turn, a tight alleyway of stone beneath another archway. Here, beyond the final houses, it was deserted.

"Maybe we should ask somebody," said Benjamiah. "Before we go any farther. Hansel said . . ."

"Oh, who cares what Hansel says?"

Elizabella strode forward and out of sight. Benjamiah took a deep breath and hurried after her.

The alleyway was dark and claustrophobic, clammy stone walls rising high to the sky. It twisted and deviated, igniting panic in Benjamiah. Then he saw a splash of light at the next junction.

He emerged into a wilderness, a panorama of trees— not the wraithlike bonewoods that lined the cobbled streets, but trees of glorious green, with smoke-colored berries bunched at the tips of their branches. The canopy was a mosaic of leaves and early-morning sunlight. Sunshine fell in columns, where butterflies of all colors drifted in terrific numbers. The forest floor was a scatter of leaves, twigs, and fallen smokeberries.

There were toadstools as tall as Benjamiah, enormous and incandescent flowers growing upside down from mossy branches, walls of bracken with thorns as big and deadly as tiger teeth. The forest was charged with birdsong, too, the first Benjamiah had heard in Wreathenwold. According

to Archscholar Wolfsdaughter, most of the animals and insects of Wreathenwold took shelter in Root Folk streets.

Along the edges of the forest were enormous, ancient trees cloaked in lichen. Hewn into the trees were doors and windows.

The Root Folk were nothing like the dollcasters. These people wore shawls and bangles and beads, with glyphs etched all over their skin, their eyes muddy and swampy. Benjamiah saw a slender woman whose left arm ended in a spray of sticks instead of a hand. Sitting dreamily on a fallen tree was an old man whose left leg had become the trunk of a tree, planted in the earth. He didn't seem at all concerned.

"Let's ask somebody about the key," said Elizabella.

"Are we allowed to be here?" said Benjamiah.

"Of course," said Elizabella, though she didn't sound completely sure. "Root Folk are peaceful. Just don't upset them."

How was Benjamiah supposed to know what might upset the Root Folk, though? Before he could ask, Elizabella was on her way, tracking a path through the forest. Butterflies looped and drifted like radiant snowflakes. A woman with moss covering half her face was having an argument with a large indigo flower. Other Root Folk were in the canopy, stowing the ripest smokeberries in baskets.

Elizabella approached the man whose leg was rooted in

the mud. Sunlight lay across his face. He looked incredibly peaceful.

"Excuse me," she said, and the man lazily opened his eyes.

"Beautiful morning, isn't it?" he said, his voice earthy. "What are you two doing here? Up to no good?"

It was said with a mischievous smile.

"Of course not," said Elizabella, looking as sweet as it was possible to look. "We're searching for a key-maker. Somebody who can tell us about this."

She handed over the silver spoke.

"Ah, been a long time since I've seen one of these," said the old man. "It wasn't made here, though. It's from the Whispering Wood."

"And where's that?" said Elizabella, looking excited.

"How should I know?" said the old man. "I've been planted here for thirty moons now. You could ask around, but I expect nobody knows. That's the way it is, after all."

Benjamiah saw the dejection on Elizabella's face. She took the key back, thanked the old man, and walked on. She asked a dozen or more Root Folk if they knew the way to the Whispering Wood. None did. There was an elderly woman with a mane of holly for hair, a man with a tree knot for a nose, a boy with flowers blooming behind both ears. To Benjamiah, the forest was fantastic and impossible, the people at various stages of becoming a part of it, but to Elizabella there was nothing but disappointment.

Around them, the Smoking Orchard had grown busier, a festival of butterflies and Root Folk up in the trees picking smokeberries. Some of them were chewing something that Elizabella said was called moon leaf, which seemed to make them happy. Occasionally songs broke out amid the canopy.

Elizabella wouldn't give up. She spent hours wandering the orchard, asking for help while Benjamiah trailed behind. Sadly, it seemed the Root Folk were no more adept at navigating Wreathenwold than the dollcasters.

Finally Benjamiah could see that the truth sank in for Elizabella—nobody knew how to find the Whispering Wood. Thoroughly crestfallen, she led the way out of the Smoking Orchard.

On returning to the previous street, they were accosted by a desperate, disheveled man. He was bearded, dressed in rags, scraped and bruised and wild-eyed. He fell to his knees in front of Elizabella and Benjamiah.

"Please!" he howled. "Please! I'm lost. Help me. Do you know the street with Scaramouche's Circus? Have you seen it? Please . . . My family . . . It's been years now . . . My children, they must be all grown up . . . The street with the circus? And there's the Violet Bank, and . . ."

It was one of the saddest and most frightening things Benjamiah had ever seen. And, worse still, he knew how the man felt. Was he any more lost than Benjamiah? Tears rolled from the man's red, swollen eyes.

"Come," said Elizabella softly in Benjamiah's ear. "There's nothing we can do."

Benjamiah wanted to argue, but he was too afraid, and they walked away, both thoroughly shaken. The lost man threw himself at the feet of two women, repeating his frantic pleas.

Dejected, Elizabella and Benjamiah went into a nearby tearoom. They ordered cups of treacle tea and sticky pastries and sat at a corner table. The tearoom smelled of honey, the window steamed up. At the next table was a woman reading a newspaper, a hairy green tarantula with crosses for eyes resting on her arm.

Having paid out of his playing cards, Benjamiah set the remainder of the deck on the table. Unable to take his mind off the lost man, he asked, "Does that happen a lot?"

"All the time," said Elizabella, shrugging. "I told you, you should have stayed at Follynook."

Benjamiah tried to swallow, but couldn't. His body had run cold. Could that man be him one day, wandering Wreathenwold, pleading for help? Elizabella must have glimpsed Benjamiah's terror because she slid the rest of her pastry across the table for him to finish. It helped—and not just because it tasted delicious.

"What now?" he said, brushing flakes from his waistcoat. "How do we get to the Whispering Wood?"

"Edwid *must* have had a method for finding his way," said Elizabella. "How else could he have got all the way to the Whispering Wood and back?"

"Did you bring his notebook?" asked Benjamiah. "I peeked inside, before you caught me. . . ."

"I remember," said Elizabella, as icy and dangerous as a glacier.

"Well," said Benjamiah, blushing, "the drawings looked like maps. . . ."

From her bag, Elizabella pulled out Edwid's tattered notebook. She also withdrew the small box wrapped in red thread, held shut by a tiny silver latch.

"That's the insignia of the Company of Mapmakers," she said, tapping the labyrinth carved on the lid.

"Do you think there was something inside? Like a compass or something?"

"Maybe. Although I've never heard of *anything* that can help people find their way in Wreathenwold."

"Where has it gone, then?" asked Benjamiah, opening the box to find it empty.

Elizabella didn't know.

"Weird," said Benjamiah.

"What is?"

"Why would it be tied with a thread when it also has a latch?"

"What's your point?" said Elizabella, frustrated.

"I don't know."

"Well, wonderful!"

Ignoring Elizabella's sarcasm, Benjamiah drew Edwid's notebook across the table and leafed through it. On each page were sketches of connected streets, like the threads of a spiderweb. Alongside were notes, details of various buildings and features. None of it made much sense— Benjamiah certainly couldn't see anything that might lead them to the Whispering Wood.

"So Edwid was trying to draw maps," he said.

"Looks that way," said Elizabella stiffly.

"Isn't that illegal?"

"Are you calling my brother a criminal?"

"No, just . . . ," began Benjamiah, before thinking twice.

"Anyway, it's impossible to map the city," said Elizabella.

"What do you mean?"

"Just ask the Company of Mapmakers," she said. "They've been trying for nearly a thousand years. Wreathenwold doesn't *want* to be mapped. Sketches change in the night. Descriptions alter. Every time you look in that notebook, it's different. And that's before you think about all the bad luck that falls upon Mapmakers. They always end up mad, ill, murdered, or eaten. . . ."

Benjamiah shuddered, closing the notebook. *Eaten by what?*

"Maybe we should just go home," he said.

Elizabella's eyes narrowed. "It's *my* home, for a start," she said. "Not yours. And secondly it isn't home without Edwid. I'm not going back there without him. Ever."

Benjamiah looked down, playing with the last flakes of pastry on his plate, waiting for the burning coals of Elizabella's fury to cool. Across the table she brooded, her expression one of dangerous, destructive single-mindedness that couldn't possibly be reasoned with. Just like she'd been when she was plotting to leave.

It happened quickly. Elizabella snatched up the box and the notebook and—crucially—Benjamiah's playing cards, shoved everything into her bag, and stormed out of the tearoom. In a blur, she was rushing up the street and out of sight.

Benjamiah ran after her, Nuisance the dormouse scampering alongside.

Elizabella tore through the rain in the direction of Where We Live. For a moment, Benjamiah prayed she was heading home. Then she veered to the left, weaving between angry comers-and-goers, then down a sudden right turn that Benjamiah hadn't seen before. It didn't lead to Where We Live, nor did it lead back to the Smoking Orchard. Try as he might, Benjamiah was too slow—Elizabella disappeared beneath the archway.

The new street was icy cold, aflutter with snow.

Benjamiah was forced to stagger out of the path of a monumental clockwork elephant trawling a train of wagons loaded with steel beams. When it was gone, Benjamiah cast around for Elizabella. The street was hectic, with carts and carriages going in both directions, streams of people hurrying one way or another, all scowls and mutters and tailcoats.

Benjamiah ran breathlessly onto a misty street that curved and meandered. It was so gloomy that oil lamps had been lit, burning holes in the fog. He saw Elizabella up ahead—she'd slowed to a walk. He called out her name, but it only made her run again. Street after street, Benjamiah followed, only catching up when they were absolutely, irrevocably lost.

They came to a drizzly street. Market stalls lined the pavements, traders and merchants and customers creating an almighty din. A heavily scarred man fried lime-smelling nuts in a big steel bowl.

Behind it, Benjamiah cornered Elizabella. She had squeezed herself between two barrels, knees drawn into her chest, breathing ragged and hair and eyes wild. With great caution, he sat down next to her, and the two of them caught their breath.

"Can you remember the way back?" he asked. Elizabella shook her head.

Benjamiah let this sink in. He recalled the lost man

from earlier, raving, desperate. Fear spread through his body. That would be him in ten years. Never mind just finding the way back to Follynook, how was he ever getting home? The terror of never seeing Mum, Dad, and Grandma again rose through his body, blotting his mind.

"We're lost, then," he said, barely holding it together.

"We'll just have to find the Whispering Wood. However long it takes."

How were they supposed to do that?

"Keep the cards," said Benjamiah. "I'm still staying."

"Here," she said, handing them back. "I'm sorry I took them. I don't know what I was thinking."

He took the deck from her trembling hands.

"Can I see that box again?" he asked. "The empty one, from the Company of Mapmakers."

Elizabella handed it over, dazed. Benjamiah undid the thread, toyed with the latch, opened and closed the box. Then he set it down in his lap and lifted the thread, which was about fifteen inches long. He stared at the labyrinth carved into the lid of the box.

"Strange," he muttered.

"What is?"

A labyrinth. A thread . . .

"It's like that Greek myth," said Benjamiah. "With the labyrinth and the Minotaur."

"What are you *talking* about?"

"Nothing," said Benjamiah. "Just a stupid story my dad read me once. King Minos built the labyrinth to hold the Minotaur, because he had become so monstrous, and anyway he was offensive to King Minos. The idea was that the monster would never find his way out."

Elizabella stared at him blankly, not paying much attention.

"There were wars," said Benjamiah. "King Minos's son was killed by the Athenians. After Minos defeated them, he demanded that seven men and seven women be given as a tribute every seven years. They were sent into the labyrinth, where the Minotaur devoured them."

"Has this got anything to do with anything?" asked Elizabella.

"Probably not," said Benjamiah. "Anyway, an Athenian named Theseus volunteered to slay the Minotaur. He would go into the labyrinth and kill the monster. But killing the Minotaur was only the first challenge. The bigger problem was finding a way back out of the labyrinth, which after all had been built to ensure the Minotaur himself never found his way out. But Theseus was given a ball of thread by somebody who loved him. A woman. Actually, I think she was the daughter of King Minos."

"It isn't a ball of thread," said Elizabella. "It's a piece of thread, for tying the box."

"Maybe," said Benjamiah. "But why tie the box if it

has a working latch? Maybe the thread was *in* the box."

He lifted the length of thread again. It snaked gently in the breeze. Then he set it down on top of the box in his lap, where it lay coiled.

"What was her name?" he said, racking his brains.

"Whose name?"

"The woman who gave Theseus the thread."

"What does it matter?" said Elizabella.

"I just want to remember," said Benjamiah sulkily.

"Where did you even hear all this rubbish?"

"Dad read the story to me. He's always trying to get me interested in the stuff he likes. Never read me anything serious."

Although, considering the world in which Benjamiah now found himself, maybe Dad had been right all along. That was a strange thought.

"At least he read to you," said Elizabella. "Sounds like you could do with some fun in your life. Anyway, can you just be quiet for a minute? I need to think."

That would be a first, thought Benjamiah ruefully.

He hadn't seen Elizabella do any thinking so far. She'd just blundered forward without a plan, and now they were lost. Benjamiah kept it to himself, watching Elizabella as she clamped her eyes shut, rubbing her temples with her fingers.

Right then, the name came to Benjamiah.

"Ariadne!"

Two things happened. Elizabella jumped out of her skin. And the thread on top of the box came to life.

It lifted itself up like a tiny snake, one end neatly coiled, the other raised like the rocking head of a dancing cobra. Elizabella and Benjamiah gaped. The thread turned its head, its tail flickering, looking at them both in turn. Not *looking*, Benjamiah reminded himself—it had no eyes, after all.

"Is that . . . Is Ariadne your name?" whispered Benjamiah.

The thread nodded eagerly.

Elizabella shoved Benjamiah out of the way. She lowered her head, drawing as close as she could to Ariadne.

"*You* were in the Mapmakers' box," she said.

Ariadne nodded.

"Do you know my brother, Edwid?"

Again Ariadne nodded keenly.

"Did you help him find his way round Wreathenwold?"

For a third time, the magic thread nodded.

"How?"

"I don't think she can talk," said Benjamiah.

"I can see that!" snapped Elizabella, before turning her attention back to Ariadne. "Can you lead us to Edwid?"

Ariadne drooped her head and shook it.

"Well, what good are you, then?" demanded Elizabella.

Now it was Benjamiah's turn to shoulder Elizabella out of the way.

"Can you lead us to the man who took Edwid?" he asked.

Ariadne shook her head.

"Stupid string," muttered Elizabella.

Ariadne looked offended—at least, as offended as a piece of thread could look.

"Ariadne, can you only find places?" said Benjamiah.

Another nod of the head.

"Can you lead us to where Edwid is?" said Elizabella.

Ariadne shook her head. Already she looked wary of Elizabella's temper. Benjamiah knew how she felt.

"That's not how it works," he said. "That's the same as finding a person, which obviously she can't do. But she can find things that don't move. Ariadne, do you know the way to the Whispering Wood?"

This time, Ariadne's nod was proud and theatrical, as though offended by any suggestion that she *wouldn't* know the way.

"Can you lead us there?" said Benjamiah.

With a bow, Ariadne the thread shivered, flourished, and rose. One end looped gently round Benjamiah's finger, like a monkey's tail on a branch, and then her other end came up and looped round the bridge of Elizabella's despectacles. Up and up she swung, from Elizabella's despectacles to her straw hat, onto the barrel beside her, up a pipe, onto the stone of the building behind them.

Elizabella looked alive again, all the color returned to her face, incandescent with renewed hope. She gave a real laugh, the first Benjamiah had heard. He knew how she felt. Moments before, he'd been paralyzed by fear and panic, hopelessly lost. Now there was hope again, and the relief was dizzying.

From above, with a flick of her tail, the marvelous Ariadne beckoned them on.

ELEVEN
WITH THE WHISPERING WOOD

Folklore holds that the bonewood trees lining our streets were once a tribe of Root Folk. Seeing the dollcasters' disregard for the natural world, they planted themselves and became bonewoods with the promise of forever keeping watch. A version of this story is a charming favorite from Mildred Fogge's fabulous *The Book of Barely Believable Stories.*
—*A Brief History of Wreathenwold*,
Archscholar Collum Wolfsdaughter

ARIADNE LED THEM through the market, swinging from one end to the other, hooking onto the rims of top hats and pince-nez, the fingers of bonewoods and the awnings of stalls. Nobody else saw her—she was too deft and swift amid the chaos of Wreathenwold.

"I can't believe it," said Benjamiah, watching her.

"So this is how Edwid found his way around," said

Elizabella. "This thread . . . I've never heard of anything like it. Do you know how valuable she must be? What people would pay for her . . ."

Benjamiah was thinking of home. Could Ariadne show him the way back? She could certainly lead him back to Horis & Hoggish Books, at least, after they'd found Edwid. But would the door be there?

"Edwid must have got her from the Company of Mapmakers," he said.

"But how? How could he have even found the House of Mapmakers? Edwid and I always talked about visiting there one day, to see the Mapmakers. But it's impossible!"

"Edwid must have found a way," said Benjamiah. "Maybe that's where he went, the first time he ran away?"

Elizabella lapsed into deep thought. Benjamiah recalled Hansel saying that Edwid had become distant from Elizabella after he first ran away and returned with color-less eyes. No doubt she was still hurt and confused about it.

So drastically had Elizabella's mood improved that, before leaving the market, she suggested buying some sweets. Benjamiah thought that was the best idea she'd had so far. They headed toward a huge, carnival-like tent embla-zoned with the words MISS BLISS'S CONFECTIONS. Ariadne took refuge in Benjamiah's breast pocket.

Stepping inside, they found paradise. Even the air tasted of sugar. Benjamiah's head swam with the wave of delicious smells—honey, caramel, sticky fruit. Mountains of strange sweets surrounded them, stalls crammed with jars, piles of sticky pastries gathered in baskets. Throughout the tent, bug-eyed children—giggling and charged with sugar—chased fat, fluttering insects, trapping them in their hands and shoving them in their mouths. Some had cast their poppets as birds to help catch them.

"Sugar-flies," said Elizabella. "Maybe the best thing ever, if you can grab one."

Miss Bliss wore a headscarf, walked with a cane, and had a smile as sweet as her shop. For four pieces each, Elizabella and Benjamiah could sample sweets to their heart's content. Benjamiah still hadn't worked out the value of the playing cards, so it was Elizabella who handed over a five of spades. Miss Bliss returned two aces of clubs in change.

Benjamiah didn't know where to begin, so Elizabella took the lead. They tried melts, which hit the tongue in a flood of dreamy sugar. Nuisance the nightjar brought Benjamiah a sugar-fly, which despite his reservations did turn out to be one of the best things he'd ever tasted. They shared opple swirls, plumpkin laces, small sweets called wyrm's eggs that hatched on the tongue in an eruption of fizz and flavor.

"Oh, these are *amazing*!" said Elizabella, pressing a marblelike sweet upon Benjamiah.

Unlike everything else he'd tried, this one was bland and disappointing.

"Doesn't really taste of anything," he said.

But something was wrong. His voice had become high-pitched as though he'd inhaled helium.

"What have you done?" he squeaked.

Elizabella lit up with laughter.

"Stop laughing! Make it stop!"

Which only made it funnier for Elizabella.

"They're called tweet-tweets," she said. "It will wear off soon."

"You're making me very cross!" squeaked Benjamiah, at which Elizabella only laughed harder.

Finally the effect faded. Elizabella stared at the tweet-tweets in her palm, suddenly wistful.

"Edwid and I used to slip those into Hansel's food," she said. "So, when he told us off, it would come out all high-pitched, and he wouldn't know why. We'd laugh so much it hurt."

Benjamiah took the sweets from Elizabella's hand, wrapped them in a handkerchief, and stowed them in his bag.

"Let's save them for Edwid," he said. "He'll need some-thing after we rescue him."

Something about that alarmed Elizabella. She looked at Benjamiah, opened her mouth to speak, and then decided against it. Now she looked serious again. Benjamiah thought that there was one Elizabella wrapped in another— the real one he'd glimpsed eating sweets, now cloaked in a different one.

"We're wasting time," she said. "Let's go."

On they went, jittery from the sugar overload. Ariadne swung from an umbrella to the collar of a woman. There she stayed, a tiny snake hitching a ride, gesturing at the children to follow.

"You mentioned the Minotaur," said Elizabella quietly.

"Just a Greek myth. I guess you don't know about Ancient Greece."

"You shouldn't mention him," said Elizabella. "It's bad luck."

"What do you mean?"

"You really don't know?" she said, one eye cocked at him in disbelief.

"I've told you," said Benjamiah. "I'm not from here."

"*Everybody's* from here," she said. "There is only the labyrinth going on forever. You must be from somewhere in Wreathenwold. Come on, stop pretending. You can fool Hansel, but you can't fool me."

"Why would I want to fool Hansel?"

"Another lost boy," said Elizabella with a shrug, "looking for a home. And a family. Or maybe you're in trouble. A criminal. A pocket-picker or a color-poacher. Or a smuggler for the Crowe twins. Come on, just admit it."

"You're wrong," said Benjamiah. "I would never do that. If you don't believe me, that's up to you. If I hadn't come, we wouldn't have Ariadne. You'd still be squashed between those barrels with no clue where to go."

Elizabella went quiet, seeming to accept the truth of what he said—not that she'd admit it.

"What did you mean about the Minotaur?" said Benjamiah eventually.

"Who do you think lives at the center of the labyrinth?"

The labyrinth. The bull-head clips of the Hanged Men. The grotesques with the heads of bulls. It dawned upon him slowly. . . .

"The Minotaur is *real*?" said Benjamiah.

"You are so strange," said Elizabella. "Of *course* he's real. Who do you think rules Wreathenwold?"

"A monster . . . rules Wreathenwold?"

A long stare followed, in which Elizabella seemed to grapple with the possibility that Benjamiah really was a stranger to her world.

"People don't talk about him," she said. "Nobody ever sees him. All the innermost streets of Wreathenwold are his, surrounding the Shrouded Palace where he lives. That's the castle built by the magi who formed the labyrinth, before they were murdered. Nobody goes anywhere near it. They say the Minotaur eats lost people—anybody who wanders too close. Children are his favorite."

Benjamiah felt dazed, a chill spidering down his spine.

"So did the Minotaur murder the magi?"

Elizabella looked around anxiously, wary of eaves-droppers.

"No," she hissed. "Somebody else did. But we can't talk about that here."

"How does a monster rule Wreathenwold?" said Benjamiah.

"He doesn't do much ruling," said Elizabella. "The Captains of the Companies do that for him. There are ninety-eight Honorable Companies, some more powerful than others. But the Hanged Men ultimately serve the Minotaur. Which means he's in charge."

"And what's the Viper?" said Benjamiah.

"Where did you hear about her?" said Elizabella, looking grave.

"The House of Hanged Men."

Before Hansel had rescued Benjamiah, he recalled the man being dragged into the House of Hanged Men. He'd been deranged with fear and howling about the Viper.

Elizabella looked around warily again. She'd paled at the mention of the Viper.

"The Viper is Odith Murdstone," she said, so quietly that Benjamiah had to lean in. "Captain of the Company of Colornomics. One of the most powerful people in

Wreathenwold. She's in charge of all the color and money, which she mostly hoards for herself. She taxes the poor until they're ruined. She gives loans that she knows people can't repay, only to demand ten times the amount in interest. She's *obsessed* with money. People say most of the color-poaching leads right back to her. And she's obsessed with extracting and collecting eye colors, especially from children. Even does the procedure herself, apparently."

Elizabella finished with a shiver. Odith Murdstone sounded despicable, though she didn't trouble Benjamiah nearly as much as the Minotaur. What if they took the wrong turn, or lost Ariadne, and found themselves in the path of that terrible monster?

Luckily, nothing of the sort happened the rest of the day. Guided by Ariadne, they threaded a street where lightning blazed in the moody sky above rows of Gothic marble buildings guarded by Hanged Men. They battled through a street where the snow was knee-deep and whipped against their pink cheeks, gathering in their hats and stiffening their fingers.

Along a street of taverns and theaters they followed Ariadne, their feet becoming so sore that eventually they paid for a hansom cab to take them from one end to the other, and they did the same on the next street, and the street after that. It proved a more agreeable way to travel—both children read while the clockwork horses pulled them onward. Benjamiah continued with *A Brief History of Wreathenwold*, and Elizabella read *Jamima Cleaves and the Secret Deaths*.

"Don't you find that boring?" she asked.

"Facts are never boring," said Benjamiah.

Elizabella looked baffled.

"What's it about, anyway?" he said, gesturing to her book.

"Oh, Jamima is solving a series of deaths caused by a secret," said Elizabella. "Secrets in Wreathenwold can be cursed so that anybody who hears them will die shortly afterward. But secrets want to live and want to be told. They're like a virus. It takes a dark kind of magic to curse a secret, though. You'd only do it to the most dangerous kind."

Benjamiah shook his head. He would have put it down as more nonsense had he not soon reached a section in *A Brief History of Wreathenwold* that confirmed what Elizabella had said. Archscholar Wolfsdaughter said witchcraft could be used to curse the most dangerous secrets so that whoever heard them would become ill and soon lose their life. It was supposed to stop the secret from spreading. But like Elizabella said, secrets wanted to be told, wanted to be found. Whoever harbored the secret would be desperate to tell it—before the secret killed them.

On a sunny street, they had lunch sitting outside beneath the boughs of a bonewood tree. Nuisance, now a capuchin, was playfighting with Ariadne under the table. They had sweetdough sandwiches and milk punch. The two meals cost seven pieces, which Elizabella had paid for with an ace of diamonds and a two of spades.

"Hearts are worth the most, then diamonds, then spades, then clubs," she'd said, as though talking to a dimwit. "An ace is worth the least, a king the most. An ace of clubs is one piece. A king of hearts is thirteen bits. I've never even seen one."

Benjamiah had one in his deck. He gave it to Elizabella.

"Now you have," he said. "Keep it."

This act of casual generosity seemed to embarrass Elizabella, who finished her milk punch in a daze while Benjamiah read. He could have sworn she was trying not to smile.

Their strength regathered, Ariadne led them on. Streets of rain, streets of cloud, streets of dazzling sunlight. Warm streets, cold streets, streets that went on forever and streets no longer than a Wyvern-on-the-Water lane. A woman in a shabby waistcoat offered Benjamiah two hundred bits for each of his eye colors. It frightened Benjamiah enough that he wore his despectacles all the time afterward.

In a fountain—a great stone rendering of the Minotaur at its center—a group of children raced their poppets, an array of varicolored fish doing laps as the children hooted and bickered.

They walked an entire street filled with soulblooms, flowers of dazzling color atop glassy stems, rising from the soil behind inscribed marble plaques. Names, the year the person died, epitaphs—some of them lost to moss.

"The color is the color of our soul," whispered a respectful Elizabella. "The most radiant soulblooms were the most radiant people."

Benjamiah thought back to the mesmerizing purple of Elizabella's mother's soulbloom. She must have been wonderful.

Evening drew in. The two children were exhausted. They walked a street beneath a turquoise sky falling into layers of violet, tangerine, and indigo toward the horizon. Smoke unfurled dreamily from chimneys. A shabby young boy was lighting oil lamps with his flaming poppet.

"I wonder how much further it is," said Elizabella. "Shame she can't talk."

Even Ariadne seemed tired. She was coiled on Nuisance, who was a nightjar again. The bird could apparently interpret Ariadne's increasingly weary directions.

"Edwid won't be able to help you get home," said Elizabella suddenly.

"We can ask him," said Benjamiah.

Elizabella was silent, struggling with something unseen.

"Ariadne will, anyway," said Benjamiah. "After we've found Edwid. Everything can be fixed. We can get Edwid home safely. I can find my way back. That's how life is: everything has a solution if you work hard enough to find it."

Elizabella shook her head. "No, life isn't like that," she said, sounding sad. "Not everything can be fixed. Or solved. I wish it were like that."

Something squirmed in Benjamiah's stomach. He thought of Mum and Dad, their marriage. There had to be a way to fix it all. There were answers to every problem, weren't there?

The street ended in a wide stone staircase trailing downward and turning out of sight. Elizabella, Benjamiah, Nuisance, and Ariadne followed it until they emerged in the next street.

Before them was the Whispering Wood—and it was breathtaking.

A dusting of delicate snow lay over everything, drifting in dreamy flakes. Trees were sparser here than in the Smoking Orchard, undressed of leaves, shorter and stouter with boughs that flowed in a bell shape like weeping willows. Hanging from the branches were lanterns of all different sizes and designs, flames flickering within. There were thousands of them, a galaxy of candle flames—constellations and nebulae, myriad hypnotic patterns as far as the eye could see, glorious in the gathering dark. It was serene and astonishing.

Their boots crunched in the snow as they edged forward, passing beneath the first tree. Above them, the lanterns glowed, rocking gently in the breeze, sprinkled with snow.

"What is this place?" said Elizabella.

Benjamiah had no answer. Even Nuisance was behaving, rendered solemn by the scene before them. Ariadne was coiled nervously on the nightjar's back.

Soft feet approached from behind.

"Good evening, children. I am Honeysuckle. Can I help you?"

One of the Root Folk loomed over them. Honeysuckle was tall and lean, olive-skinned, and wrapped in shawls of silver and blue. Her hair was a wreath of flowers, meadow-smelling, her eyes muddy and somnolent. She had a smile as bright and gentle as a candle flame. Rattling on her wrists were bracelets of dice.

Having introduced themselves, Elizabella handed over the key. Honeysuckle took it in patterned hands, rotating it gently, before lifting her gaze to Elizabella.

"I remember this one," she said. "I made it myself. And I remember your face."

"My face . . . ?"

"You are identical," said Honeysuckle, smiling.

Elizabella's face lit up. "You remember Edwid?"

"I do," said Honeysuckle. "It isn't every day that a child

comes here. And I can't remember any child buying four whisperwicks at once."

"Whisperwicks?"

Honeysuckle gestured to the lanterns.

"What are they?" asked Benjamiah.

"Messages," said Honeysuckle. "Memories. Words left behind. Every candle flame is a voice. People leave them for their families, so that one day they can unlock the lantern and hear the words of their loved one again. Only once, though. When the lantern is open, and the message is heard, the candle goes out forever."

"Why would Edwid do that?" said Elizabella, face creased in confusion. "Did he tell you?"

"It's not my place to ask why," said Honeysuckle.

"So this key opens four different whisperwicks?" said Elizabella.

Honeysuckle nodded. "You see the four threads trailing to the tip? Each opens a different lantern."

"Can you show me which ones?"

"I cannot."

This shocked Elizabella. She stared open-mouthed, snow fluttering upon her straw hat. Darkness was setting in, the forest of candles burning bolder.

"Why not?" she said quietly.

"Because it isn't my place," said Honeysuckle. "I make the whisperwicks and the keys. Beyond that, I play no part.

It is up to whoever left the whisperwick to instruct their loved ones on how to find them. I cannot interfere."

"You don't understand," said Elizabella, trying to keep her cool. "My brother has been taken, so he can't tell me. What he hid in the whisperwicks will help us find him."

"I am sorry to hear that," said Honeysuckle. "Truly. But I cannot help."

Elizabella's temper sparked. She glared up at Honeysuckle.

"I want my brother back," she said, hands on hips, voice low. "You have to help me. You *must*."

"If I could, I would," said Honeysuckle. "I am governed by greater obligations. I cannot interfere. Not under any circumstances."

"So you don't even care?"

Quiet fell, broken only by the feathery fall of snow, the creak of branches and lanterns in the breeze. Elizabella glowered, but Honeysuckle was adamant.

"Your love makes you fierce," she said. "Your love brought you here. It is a map. Let it be a guide here too."

"It's impossible without your help," said Elizabella, now a picture of despair.

"It is no such thing," said Honeysuckle. "Look more closely at the lanterns."

Benjamiah joined Elizabella in examining the whisperwicks hanging from the nearest bough. No two were alike. One was shaped like an opple, with a trim of silver and a strange coat of arms. Another was the head of a hound, another a cornucopia of gold.

"The lanterns are made precisely as instructed," said Honeysuckle. "Your brother chose everything. Shape, color, detail. If you know your brother, perhaps there is hope."

With that, she left, drifting through the trees. Elizabella, confronted with this most peculiar of enigmas, looked bereft.

"How will we ever find them?" she said.

Benjamiah took out Edwid's notebook. Elizabella had been correct—all the little drawings of maps had shifted, as though every stroke of the pencil were a snake that had slithered and settled in a new configuration. Even words seemed to have changed, or crept across the page, now attached to different features. There were several sketches of great complexity—smaller tangles of streets, not the great sweeping arcs of Wreathenwold—which looked less like maps and more like oddly shaped, self-contained labyrinths. Edwid had added no notes beside these.

While Benjamiah flicked through, Elizabella wandered the forest, muttering to herself as she walked, key in hand. From where he stood, Benjamiah heard random words like "Prendelgast" and "opple" and "treacle tea." He watched

Elizabella try random lanterns, saw her disappointment renew itself with every failure.

"It looks like a tree," said Benjamiah, showing one page to Nuisance and Ariadne.

And it did. It was a series of streets whose overall shape, if Benjamiah squinted, resembled a bell-shaped tree. More time passed in which Benjamiah tried to make sense of the notebook, and Elizabella looked increasingly cold and dispirited among the candlelit trees.

Benjamiah joined her. "What animals does he make?" he asked.

"I don't need your help."

"You can't just try every lantern. We'll be here for months."

Elizabella glared. "He cast all kinds of spells," she said, hands on hips.

"Does he have a favorite? The Hanged Men always seem to cast tigers. There was that woman in the tearoom with a tarantula on her arm. Do people cast some spells more than others? Don't you?"

Elizabella nodded. "A bear."

"What about Edwid?"

"He liked to cast an owl," she said, "when he was thinking about stuff."

"Let's start there," said Benjamiah. "Find any that look like owls. We'll check every tree if we need to."

Not for the first time, Elizabella seemed moved by

Benjamiah's determination to help, though she was unable to articulate it. He didn't mind. He went one way and Elizabella the other, and they investigated tree after tree, branch after branch, lantern after lantern. Staring at the candles—set against the dark air—stung Benjamiah's eyes. A desire to sleep pulled at him.

Between them, they found several lanterns resembling owls. Edwid's key fitted none of them. Elizabella slumped on a fallen tree and buried her face in her hands.

"Don't give up," said Benjamiah. "What else does Edwid like? He would choose something meaningful."

So Elizabella talked about her brother, summoning random facts and memories in the hope it would inspire something. He liked treacle tea and wyrm's eggs and plumpkin soup. They couldn't envisage a lantern shaped like any of those. He liked adventure books, racing poppets with Wilfrid Shiren and the other boys from the street. He was interested in puzzles, clockwork animals, steam engines.

"Those things are too generic," said Benjamiah. "Not personal enough. What about Edwid as a person?"

Elizabella crafted a picture of him that was similar to Hansel's, though with a softer edge. Like Hansel, Elizabella talked movingly of his mischief, his determination, his single-mindedness. But she also described a twin brother who cared, who never let her down. Who stayed up all night with Elizabella when she was frightened of Agatha Drake—an ancient witch said to visit children during the Festival of Midsommer. Edwid helped Elizabella with her dollcasting, always shared his milk punch, never failed to light a smile on her lips whenever she was sad.

"Who's his favorite person?" said Benjamiah.

Elizabella's cheeks filled with color, her eyes glistening.

"Probably me," she said, sounding terribly sad.

The answer dawned on them both at the same time. They weren't looking for an owl, Edwid's favorite spell. They were looking for Elizabella's—a bear.

The excitement provided new energy.

"There's one here!" Elizabella shouted.

"Here, too!" Benjamiah shouted back.

Some were shaped like a bear's head. Others were shaped like an entire bear sitting on its haunches. Some were white, some silver, some gold. They had tried many, hope rising and falling, when Nuisance the nightjar fluttered into Benjamiah's face, was swatted away, and retreated to a small lantern nearby—unassuming and coppery and shaped like a bear's face.

"Here," said Benjamiah, breath smoking.

Elizabella joined him. It felt like their last chance. With a trembling hand, she lifted the key. Benjamiah had his arms wrapped across his chest, shaking with the cold, his hair wet and feet aching. Elizabella's cheeks were red-raw.

The key slotted in with a click. Then one of the threads on the needle began to wriggle, crawling into the keyhole like a caterpillar, disappearing within. There was another click and the lantern unlocked. Elizabella and Benjamiah swapped a glance—one that muddled relief, excitement, nervousness. Elizabella opened the glass door. A boy's whisper poured out:

> *A door that moves not out nor in,*
> *And guarded by our every sin.*

Then the candle went out, and silence fell.

"Edwid . . . ," said Elizabella.

Unexpectedly, she covered her face with her hands. Benjamiah had the distinct impression that, behind her fingers, she was crying.

Embarrassed, he committed the couplet to memory, then took out Edwid's notebook and scribbled it down. He held it in front of Elizabella's face.

"Any idea what it means?" he said, waiting for her to lower her hands.

She read the words with dazed, bloodshot eyes. Gradually they came back into focus.

"Absolutely none," she said. "No idea at all. What could that *possibly* mean?"

"Maybe it's where we'll find Edwid," said Benjamiah. "Or at least where we might find some answers."

"But it means *nothing*," said Elizabella, sighing.

She grabbed the notebook from Benjamiah's hand, pulling it closer to her eyes, as if trying to force it to reveal more.

"Remember what Honeysuckle told us?" said Benjamiah. "Edwid paid for *four* whisperwicks. Maybe they mean something *together*."

A moment of consideration, then Elizabella dashed off. Benjamiah followed. They found Honeysuckle in the hollow of an enormous tree. She was singing softly, sketching out an elaborate lantern on a great sheaf of papyrus. A log fire burned beside her. Spread across her workbench were half-made lanterns, pots of wax, an array of tools. Candles burned, giving off cloying perfumes, weaving trails of heavy and fragrant smoke.

"Help us find the others," said Elizabella, breathless. "Edwid's other lanterns . . . We found one . . . The bear . . . Where are the others? Please, you have to help. *Please . . .*"

"Calm down, my child," said Honeysuckle, rising. "Be still a moment. Warm yourself. Would you like a drink?"

Elizabella was a hurricane in a bottle, ready to burst. But Honeysuckle's voice was soothing and musical. She led Elizabella and Benjamiah to stools beside the firepit, and laid blankets round their shoulders. The welcome warmth prickled Benjamiah's skin. Honeysuckle gave them each a wooden tumbler of hot treacle tea, spiced with something exotic. Its warmth and flavor flooded Benjamiah.

Honeysuckle sat on the other side of the firepit. Flames danced and twisted in her eyes.

"Your brother paid for four whisperwicks," she said. "And I made them."

"Yes, but please can you help us find the others? We've been looking for ages and only found one. We think the message will only make sense once we've found them all—"

Honeysuckle lifted a hand, and Elizabella fell silent.

"The other three are not here," she said softly. "Your brother left one in the Whispering Wood. He took the others with him. I have no idea where they are. I'm sorry."

It struck Elizabella like a punch to the gut. Her body emptied of breath, her face blanching.

"You mean . . . ," she whispered, "you mean they could be *anywhere*?"

Honeysuckle gave a melancholy nod. "I can only repeat what I said earlier. Your love for your brother is your map. It is formidable. It could slay monsters. Do not underestimate it. Love knows no labyrinth. Love can guide us out of the darkest of places."

Benjamiah eyed Elizabella—she looked blank, like her mind was a thousand miles away.

"Are all Edwid's lanterns the same?" Benjamiah asked Honeysuckle.

"Yes," she said. "Four identical whisperwicks. A tribute to his twin sister."

It was too much for Elizabella. She set her cup down and unwrapped herself slowly from the blanket. Then she stood, a fragile grip on her composure, and left the tree.

"Your friend needs you," said Honeysuckle. "Go after her."

"I'm not sure she wants me to be her friend," said Benjamiah.

"Not yet," said Honeysuckle. "But she will not make it without you. She is more lost than you know. She cannot yet say what must be said. Do not give up on her."

What did that mean? What needed to be said? Benjamiah wasn't convinced Elizabella would ever need him. He had no friends at home. Why would he have any here?

"And one other thing," said Honeysuckle. "Do not refuse it."

"Refuse what?" said Benjamiah, bewildered.

"The connection you feel with this poppet," she said, gesturing to Nuisance, now a capuchin. He was dipping a furry finger into Honeysuckle's pots of wax.

"But he isn't mine," said Benjamiah.

"Not until you let him be," said Honeysuckle. "Do you feel nothing when you look at him?"

Benjamiah stared at the mischievous monkey. Nuisance turned his gaze to Benjamiah, black-and-red fur, big buttons for eyes. Something beat in the dark reaches of

Benjamiah's mind, like a muscle he'd never accessed. He found it terrifying and thrilling at the same time.

"I know you're afraid," said Honeysuckle. "It will not do. You and your friend will not make it if you live in denial. A terrible darkness follows this missing boy and his lanterns. I feel it gathering, pressing upon us all. Now go. You are needed."

Unsure what else to say, Benjamiah said goodbye and left Honeysuckle's hollow. Elizabella had picked up her bag and slung it over her shoulder. Her eyes had a glassy, far-off quality. Ariadne was dangling lazily from a branch.

"It's a start," said Benjamiah.

"It's nothing," said Elizabella. "We have nothing. A message that means absolutely nothing. The other three whisperwicks could be hidden anywhere. Wreathenwold is a labyrinth, remember? Even with Ariadne, it's completely hopeless."

"Maybe not," said Benjamiah.

"Just accept it."

"We might have something," he said. "In Edwid's notebook."

Elizabella's attention snapped onto him, as swift and hard as an elastic band.

"What do you mean?" she said.

Benjamiah took out the notebook and showed Elizabella the self-contained maze that resembled a tree.

"We found one of the whisperwicks in a tree," said Benjamiah. "Look here, on this page. This isn't a map. This is a drawing made to look like a map. Edwid kept a record of where he hid them. I think there might be others that show where the lanterns are hidden."

Elizabella snatched the notebook out of Benjamiah's hand, racing through the pages, tutting and griping as she examined page after page beneath the weak light of a lantern. She was too frustrated to absorb anything.

Gently Benjamiah drew the notebook from her hands.

"Nothing!" she said despairingly.

"Look, we're exhausted," said Benjamiah. "Let's get some sleep. We can start again in the morning."

Elizabella, her face drained and gaunt, conceded.

TWELVE

WITH EDWID'S CLUES

Theoretically, there are only two limiting influences on the practice of dollcasting—law and taboo. Law prohibits the casting of lethal spiders and snakes, as well as various monsters that are considered too dangerous. Casting one's doll as a human is the most unpalatable taboo, reviled and deeply offensive.

—*A Brief History of Wreathenwold*,
Archscholar Collum Wolfsdaughter

BENJAMIAH PAID four bits and four pieces for two single rooms, including dinner and breakfast. Slowly he was getting the hang of how much each playing card was worth, though he still needed Elizabella's help in settling on the seven of diamonds and four of clubs to meet the bill.

The inn was called The Snug. It was cozy enough, the rooms small with dark beams and bonewood wainscotting and hearths with roaring fires. On the walls were various ghoulish paintings: one showed a monstrous serpent with baleful eyes called the Greatslang, hooded like a cobra with tusks curving from its lower jaw.

After dinner and a quick wash, Benjamiah climbed into bed, exhausted. Nuisance lay on the wobbly bedside table, in doll form. Before closing his eyes, Benjamiah reached out and rested his hand upon him. Though Nuisance had led Benjamiah into this mess, Benjamiah felt increasingly close to the poppet—and found he wanted Nuisance nearby at all times.

His last thoughts, before drifting off to sleep, were of Grandma, Mum, and Dad. They would be sick with worry, frantic and bewildered. He wished he could write them a letter. He'd tell them he was safe, that he'd be home soon, and that he missed them all enormously.

Benjamiah woke to sunlight poking through the curtains, a capuchin hooting on his headboard and a fist pounding on his door.

Throwing on some clothes, he flapped a hand at Nuisance and blundered over to the door. Visions of Hanged Men come to arrest him quickly gave way to reality. It was, of course, Elizabella, smartly dressed, bright-eyed, and extremely cross.

"Finally," she said. "Were you planning on sleeping all day?"

She bundled past him. A glance at the clock told Benjamiah it had been daylight for about ten minutes. Elizabella had brought sweetdough rolls and smokeberry juice. She had also brought Edwid's notebook, and a demand that Benjamiah get immediately to work.

"I can't see anything in here," she said, slapping the book down on his bed.

They spent the entire morning in Benjamiah's room, him flicking through the scores of maps and configurations, Elizabella pacing and complaining.

"I knew it was too good to be true," she snapped after an hour with no success. "There's nothing there. It's hopeless!"

"It just needs patience," said Benjamiah through gritted teeth. "Have you ever heard of patience? We need to check all the drawings. *Carefully.*"

This quieted Elizabella's objections, but did nothing to ease her restlessness. She paced, lay on the bed, sprang up, and sat in the armchair by the bookcase, sighing and clicking her tongue and breathing noisily out of her nose. Combined with Nuisance fluttering about and Ariadne swinging along the curtain rail, it would be a miracle if Benjamiah made any progress at all.

As if she weren't being distracting enough, Elizabella unhitched her poppet and sent the midnight blue doll cartwheeling through the air. Barely an inch above the rug, Emba's head blossomed and a snout poked out, the marble eyes swelling, the dark blue leather expanding in a wildfire of muscle and fur. In an instant, Emba was a bear with bluish fur, tinged with white on the throat, round, smoky eyes turning one way and another. She was not much bulkier than a large dog.

"That bear isn't very big," observed Benjamiah.

"I'm *eleven*," said Elizabella. "You can't expect my spells to be fully grown. Now focus."

How was he supposed to focus? There was a juvenile, marble-eyed bear roaming the little room, sniffing, knocking things off the mantelpiece.

"How does it work?" asked Benjamiah.

"How does *what* work?"

"Casting spells," he said. "Is there an incantation you say in your head?"

Elizabella snorted. "No, there's no *incantation*," she said, as Emba stood, as tall as Elizabella, and patted Elizabella's hands with her paws, left and then right. "You learn from spellbooks. You learn about animals' body shapes, their muscles, their organs. Their habits and personalities. You have to commit it all to memory."

That explained the spellbooks Benjamiah saw in Follynook.

"But how do you control them?" he said.

"It's . . . I can't explain," said Elizabella. "Only a dollcaster could understand it. It's like your poppet is a muscle—a set of muscles—that you can flex and relax. In your mind."

To demonstrate, Emba became a capuchin. The capuchin did a handstand. Benjamiah thought both Emba and Elizabella were show-offs, though he kept it to himself.

He watched Nuisance, who was doing his best to irritate the dignified and obedient Emba. As he had before, Benjamiah felt something twinge at the shadowy edges of his mind. A sensation he felt he could access if the thought weren't so terrifying. Was that the muscle that Elizabella was referring to? But how? Nuisance wasn't his poppet. But then hadn't Honeysuckle warned Benjamiah about refusing the connection?

"There's something called aether," said Elizabella. "Aether is like . . . It's hard to explain. It's like the air *beneath* the air. Like every speck of aether is a space that air or dust or wood occupies. The material of the doll, in this case. Our poppets are our little parcel of aether. Do you understand?"

Benjamiah wasn't sure. Not understanding was new to him, and he didn't like the feeling. He remembered explaining triangles to Lucy Thompson when she was struggling. Now he had a glimpse of how she must have felt.

"Anyway, we're getting distracted. Concentrate."

Benjamiah went back to work, swallowing some rude replies. While Elizabella cast spells round him, Benjamiah painstakingly identified three more concentrations of streets that resembled broader shapes. By this point, Emba was a cat and had trapped Nuisance the dormouse between her paws.

"Look at these," said Benjamiah, prying Nuisance from Emba's grip.

Elizabella dashed over. Benjamiah showed her the three shapes in turn. Her face remained expressionless.

"Do they look like anything to you?" said Benjamiah.

"No. Nothing."

"This one's like a bird. Here's its head, the beak . . ."

Benjamiah pointed everything out. Elizabella's lips were pursed, her eyes blank.

"I think it's a raven, to be more precise," said Benjamiah. "Could be a crow. The dimensions would fit. More like a raven. They have bigger, curvier beaks."

"What about the others?" asked Elizabella.

"This one," said Benjamiah, finding the page, "looks like the head of a snake with its mouth open. These are fangs. . . ."

Elizabella looked unconvinced. "And the other one?"

Benjamiah took a deep breath, turning to one of the last pages in the notebook.

"It's the head of a bull," he said. "Which probably means . . ."

"The Minotaur." Elizabella finished the sentence for him.

She sat on the edge of the bed. Ariadne was spiraling up and down the headboard like a bored, sleepy snake. Dust swam in the sunlight coming through the window.

"A raven. A snake. The Minotaur."

"Maybe they aren't where the whisperwicks are hidden," said Benjamiah.

"What else could they be?"

Benjamiah shrugged.

"They have to be," said Elizabella. "They *have* to be. One was shaped just like a tree from the Whispering Wood!"

"It could be a coincidence," said Benjamiah.

"No, it has to be Edwid's record of where he hid them."

"Only because you want it to be," said Benjamiah, wary of Elizabella's temper. "Because if they aren't, we have nothing else."

"Fine," she said. "They have to be because we have nothing else. They're all we have. So I'm going to assume they are."

"Well, what do they mean?" asked Benjamiah.

"The tree we found," said Elizabella, "in the Whispering Wood. The Minotaur is obvious, though could Edwid really have hidden one *there* . . . ? Perhaps the Minotaur means something else. We'll have to figure that out later. I have no idea about the raven. But the snake . . ."

Elizabella lapsed into thought, shaking her head.

"Look at it," she said. "It's a particular kind of snake. A viper. Which can only mean *the* Viper. There are no other vipers in Wreathenwold. Even casting a viper is forbidden, precisely because of *the* Viper. Odith Murdstone. Captain of the Company of Colornomics. She lives at the Magimmaculum, where they trade color. Though why Edwid would risk going there . . ."

Elizabella's dire warnings about the character of the Viper rang through Benjamiah's mind. His stomach twisted, all barbs and edges.

"Why would Edwid leave a whisperwick anywhere near Odith Murdstone?" he said, finding his voice had thickened.

"It's *obvious* he didn't want the whisperwicks to be found," said Elizabella. "Hence hiding them at all. If he didn't want them to be found, perhaps he thought the best option was to hide them where nobody would dare to look. Before Edwid . . . Before he *left*, he told me to burn the notebook."

That was new information. "Why didn't you?" said Benjamiah.

"I didn't want to lose any more of him."

It was a moment of bare honesty that surprised, and saddened, Benjamiah. Elizabella fidgeted, apparently embarrassed. But the idea that Edwid had asked his sister to burn the notebook worried Benjamiah.

"Then why are we trying to find the whisperwicks?"

"Because we have nothing else!" snapped Elizabella. "Nothing! The whisperwicks might hold the key to why somebody would want to take Edwid in the first place. If we find that out, we might find *him*. We have to find them, no matter what Edwid wanted."

Benjamiah didn't look convinced. Neither, in truth, did Elizabella.

"Honeysuckle told me something before we left the Whispering Wood," he said.

He recited her warning about a darkness following Edwid and his whisperwicks. Elizabella was unmoved.

"I don't care about any of that. As I've said, you're welcome to leave," she said. "But I'm going. Ariadne?"

The thread stood to attention.

"Take me to the Magimmaculum."

Twenty minutes later, Elizabella was back in her coat and straw hat, bag on her back and poppet hitched to her hip, following Ariadne down the street.

Behind her trailed Benjamiah and Nuisance.

They traveled the entire day, through sun and mist, rain and hail. For the most part, they walked, though they took some streets in hansoms when their legs ached or the weather was too inclement. A stiffness remained between Elizabella and Benjamiah, their exchanges terse and businesslike. Mostly Elizabella was swamped by her own thoughts, worries playing out on her face, muttering to herself. Benjamiah kept himself to himself, taking in the wonders of the city when they walked and reading *A Brief History of Wreathenwold* at every opportunity.

Occasionally, they encountered people who had cast their dolls as horses, on which they rode.

"Couldn't we do that with Emba?" said Benjamiah.

"I'm too young," said Elizabella. "She'd be too small. Wouldn't be able to carry us both."

Night came with no apparent prospect of reaching the Magimmaculum, so they found rooms at a dingy tavern and continued their journey the next morning. The following day was much the same—a palette of varying weather, long streets alive with sights that continued to bewilder Benjamiah. They saw carnivals and clockwork chess players like the Mechanical Turk in booths (Elizabella wouldn't let Benjamiah play them). They passed the vast marble mausoleum of the Company of Dying, Death, and the Dead, guarded by two ominous robed figures wearing plague-doctor masks and armed with scythes.

"What is the Magimmaculum?" Benjamiah asked over lunch at a tearoom.

Elizabella looked up from her plumpkin soup. She hadn't eaten much—she seemed thinner every day.

"Doesn't taste like Hansel's," she said, pushing the bowl away.

"Do you miss him?"

Elizabella's eyes narrowed, unwilling to answer.

"The Magimmaculum is where we'll find the Viper," she said. "She lives there."

"How do you know she lives there?" said Benjamiah.

"Everybody does," said Elizabella. "Well, *almost* everybody."

Benjamiah ignored that and went back to his book.

It was then, reading *A Brief History of Wreathenwold*, that he found the answer to a question he had asked both Hansel and Elizabella. Both of them had avoided answering it, he recalled. What had happened to the last of the magi? Who had murdered them?

This is how the story goes.

There were twelve magi left. Their numbers had dwindled over the centuries. Mad and paranoid, they had twisted Wreathenwold into a vast labyrinth and lived in a palace at its center. From there, they ruled, venturing out only to inflict cruelty upon the dollcasters.

They had servants at the palace,

dollcasters forced to serve or entertain them. One was a maid named Osmeralda.

Little is known about Osmeralda prior to these events. It is understood that she fell in love with another dollcaster, likely another servant at the palace. They were deeply in love and wonderfully happy, despite the cruelty of their masters.

But then Osmeralda's beau fell gravely ill. When nothing else could save him, Osmeralda begged the magi for help. The magi—who had the entire aether at their command and whose power was immense—could not or would not help.

Osmeralda's lover died. The precise facts of what followed are uncertain, but it is understood that Osmeralda—deformed by pain and fury and drawing upon some wicked, unknown sorcery of the like no dollcaster should possess—slaughtered the magi in their palace. Rumors persist that one of the twelve magi betrayed his kin and helped her, perhaps himself in love with Osmeralda—this has never been proven.

With the magi murdered, Osmeralda christened herself the Widow and renamed her doll Grief. Her fury did not subside with the killing of the magi. Upon all of Wreathenwold she wreaked a devastation and slaughter the like of which surpassed the worst deeds of the magi. Never had there been a dollcaster as powerful as the Widow, nor has there been since.

For twenty-one years, the Widow ruled and razed Wreathenwold—doubtless the darkest age in recorded history. Her fury was apocalyptic, her savagery without parallel. Entire streets were burned, families slaughtered. All was darkness and ash and terror.

Then came the Minotaur, who finally overthrew the Widow. It is said the grotesques that adorn Wreathenwold to this day were his army. Nothing is known of the Minotaur prior to these events, and still little is understood about him.

The Widow was executed, and the Minotaur remains our ruler, though naturally the ninety-eight Honorable Companies handle all actual governance. Although almost a hundred years have passed since the Widow was executed, the scars of her

reign remain throughout the labyrinth, and
she is seldom spoken of.

Wolfsdaughter's brief description of the Widow's reign
was enough to make Benjamiah's blood flow cold. Entire
streets burning, smoke and screams and blood. Grief was
like no other poppet—the Widow could split her into
thousands of individual spells, raining plagues of bats,
locusts, and spiders upon the city.

Benjamiah had to stop reading. Elizabella noticed how
quiet he'd fallen, looking faintly sick.

"What's wrong now?" she said, slightly annoyed.

"I was reading about the Widow."

Elizabella paled. "Isn't there something more cheerful
you could read? Try a Jamima Cleaves."

But Benjamiah, for perhaps the first time in his life,
had lost all appetite for reading.

At long last, when Elizabella was ready to explode and even
Benjamiah had begun to wonder if Ariadne was leading
them astray, they reached the Magimmaculum.

The street itself was wide and lined with grand, officious
buildings hewn from marble, all stone gables and colon-
nades and elaborate friezes depicting centaurs and fairies.
Fountains splashed in courtyards of checkered slabs. This
was a street of fabulous wealth, where their shabby attire

and travel-weary expressions marked them out. The people wore fancy frock coats, sparkly waistcoats, pinstriped trousers, dresses, cravats, and umbrellas of bright, bold colors that were therefore worth a small fortune. Gone was the hustle and bustle—here people moved slowly, with all the time and liberty that wealth brings, regarding Benjamiah and Elizabella like something rotten that needed mopping up.

Here the sky was brooding and moody, the clouds bunched and blackish as though on the brink of a thunderstorm. Indeed, sometimes a great throaty thunderclap sounded, and the air was hot and charged. Occasionally, a gunshot of rain fell and burst. Once or twice, lightning lashed.

"Show us the Magimmaculum," Elizabella said to Ariadne.

In truth, it was impossible to miss, a great Gothic building that reminded Benjamiah of the Sagrada Família in Barcelona. He'd visited with Mum, Dad, and Grandma two summers ago. The memory was a sudden, sharp reminder of how much he missed them all. High above were six spires puncturing the sky, each streaked with a spiral of colored glass that twisted to the top. The tallest three were red, blue, and yellow, the shorter three orange, green, and violet. The entire building was of a dark, dreary stone, supported by ornamented flying buttresses adorned with curlicues or whorls, or else the shapes of prancing beasts. Perched at

corners, on ledges, and upon columns were bull-headed grotesques.

Imposed upon the stormy sky, it looked a dreadful, insurmountable place. A wide flight of stone steps joined the street to the great doors of the Magimmaculum. There were Hanged Men everywhere. Impeccably dressed people came and went, waving passes to enter.

"The glass on those spires is worth more than our whole street," said Elizabella bitterly.

"We'll never get in there," said Benjamiah.

"Edwid must have," said Elizabella. "There's got to be a way in. Let's wait and see."

They did so, monitoring the front of the Magimmaculum from the far side of the courtyard through the playing water of an enormous fountain. Water spouted from the horns and mouth of a great stone Minotaur, looking monstrous and mighty. They watched the Magimmaculum for almost two hours. Nuisance frolicked noisily in the water, much to Benjamiah's embarrassment and Elizabella's ire.

"The Hanged Men never leave," said Benjamiah. "There's at least six of them there all the time. They check everybody who goes in and out."

"Maybe we should use our money to buy some expensive clothes," said Elizabella. "And say our parents are inside."

"What if they ask for names?" said Benjamiah. "Or just

tell us to wait? Then we'll have wasted all our playing cards. Maybe there's another way in."

Doing their best not to look suspicious, Elizabella and Benjamiah crossed the courtyard. Thunder trembled, and a smile of blue lightning briefly flared. They sidled along the front of the Magimmaculum and peered down the first gap between the building and an austere-looking library. They saw a courtyard full of tables, where fancy-looking people sipped rosewater or poppysyrup and Hanged Men patrolled.

The gap on the other side was far more promising—a gloomy alleyway, dark and empty, save for a single Hanged Man sitting on a chair. He was stationed next to a door.

"We could take him," said Elizabella. "Emba and I."

"Sure you could," said Benjamiah, rolling his eyes.

"You could distract him and I'd sneak in," she said.

"And then what? Just hope nobody sees you while you spend hours looking for Edwid's whisperwick?"

"It's the best we can do!" snapped Elizabella.

Then the door beside the Hanged Man opened. Two children stepped out, a boy and a girl dressed in flat caps and rags, their faces streaked with soot and their hands grubby. The Hanged Man nodded as they left. Elizabella smiled.

They followed the children down the street. Then Elizabella cornered them. The children looked terrified, even more so as Elizabella shepherded them into an alleyway with a big, dangerous smile on her face.

The children were clearly brother and sister, thin and pale and knobbly. Poppets, frayed and shabby, dangled at their hips.

"What are your names?" said Elizabella.

"Clora Spooler," said the girl. "And this is my brother, Odgar."

"Do you work at the Magimmaculum?" said Elizabella.

Clora and Odgar nodded.

"What do you do there?"

They swapped a glance, swallowed in unison.

"It's okay," said Benjamiah. "We just need to get inside."

"We can't help with that," said Clora, looking terrified. "We'd get in trouble. Terrible trouble . . ."

"How much do they pay you?" asked Elizabella.

"Two bits and seven pieces," said Odgar.

"Each?"

The siblings shook their heads.

"A day?"

"A week," said Clora sadly.

Elizabella took the king of hearts out of her pocket. It was worth thirteen bits. It would take Clora and Odgar nearly five weeks to earn that much, according to Benjamiah's calculations.

"I'll give you this," said Elizabella, "if you do two things for me."

"What things?" said Odgar warily.

"Number one, you take tomorrow off," she said. "And, number two, tell us everything about the Magimmaculum. Everything you know. Everything you can think of. Everything you do there. Every little detail. Do we have a deal?"

Clora and Odgar looked at each other again with their colorless eyes, then cupped their hands and whispered into each other's ears. Eventually they nodded. Elizabella handed over the king of hearts with a smile. Clora took it like it was the most fragile and precious thing in the world.

"Okay," said Elizabella. "Tell us everything."

They sat in the alleyway while Clora and Odgar gave up every detail about the Magimmaculum, starting with their daily duties and moving on to the layout of the building itself. They described the great vaulted trading floor, swarming with color-traders and clerks who howled and bartered. There were the many smoking rooms and bars, with fireplaces to be lit and tended by Clora and Odgar, and offices and studies to be tidied, the corridors that needed sweeping. Benjamiah made notes while Elizabella simply nodded, apparently absorbing information with no need of a record.

"What about the Viper?" she asked.

The siblings shared a mournful look.

"Sometimes we see her," said Odgar, staring down at his tattered shoes. "Sometimes she watches the trading floor. She . . ." He trailed off.

Clora simply added, "Stay out of her way. Just *stay out of her way*, or . . ."

The sentence hung in the air, unfinished and sinister.

After an age, in which Elizabella plied Clora and Odgar for every conceivable detail, the siblings were allowed to leave.

Benjamiah met Elizabella's eyes. She'd taken her despectacles off and her eyes shone, not a single color but an elaborate complex of every imaginable green and strands of brown. They were electrified with purpose.

"We'd better find a bed for the night," she said. "Busy day tomorrow."

Benjamiah's stomach churned. Tomorrow *was* going to be busy—they were breaking into the Magimmaculum.

THIRTEEN

WITH THE MAGIMMACULUM

Color is the standard for the Wreathenwold economy. The primary colors of red, yellow, and blue are most valuable, followed by the secondary and tertiary colors, and so on. With the help of a serum and a ghoulish instrument called a spectractor, color can be extracted from almost all surfaces and materials. Poppets are the only known material from which color cannot be lifted.

—A Brief History of Wreathenwold,
Archscholar Collum Wolfsdaughter

BENJAMIAH BARELY SLEPT. All night his belly was a snake pit. What little rest he got was fleeting, full of slithering, coiling shadows and the hissing of snakes. He woke exhausted, Nuisance the nightjar twittering above him.

Benjamiah studied the happy bird. Why had Nuisance chosen him? Who did Nuisance really belong to? Staring into his small button eyes, Benjamiah felt again that twinge of some impossible connection. If Benjamiah really tried, if he really allowed himself to believe in magic, could he cast Nuisance the way Elizabella cast Emba?

His mind was drawn back to the dreaded Magimmaculum. Were they really going to do this? What if they were wrong about Edwid's drawings? Their only guide was Elizabella's brute-minded determination. As if sensing his fear, Nuisance fluttered down and nuzzled Benjamiah with his beak. Benjamiah was shocked by how much better it made him feel.

Elizabella arrived in Benjamiah's room, looking fresh, composed, and well rested.

"We can't take him," said Elizabella, gesturing to Nuisance. "He'll have to stay here."

The nightjar seemed offended, cocking his head and loosing a sorrowful skirl.

"I'm sorry," Benjamiah said, scratching his feathers. "She's probably right."

Still, Benjamiah would miss him. Being apart from Nuisance felt wrong. And, to make matters worse, Elizabella now held out a shabby doll of lifeless gray, smaller than a real poppet and devoid of any character or features.

"You can't go without a doll," said Elizabella. "Everybody has one."

Benjamiah took it from her. "Where did you get this?" he said, wrinkling his nose. "Is this a real poppet?"

"Of *course* not. There's a toy shop along the street. Nobody will pay any attention to us, so don't worry. Besides, it's not like you can do anything useful with your *real* poppet."

Muttering grumpily, Benjamiah attached the toy poppet to his hip. Nuisance, mortally offended, squawked and fluttered off to sulk. Benjamiah wanted to apologize, but felt sick with nerves.

"You look tired," said Elizabella.

"You don't."

"Slept like the dead," she said. "Are we clear on the plan?"

Benjamiah nodded, then sat on the bed, taking a deep breath.

"You don't have to come," she said.

"You can't do it alone," said Benjamiah.

"I'll work something out."

"I'm coming."

"Fine," said Elizabella. She stood with her hands on her hips, studying Benjamiah. "We don't look shabby enough."

Without warning, she ripped the breast pocket off Benjamiah's waistcoat, and loosened seams here and there. She used soot from the fireplace to grubby up his skin, clothes, and shoes. She did the same to herself.

"Don't lose your despectacles," she said. "Children who live in orphanages don't have pretty brown eyes. If anybody sees yours . . . Well, *just don't let anybody see your eyes.*"

Benjamiah had no response, save for an awkward swallow.

Seeing his terror, Elizabella said, "We can do this. We have Emba. And we're clever."

Benjamiah nodded, pushing the despectacles as tight as he could against the bridge of his nose.

They walked in silence to the Magimmaculum, the streets eerie and empty. A few stars were scattered across the sky, not yet swallowed in the gathering dawn, arranged in constellations alien to those Benjamiah knew so well. What he would give, in that moment, to be gazing at the stars of his own world, far from this crazy plan.

All too quickly, they emerged on the street of the Magimmaculum. Wind scythed, the dark air hot and electrified, the stormy sky all the more disturbing in the murky dawn. A tail of lightning lashed, like Scylla in the black waters of her strait.

"Last chance to go back," said Elizabella.

Benjamiah said nothing. The Magimmaculum rose ahead of them, all spires and spikes and grotesques. Color-traders were dotted around, some smoking pipes beneath the gas lamps. Hanged Men patrolled the front steps. Elizabella and Benjamiah kept their heads down, moving quickly toward the side door.

Approaching the Hanged Man at the servants' entrance

had, for Benjamiah, the slow and dreadful quality of a nightmare. Elizabella had no such reservations.

"Clora and Odgar are unwell," she said confidently. "We're covering for them."

The Hanged Man, face wrapped in sackcloth, was still. Had he rumbled them already? His silence seemed to stretch forever. Benjamiah stared at his silvery gloves—Elizabella had explained that they were coated in fine, para-lyzing prickles that rendered poppets limp and lifeless. If he suspected them, and suddenly snatched Emba . . .

"In you go," he finally said.

Relief flooded Benjamiah. Feeling light-headed, they hurried inside and closed the door, finding themselves at the top of a cold, narrow staircase of dark stone. On the walls were torches in brackets, making minerals in the stone sparkle. Both stood for a moment, catching their breath. They were inside. The door was closed. Forward, for all its terrors, was the only option.

"Let's go," said Elizabella.

Benjamiah nodded. "The cleaning supplies are in a little room on the left. The coal and kindling for the fires are in buckets by the fireplaces."

Elizabella didn't seem to be listening. They headed down the stairs, into a warren of dark corridors where Benjamiah found the room with the cleaning supplies. He grabbed Odgar's polishing accoutrements—cotton pads, a bottle of oil, and a vial of serum that made his eyes water.

"We'll look around down here first," said Elizabella. "Then make our way upstairs. Remember, the whisperwick must be hidden somewhere nobody goes, or somewhere it wouldn't look out of place."

They searched the dark corridors beneath the Magimmaculum, investigating storage rooms and cellars full of barrels and wine, boxes and sheeted furniture, empty rooms at the bottom of little staircases and pantries and larders near the kitchens. Around them the Magimmaculum was coming to life, the sounds of feet and voices muffled through the stone, cooks and housekeepers and servants beginning their day.

"There's nothing down here," said Elizabella. "And I can't imagine Edwid hiding the whisperwick in the kitchens. We need to go up."

Clora and Odgar had described the servants' staircase, which would deliver them to the higher floors of the Magimmaculum. The staircase was narrow, hewn out of gray stone. They passed a barmaid carrying a great barrel on her shoulder, and a scuttling housekeeper with an eye patch. Neither paid them any attention. Through closed doors, they heard movement, voices—the gears of the Magimmaculum were starting to turn.

"We need to search the atrium," said Elizabella. "I'll deal with the fireplaces. Do some polishing or something.

Look busy. But *keep an eye out for the lantern.*"

She took a deep breath, steadied herself, and pushed open the door.

The atrium of the Magimmaculum was breathtaking. Its great ceiling was dome-shaped, inlaid with magnificent frescoes depicting poppets, people, and monsters in fierce, erratic colors and irregular shapes. Windows taller than houses streaked down either side. The floor tiles were like dark mirrors, alive with flecks of color that swam and darted like shoals of tiny fish. At the back was a corridor, lined with velvet and paneled wood, leading to the trading floor. In the center was a grand helical staircase round a great stone tower rising from floor to ceiling. The largest chandelier Benjamiah had ever seen, lit with a thousand candles, hung above them. It was like a monumental upside-down oak tree, rooted in the ceiling, every leaf aflame.

"Could it be hidden in that?" he asked.

"How would Edwid get up there?" said Elizabella, though she looked worried.

"Well, we can't just stand here, gawping," said Benjamiah. "We need to work while we search."

Already he had spotted two Hanged Men by the doors, staring in their direction from across the atrium. Smartly dressed color-traders wrinkled their noses at the mere sight of them too, muttering words like "filthy" and "pitiful."

So Benjamiah buffed and polished whatever wooden

surface he could find, soaking a cotton pad in the oil and the serum and bringing out a sparkle in banisters, wainscotting, and the grandest piano he'd ever seen. Elizabella, meanwhile, tended to the four enormous fireplaces in the atrium, piling up kindling and coal and then lighting batons of rolled-up newspaper with Emba catching fire in her hand. While they worked, they shot glances up at the chandelier and its countless candles, scouting for Edwid's whisperwick.

The atrium grew busier. Color-traders and clerks flowed in greater numbers, the former hum now a din of boasts and greetings and laughter.

Elizabella sidled over to Benjamiah when the fires were lit.

"It isn't up there," she said, looking half-frustrated and half-relieved.

"Good," said Benjamiah. "Let's get out of here."

They hurried between smoking rooms and parlors on the upper floors, lighting fires, wiping, sweeping, and feeling thoroughly miserable. There was no sign of Edwid's lantern anywhere, nor did there seem any prospect of finding it with so much work to do.

Their luck finally changed in yet another smoking room. A pall of smoke hung in the air, fruit-smelling plumes rising from the pipes of color-traders and clerks lounging in squashy armchairs. Elizabella was lighting the fire, Benjamiah buffing the mantelpiece. Two clerks, chubby and smartly dressed, lazed in armchairs nearby, smoking and looking pleased with themselves.

"Have you met the new chap?" said the blond clerk on the left. "Tall fellow. All pale and slick. The Viper likes him."

"I heard he hasn't made many friends," said the brown-haired clerk on the right. "Peculiar chap. Nobody seems to know where he sprang from."

"Curious," said the blond clerk, smoke pouring from his mouth.

"I saw the Viper heading for the trading floor just now," said Brown Hair. "She's keeping a close eye on things at the moment."

"Probably that business with the indigo," said Blond Hair. "Who could have predicted a fall like that?"

"She hasn't been in this foul a mood since her mother died," said Brown Hair, lowering his voice. "What a vicious woman she was too."

"I heard the Viper has a shrine in her suite," replied Blond Hair. "Candles, gifts, flowers. Tributes to the old snake. People leave them to get in Murdstone's good books. Like she has any good books."

The clerks laughed. Elizabella's head cranked toward Benjamiah, her eyes wide.

Candles . . . , she mouthed.

Before Benjamiah could say a word, Elizabella darted off.

He followed. Not bothering to wait for Benjamiah, Elizabella hurried through the door on to the servants' staircase. She tore up the stairs, Benjamiah chasing her, all the way to the top.

"*Elizabella . . . ,*" he panted as she twisted out of sight again and again, shoes slapping on the stone. "*Wait. Elizabella . . .*"

Only at the very top did Benjamiah catch up. Before them was a door marked STRICTLY AUTHORIZED PERSONNEL ONLY, a coiled viper carved into the wood.

"We can't," whispered Benjamiah, breathless. "Clora and Odgar don't tend to the Viper's suite. She has her own servants. If we're seen . . ."

"You heard what they said," said Elizabella, a dangerous light in her eyes. "The Viper has a shrine to her mother. Full of gifts and tributes and *candles*. It's the perfect place for Edwid to hide the whisperwick."

"We'll be caught!" moaned Benjamiah.

"Follow my lead," said Elizabella, opening the door.

Ahead was a corridor, a carpet of moody purple laid on dark, gleaming floorboards. It was dimly lit, the wall panels somber and varnished, huge paintings on either wall—the colors fabulous and the images strange and chaotic, each one signed by an artist named Matador. There were busts and sculptures, too, all of vipers in various positions, fangs bared, eyes popping. It was eerily quiet.

Elizabella scurried forward, Benjamiah following. They saw vipers everywhere—not just the stone sculptures, but woven into the purple carpet, carved into the wall panels, cut into the gas lamps. Even the paintings, among all their hectic sprays of color and uncertain shapes, revealed hidden vipers biting flesh, venom dripping from their jaws.

"The Viper could be here," whispered Benjamiah, feeling faint.

"You heard them. She's on the trading floor."

The corridor ended in a flight of steps swathed in blood-clot purple, which led to the Viper's suite. It was enormous and open-plan, the theme of dark wood and purple repeated everywhere. Windows on every side, overlooking the wreathed streets below, were filled with the stormy sky. In the main sitting room were settees, columns of books whose leather was bright and striking, an enormous desk by the largest window. Everywhere there were artifacts and paintings of fabulous color. It was more color than Benjamiah had seen anywhere else in Wreathenwold. A fire crackled in the hearth.

"Find the shrine," whispered Elizabella.

They found bedrooms, and studies, and parlors. On the Viper's vast desk, they found an elaborate metal instrument with rubber grips, a sinister needle at one end and an empty vial at the other.

"A spectractor," said Elizabella, shivering. "For extracting color. You apply a serum, and then the needle sucks the color into the vial. You can use it on anything except poppets. Books, clothes, flower petals. Eyes."

Benjamiah put it down, feeling sick. Next they found a huge room filled with cases of marbles, except the marbles were single colors—brilliant blues, blood reds, daffodil yellows. The cases were stacked to the ceiling, thousands of them.

"Do you know how much money this is?" said Elizabella, furious. "Just sitting here doing nothing."

They went up another flight of purple stairs. At the top was a door. And beyond the door was the shrine.

On the far wall was an enormous portrait of a squat, gloomy woman in a dark gown, with a puffy white frilled collar and sunken eyes. From a garish jug rose a soulbloom, an ugly, drooping flower of mucus green. Surrounding it was a sea of candles, flowers of extraordinary hues and tributes of expensive-looking ornaments and jewelry. Elizabella took one step inside.

"What are you doing here?" came a voice from behind them.

They turned, stricken with horror. Standing there was a girl around their own age, with a flat, oval face, a bloodless complexion, and quick, greedy eyes. Her hair fell in ginger ringlets, a tiara studded with gemstones perched on top. She wore the most grotesque outfit Benjamiah had ever seen—an enormous bell-shaped gown, marbled with a horrendous composite of blues and blacks and hazels. He realized, with horror, that they were eye colors. Somebody had taken them from real eyes to make this girl a dress.

At her hip was a brown poppet with a row of broken matchsticks resembling teeth.

"Who are you?" said Elizabella before she could stop herself.

The girl's eyes popped. "I am Gertrid Murdstone," she snarled. "And we do not allow *your kind* in here. Look how filthy you are! Disgusting. Mother shall have you whipped before and after you scrub your stink out of our home."

"Pardon me, miss," said Elizabella. She'd bowed her head, sounding meeker than Benjamiah had thought possible. "It was your mother who sent us, miss."

"Why would Mother send filthy servants up here?" snapped Gertrid.

"Miss, she feels bad about being downstairs so much," said Elizabella. "She said we're to be your personal servants, and do whatever you wish. To make up for it."

For a moment, Gertrid stared. Then she gave a smug smile, showing off rows of immaculate teeth.

"Finally," she said. "She must be sorry for how selfish she's been recently. Always working, never any time for me. Very well. Girl, you can brush my hair. Boy, you can rub my feet. But first you must go and scrub your hands."

Gertrid traipsed down into the main lounge of the suite. Benjamiah and Elizabella stared at each other.

"Hurry, servants," Gertrid called. "Or you shall be whipped!"

Elizabella and Benjamiah sidled into a bathroom of marble, with viper taps and vipers gilded round the mirror and plush purple decor. They washed their hands.

"What did you say that for?" hissed Benjamiah.

"Don't worry," said Elizabella. "I have an idea."

Somehow it was little comfort to Benjamiah. Their hands scrubbed clean, they joined Gertrid in the living room. She was reclined on a settee, her bare feet on a purple pouf. Benjamiah shivered.

"The hairbrush is over there, girl," said Gertrid. "Boy, fetch the mustard oil from the table. My feet are terribly sweaty. Don't press too hard on my bunions."

Stifling the urge to gag, Benjamiah did as he was told. He tried to meet Elizabella's eyes, but she was focused on the struggle with Gertrid's unruly ringlets. Gertrid's feet were smelly slabs, damp with sweat. He shuddered, trying not to retch, as he began rubbing in the foul-smelling mustard oil, all the while fearing what would happen if the Viper entered and exposed Elizabella's lie.

"What's it like to be so poor?" said Gertrid. Her feet squirmed in Benjamiah's hands.

"Not very nice, miss," said Elizabella.

"Are you orphans?" she asked.

"Yes, miss," said Elizabella.

"Were your parents poor too?"

"Yes, miss."

"It must be simply *awful* to be so poor," said Gertrid. "I'd rather be dead, I think. Do you like my dress? It's made from eye colors. Probably some of your orphan friends. Still, I'm sure Mother gave them a fair price."

Elizabella's fists were clenched behind Gertrid, her mouth tight with fury.

"Girl, why have you stopped brushing?" snapped Gertrid.

She made to swivel round, and in doing so nudged her toe upward. It knocked Benjamiah's despectacles clean off. Gertrid gasped.

"Your eyes," she said, sitting up straight. "They're brown! You . . ."

She jumped to her feet, turned, and snatched off Elizabella's despectacles.

"You aren't servants," she snapped. "Servants don't have pretty eyes like those. Why would Mother send *you*?"

"She didn't," said Elizabella.

Gertrid was confused, then furious. "I shall have your eyes, then," she said. "I can add them to my dress."

She opened her mouth, intending to let off a great howl that would summon help. In an instant, Elizabella had snatched Emba from her waist and thrown her. The juvenile bear manifested, bounding at Gertrid. Gertrid cast her own poppet as she stumbled backward. A young boar sprang up, stubby tusks sending warning jabs toward Emba. The bear and the boar squared off, prowling, growling.

Gertrid screamed. Elizabella lunged at her, clamping her mouth shut, suffocating the scream. The girls rolled, fighting, while the poppets clashed. The boar leveled its squat head, aiming its tusks at Emba's breast. But Emba was too powerful, defending against the blow and then swatting the boar aside with a devastating swipe of her paw.

The boar transformed into a lynx and sprang upon the bear, clamping her jaws on Emba's shoulder. Emba howled, flailed, and became a wolf. While the lynx and wolf grappled and snarled, Elizabella and Gertrid rolled, Gertrid striking Elizabella with a hairbrush and Elizabella smothering her mouth.

Benjamiah, helpless, recalled in that moment a passage from *A Brief History of Wreathenwold*. It was not only a precise and orderly memory that made one dollcaster superior in a poppet battle. It was the dexterity of their mind, their intelligence, their imagination, the ability to pivot in swift and tidy fashion from one spell to another.

It was obvious that Elizabella had the greater mind. When the lynx became a gorilla, Emba became one too. When Emba overpowered Gertrid's poppet again, the poppet transformed into a lion. But Elizabella was too fast— in a flash, Emba became a hawk, sweeping out of the lion's paws and then falling upon its back as a jaguar. Gertrid tried one more spell—a viper. The snake hissed, baring its slick fangs, but when it struck, Emba was already a baboon.

Emba the baboon gripped the viper beneath the head and lifted her. The snake flailed helplessly, while Gertrid squirmed out of Elizabella's grip and backed up against the wall. Her hair was askew, face blotched with red, panting and defeated.

Elizabella stood over her, scratched and scruffy. "I'd rather be poor than be you," she said, out of breath.

Gertrid pouted, casting around for help. None came. She leaped up suddenly, striking for the exit. Before Elizabella and Benjamiah could move, her head collided with an enormous marble sculpture. Gertrid fell to the purple carpet and lay still. In Emba's hand, the snake became a doll again.

"Is she . . . ," said Benjamiah.

Elizabella checked Gertrid. There was a mean-looking lump on her forehead.

"Breathing," she said. "Out cold. Let's hide her."

They dragged Gertrid into a nearby closet full of garish-colored coats, scarves, and hats, throwing her doll inside after her. They quickly tidied up the mess left behind by the fight.

"The lantern," said Elizabella, sounding calmer than she looked.

They ran up the stairs and into the shrine, into the dimness broken by a hundred glittering candles, a dizzying perfume of wax and flowers and incense. Beneath the soulless glare of the Viper's mother, they searched.

Finally, hidden behind a vase of pink flowers, they found Edwid's whisperwick. As Honeysuckle had said, it was identical to the one in the Whispering Wood.

Breathlessly, Elizabella inserted the key. Another of its roots squirmed along its length like a caterpillar, vanishing into the keyhole with a satisfying click.

After a moment to prepare herself, Elizabella opened the lantern. Out poured her brother's voice:

A path that goes not back nor forth,

A road that goes not south, east, west, nor north.

Elizabella seethed. "More nonsense," she said, as the candle went out.

Benjamiah scribbled the verse down in his notebook.

"It will make sense when we find them all," he said. "Now let's get out of here."

Elizabella nodded, looking deflated, her bonnet torn, strings of pale hair hanging out. They hid Edwid's lantern and left the shrine.

"Gertrid, buttercup?" called a woman's voice.

Horror swamped Benjamiah.

The Viper, mouthed Elizabella, looking equally terrified.

Footsteps approached. Elizabella, ever quick-thinking, yanked Benjamiah sideways. They were back in the marble bathroom, hiding behind the door. Stairs creaked as the Viper drew closer. Her voice was thin and muscular, much like a snake.

"Gertrid, my blossom? Are you here?"

Silence fell. The Viper was standing in the bathroom doorway, separated from Elizabella and Benjamiah by the flimsy door. They dared not even breathe. Any closer and they'd be found, and punished terribly. . . .

Then, mercifully, they heard Odith Murdstone retreat. The steps creaked as she returned down to the living area of the suite. What if she looked in the closet and found Gertrid? Benjamiah felt weak with terror, waiting for her outraged scream to rip through the silence.

When nothing came, Elizabella tugged his sleeve.

We have to go, she mouthed.

Benjamiah shook his head.

"No choice," she whispered. "The longer we wait, the more likely it is Gertrid will wake."

Slower than he'd ever moved, Benjamiah followed Elizabella out of the bathroom. They stood on the landing, listening, completely exposed. They heard nothing, so began their descent, one stair at a time, wincing at even the tiniest creak. At any moment, the Viper could appear in front of them. Finally they reached the bottom, giving them a view of the living room. They had to cross it to reach the servants' exit.

"Maybe she left," whispered Elizabella.

Then they saw her. They swerved behind the same marble sculpture that had floored Gertrid. The Viper was tall and straight-backed, dressed in a snakeskin frock coat and long snakeskin boots. Even her fingernails were patterned like a viper's hide. She had a prominent, strong forehead and the same reddish curls as her daughter. Her mouth was wide, dark with purple lipstick.

She crossed to the window and stood with her back to them, sipping a smoking tumbler of poppysyrup. Elizabella shifted, preparing to run. Then Odith Murdstone turned, walked over to the settee, and sat. She still had her back to them. Now was their chance.

Elizabella and Benjamiah eased out of their hiding place. The Viper drank more poppysyrup. Benjamiah's heart was a thunderstorm, one he felt sure would betray him.

"So how do you like working here, Manfred Tarr?" said the Viper suddenly.

And it was then, as Elizabella and Benjamiah froze only three feet or so behind where the Viper sat—and with the corridor to the servants' staircase within view—that they realized Odith Murdstone was not alone.

A man stood by a window that had previously been out of view, sipping his own glass of poppysyrup.

Manfred Tarr was tall and skinny, with slicked-back hair and pale skin. There were shadowy patches round his eyes, the eyes themselves dark as the ocean depths. He wore a dark waistcoat and an extravagant tailcoat. In the crook of his collar, where there might ordinarily be a tie or cravat, was a beautiful red flower. At his waist was a yellow poppet with white button eyes. In his other hand was a black cane, its head an elaborate construct of shimmering silver—it was shaped like a masquerade mask.

"Very well, thank you," said Manfred Tarr. "Very well indeed."

On turning to look at the Viper, he immediately saw the frozen figures of Elizabella and Benjamiah behind her.

His eyes narrowed, lips arcing into a bemused smile. Then he returned his gaze to Odith.

"What a wonderful establishment this is," he said. "I feel very privileged to work here."

He wasn't giving them away! It was a miracle. Manfred detached himself from the window and struck a course for an armchair to Odith's left. It would draw her gaze entirely from the children's escape path.

"No, here," said the Viper, and she pointed to an armchair to her right.

Manfred hesitated, then obliged. He sat with his legs crossed, still afforded a view of the children behind the Viper. If they made a run for it now, she would see them out of the corner of her eye. They were trapped.

"Tell me, Mr. Tarr," said Odith Murdstone. "How is it you arrive from nowhere and within a few weeks prove yourself one of the finest color-traders in my Magimmaculum?"

Manfred bowed his head, saluting the Viper with his glass.

"You are too kind, Madam Murdstone," he replied.

"Oh, Odith, please," said the Viper. "Who trained you?"

"Nobody of any note," said Manfred. "I was a humble market trader before running into one of your clerks. In a tavern, to my shame. I understand she recommended me, and here we are."

"Here we are," echoed Odith. "How fascinating. I expect you could tell all manner of stories about market life."

"I would only bore you," said Manfred. "There are few sins more terrible than being boring, I find."

The Viper's head rocked back as she unleashed a trilling, overenthusiastic laugh. There seemed a hint of romance between the Viper and Manfred. Elizabella jabbed a finger in her own mouth, miming a gag. Benjamiah was appalled. How could she joke at a time like this?

While the Viper laughed, Manfred gave Elizabella and Benjamiah a tiny flick of his head toward the exit. But it was hopeless. Odith Murdstone was at the wrong angle. Elizabella conveyed this with her hands.

Manfred stood suddenly, pacing to that side. The

Viper's head followed him. It gave Elizabella and Benjamiah a greater margin in which to edge forward. They did so painfully slowly, desperate not to make a sound.

"Forgive me," said Manfred. "I am a restless soul. Forever on the move. One of many flaws."

"I have seen no flaws yet," said Odith. "But I shall examine you closely for any glimpse of them. Rumor has it you're partial to a game of dice."

"Rumors certainly seem to thrive here," said Manfred, with a little bow. "I cannot deny it. My greatest vice."

"Just see that you don't gamble with my money," said the Viper.

"Never."

Elizabella and Benjamiah took another step. They could make a dash for it, but feared the noise they would make.

"Tell me," said the Viper, "have you heard the rumors of a magus returned to Wreathenwold?"

"I have," said Manfred. "But it's impossible. The magi are all gone. The Widow saw to that."

Odith nodded. "Still, I hear troubling things," she said. "Rumors of one last magus, imprisoned long ago, but now escaped. As you say, it must be humbug."

"I'm glad you agree," said Manfred. "I confess I've been more than a little nervous at the prospect of a magus returned to the city."

"I did not think you the nervous type, Mr. Tarr."

The children took another step. Almost there.

"Please, call me Manfred," he replied.

Elizabella and Benjamiah took one more step. In that moment, a terrible howl filled the air. It sounded like a wounded animal. Slowly, with a plunge of horror, Benjamiah understood. It was Gertrid.

"Mother . . . !" she wailed. "Mother . . . help . . . !"

The Viper leaped up and dashed across the room. It was the chance Elizabella and Benjamiah had been waiting for. Encouraged by Manfred, they bolted. They were halfway down the corridor when they heard the Viper unleash a furious scream. And, as they yanked open the door to the servants' staircase, they heard the wails of Gertrid Murdstone.

"They attacked me! Disguised as servants . . . Dirty, violent animals . . . Find them! Catch them! I want their eyes. Bright green . . . Pretty brown . . . *I want their eyes. Bring me their eyes!*"

FOURTEEN
WITH THE HOUSE OF MAPMAKERS

The Company of Mapmakers is an enigma. The magi formed the labyrinth, cursing it to ensure nobody could find their way. They also forbade the practice of mapping the city on pain of execution, a law that has remained despite the fall of the magi. The Company of Mapmakers exists today in a ceremonial capacity, though suspicions are rife that they continue their attempts to map the city in the belief that it will rid Wreathenwold of its curse.

—A Brief History of Wreathenwold,
Archscholar Collum Wolfsdaughter

BENJAMIAH HAD NEVER been an impressive athlete. At the last school sports day, he'd received a "Taking Part Is Winning" rosette after floundering in the sack race, causing a multi-child pile-up in the egg-and-spoon race, and ending up facedown in the mud during the tug-of-war. It would have been the most mortifying day of his life had

Mum and Dad not been there, leaping and whistling in support. Afterward they'd taken him for ice cream and treated him to a great book about tractors.

The fear of having his eye colors sucked out proved very effective motivation, though. Benjamiah had never run so fast, charging in Elizabella's wake, Gertrid's crazed threats chasing them every step of the way.

The stairwell was busier than before, full of house-keepers and servants hurrying up and down. The furious howls growing closer, Elizabella swung onto the banister and slid, spiraling downward while people threw themselves out of the way. Benjamiah had no choice—he flung himself after her and slid down too, thinking he might throw up as they twisted to the bottom.

Panting, they reached the dark corridors beneath the Magimmaculum. Ahead was the exit.

"Calmly," said Elizabella, out of breath and bedraggled. "Or the Hanged Man will know something is wrong."

Benjamiah felt as far away from calm as it was possible to feel. He was sure a hand would snatch them at any moment, and before long Odith Murdstone would be lowering her insidious spectractor into his eyes. They walked, steadying their breathing and tidying themselves up.

They opened the door, into stormy daylight. The Hanged Man stirred.

"Leaving already?" he said.

"We were sent home," said Elizabella. "We weren't very good."

Her cheeks were glowing, hair tumbling out of her bonnet, scratches on her jaw. Benjamiah was breathing bricks beside her.

"Is that right?" said the Hanged Man, standing.

From inside came a piercing scream. The Hanged Man looked up. Elizabella and Benjamiah bolted into the courtyard where hundreds of figures thronged, color-traders and clerks and affluent people strolling around. In the time it took for word to travel down to the Hanged Men on the street, Elizabella and Benjamiah were able to leave the Magimmaculum behind.

Beneath the archway to the next street, Elizabella stopped.

"Go and get our things," she said. "My bag's on my bed, ready to go. Here's the key. Bring Nuisance and Ariadne. Meet me in the tearoom opposite the inn."

"Where are you going?" said Benjamiah, bewildered.

"Clora and Odgar's orphanage," said Elizabella. "The Viper will go after them when she can't find us. I need to warn them."

"But you'll have to go back past the Magimmaculum!" said Benjamiah.

"I'll be fine," said Elizabella, and off she ran.

Benjamiah did as he was told. He returned to the inn,

gathered their things, and, accompanied by Nuisance (having happily ditched the toy poppet) and Ariadne, waited in the tearoom opposite. Steam fogged the glass. He had to keep wiping it to see the street. He expected the Hanged Men to arrive at any moment, Elizabella as their captive. His hands shook in his lap. Nuisance the capuchin was sipping his treacle tea, Ariadne coiling round the sugar bowl.

"Do you know where Horis and Hoggish Books is, Ariadne?" whispered Benjamiah.

Ariadne nodded. A lump formed in his throat. Would the door be there? Could he just go home and forget any of this had ever happened? His family would be beside themselves with worry. It had been days already.

The bell of the tearoom clanged. Benjamiah flinched, but it was Elizabella, looking wild and exhausted. She flopped down opposite him.

"I got there before the Hanged Men," she said. "Clora and Odgar have left. They're going to use the money to start their own cleaning business."

It was an enormous relief to Benjamiah. Something in Elizabella's expression, though, gave him pause. Her eyes stared off, and she chewed on her lower lip.

"What is it?" he asked.

"They were everywhere," said Elizabella. "The Hanged Men. Looking for us. They won't stop. They'll hunt us wherever we go now."

Benjamiah shuddered.

"I won't blame you if you leave," said Elizabella. "This is my mess. Not yours."

How far was Horis & Hoggish Books? Could Ariadne take him there, then lead Elizabella on without him? The promise of home was intoxicating. But what about Elizabella and her brother?

"I'm staying," said Benjamiah. "I'm coming with you."

"Why?" asked Elizabella.

"To help find Edwid," he said. "I said I would, so I will."

Elizabella's eyes shone, hiding another smile. They would do this together or not at all. Though Benjamiah missed Mum, Dad, and Grandma terribly, he couldn't abandon Elizabella now.

They left side by side, hurrying as far from the Magimmaculum as they could. When there were three streets between them, and then four and five, they began to relax.

"Did you hear what Manfred Tarr said?" asked Elizabella as they walked an icy street of bonewoods and crooked town houses. "About the magus?"

Benjamiah nodded. He'd read enough about the magi in *A Brief History of Wreathenwold* to feel worried. By the time they were murdered, the magi were unhinged, violent, and cruel—many of them practicing witchcraft, pushing the aether to dangerous lengths in pursuit of new powers.

"He said there were whispers of a magus returned to Wreathenwold," said Benjamiah. "Before we left, Hansel told me Edwid had been muttering about a magus. . . ."

Elizabella nodded. "He kept repeating, 'The magus . . . The magus . . . The crack in the wall . . .' I thought he was rambling because he was sick, but maybe all of this actually has something do with a magus?"

Benjamiah recalled Honeysuckle's warning—a darkness pursuing Edwid and his lanterns.

"The magi are all gone, though, aren't they?" he said. "Murdered by the Widow . . ."

Elizabella looked as fearful as he'd ever seen her. In solemn silence, they passed into a stone tunnel between two roads. Ahead was a sunlit street, but before they reached it a shadowy figure suddenly stepped in front of them.

It was Manfred Tarr.

"Don't be frightened," he said, his voice soft. "If I wanted you captured, I had my chance."

"How did you find us?" said Elizabella, suspicious.

"Your movements are not quite so careful as you think," said Manfred, smiling. "I mean you no harm. I'm only curious about what possessed you to break into the Viper's home and attack her daughter."

"We did no such thing!" said Elizabella. "She started it."

"And I rubbed her feet!" declared Benjamiah, at which Manfred looked confused.

"No need," he said, waving a hand. "I know precisely how horrid the snakelet is. But tell me: What were you doing there?"

Elizabella and Benjamiah stiffened, united in silence.

"Have I not earned your trust?" said Manfred, placing a hand on his breast.

"Why do you want to know?" asked Elizabella.

"Curiosity," said Manfred. "That cruel and demanding master."

Elizabella and Benjamiah traded a glance.

"We're looking for my brother, Edwid," she said.

"And you thought he might have been in the Viper's home?"

"Not exactly," said Elizabella, but didn't elaborate.

"Ah," said Manfred. "You keep your cards close to your chest. I respect that, as I do your bravery. And your love for your brother. It burns within you. I had a brother myself. I, too, would have done anything, and traveled anywhere, to save him."

A tear gathered in Manfred's inky eye.

"What happened to him?" asked Benjamiah.

"He died," said Manfred. "When I was nine. Ouroboros flu. Taken to a place from which no amount of courage or wit could return him."

"I'm sorry," said Elizabella.

"A long time ago," said Manfred, dabbing his eye with

a handkerchief. "And something that cannot be changed. You, on the other hand, have a chance to bring your brother home. Can I help you?"

"You already have," said Elizabella. "Thank you."

"Is there nothing else I can do?" said Manfred.

"Not unless you can find out who stole him," said Elizabella. "A shadowy figure, driving a coach pulled by clockwork mares."

"I shall investigate," said Manfred, with a little bow, "and report back."

"How will you find us?" said Elizabella. Manfred smiled but didn't answer.

"And we need to find a raven," blurted Benjamiah.

Manfred looked puzzled, and Elizabella annoyed.

"A raven?" he said.

"A dangerous raven," said Benjamiah, "knowing Edwid. It could be a real raven, or a place, or a person. Edwid hid something there. Something he didn't want to be found."

"A dangerous raven?" said Manfred, looking bemused. "I'm sorry to say I cannot help. But I can, if I may, make a recommendation?"

Elizabella nodded.

"Go to the Company of Mapmakers," he said. "Nobody keeps a greater record of this city and its people. Great mountains of records chronicling the voyages of doomed Mapmakers. The Mapmakers will never give up. Forever they toil with their scraps and manuscripts, scrabbling to form their map. If someone has come across this dangerous raven, you will learn of it at the Company of Mapmakers. I suppose the only question is how you'll find your way there. . . ."

Manfred trailed off, smiling. Ariadne was hanging unseen on the underside of the tunnel, just above his top hat. Benjamiah noticed she was quivering.

"But something tells me," continued Manfred, "that what is a problem for the rest of us is no problem for you."

Elizabella and Benjamiah stared, lips sealed. Ariadne was too big a secret to share, and they knew it.

"Is it true about the magus?" said Benjamiah.

"I fear so," said Manfred, "whatever the Viper says. Something disturbing and ancient has returned to Wreathenwold. A shadow gathers. Look after yourselves. Beware of any person without a doll. Magi have no poppets, remember. But I suspect the Hanged Men will pose a greater danger to you. The Viper is furious and won't rest until your eye colors decorate Gertrid's hideous dress. A dangerous Inspector named Cromwell is on the case, and he will do anything to please the Viper. Keep your heads down. Your eyes hidden. Keep moving. Stay on your guard."

Elizabella and Benjamiah nodded. Manfred put a hand on each of their shoulders, gave them a squeeze and a final smile, then bowed and stalked off, his cane clacking on the cobbles.

"What do you think?" said Benjamiah when he'd gone.

"I'm not sure," said Elizabella. "How did he find us?"

Benjamiah shrugged. "Where now?" he said.

Elizabella looked up at Ariadne, who had relaxed since Manfred's departure.

"Take us to the House of Mapmakers."

It took them two days to reach the House of Mapmakers, during which the character of Wreathenwold transformed. How far they had come from Follynook and Where We Live was evident in the accents, which had acquired gruff edges and dips, and in the buildings, which were older and weathered and draped in shaggy vines. They passed through two streets that had fallen foul of the Widow's violence and never been rebuilt. The charred bones of buildings rose from mounds of timber, stone, and ash.

Streets became shorter and narrower, more claustro-phobic, the cobbles broken and uneven, the arcing branches of the labyrinth tighter. There were bridges and staircases and tunnels, an endless network of unplottable turns and twists.

It was en route to the House of Mapmakers that the wanted posters sprang up. Elizabella saw the first one nailed to the front of a tavern. Emblazoned in the middle were crude sketches of them both, beneath the word WANTED in large, sinister lettering, and below this it said:

For theft, trespassing, and violence against a child. Significant reward offered for information leading to their apprehension. Girl has green eyes, the boy brown eyes. Both known to wear despectacles.

"Why did they make my nose so *pointy*?" said Elizabella, frowning, testing the shape of her nose with her fingers. "And what are we supposed to have stolen?"

"Is that all you have to say?" hissed Benjamiah.

"And how *mean* you look," said Elizabella. "Honestly, you couldn't look that scary in a million years."

It was true. Gertrid's imagination, or perhaps her pride at being overcome by Elizabella, had lent both Elizabella and Benjamiah a baleful quality. Their mouths were stretched in leers, their eyes pinched and angled, both drawn as brutish criminals. Elizabella gave a lopsided smile.

"It's not funny," said Benjamiah. "These will be everywhere. And they know about the despectacles."

"They look nothing like us!" said Elizabella.

As they walked away, she unhitched Emba from her noose. Without breaking stride, she sent Emba—cast as a hawk—soaring back to the poster. Emba shredded the paper with her talons, took flight, and caught them up farther down the street.

Benjamiah laughed. He couldn't help it.

They reached the House of Mapmakers late afternoon. It was on what seemed to be one of the oldest streets in Wreathenwold, all cracked stone and overgrown moss, several neighboring buildings fallen into ruin. Sleepy sunlight filtered through tails of wispy cloud. The House of Mapmakers itself was a great stone temple, with columns along the front supporting an ancient entablature, carved into which were prancing horses, compasses, spyglasses. A flag drooped wearily above the steps, depicting the labyrinth insignia of the Mapmakers. An inscription announced the Mapmakers as the Seventh Honorable Company of Wreathenwold. Below was another inscription:

TOGETHER, NEVER LOST.

"Ariadne, into your box," ordered Elizabella.

The thread obeyed, swinging down from a drainpipe onto Benjamiah's cap, and finally nestling in the box. Elizabella snapped it shut and pocketed it.

"Do you think Edwid stole her from here?" said Benjamiah.

Elizabella glared, unwilling to admit her brother might be a thief. Benjamiah clamped his mouth shut.

Together they mounted the steps and entered the House of Mapmakers.

Benjamiah had read about the Company in *A Brief History of Wreathenwold*. It was the magi at the center of the labyrinth who had made maps illegal, the punishment being execution. But even after the magi were gone, the Minotaur continued to forbid the practice. Attempts at mapmaking drew such misfortune and peril upon the people of Wreathenwold that it was considered too dangerous. Despite this, rumors abounded that the Company of Mapmakers continued with their underhanded attempts to map Wreathenwold, possessed by an unwavering belief that the city would only be truly free when it was mapped in its entirety.

If Archscholar Wolfsdaughter's examples were anything to go by, the Mapmakers were doomed to failure. Wreathenwold simply did not want to be mapped. Even besides the curse that made people forget their way, the city had other methods for thwarting the Mapmakers' attempts. Ernold Lacer, one of the most intrepid Mapmakers in Wreathenwold history, was lured dreamily to his death by a deceptive well-lurker. There was Motilda Twince, so haunted by the source of an unplaceable knocking sound that she went mad, sealed off her ears with Root Folk wax, and never heard the approach of a great horned spider behind her.

The entrance hall was a picture of faded magnificence. The ceiling was high and domed, flags hung limply from rusted poles. Along an elevation at one side was a raft of soulblooms of wonderful colors, popping out of vases beneath murky paintings of famous and unfortunate Mapmakers. The floor tiles were cracked, the furniture pitted and ramshackle. It was also mayhem, people rushing in every direction with reams of parchment, boxes and crates stacked in unwieldy towers everywhere. It looked like the Mapmakers were packing up.

Elizabella and Benjamiah located a long marble counter. Piled along its length were more heaps of parchment laced with cobwebs, most of it yellow and crisp and probably older than the building itself.

Through a gap they could see the flustered face of a woman with gray hair and a pointy nose.

"Excuse me," said Elizabella. "I wonder if you might be able to help us, please?"

The woman looked up, cheeks flushed, confused.

"What's that, dear?" she said, cupping an ear and squinting.

"We need some help," Elizabella half shouted.

"Help? Help with what, dear?"

"We're doing some research for a school project, and we wondered if we might access your archives? We were told . . ."

"Access our archives!" said the woman, then gave a great rattling laugh. "Dear, look around you. Our archives are *everywhere* now. Have you ever seen such a mess? And all for nothing, absolutely nothing. She's just not *here* anymore, but does anybody listen to me?"

"What are you doing here?" said a voice.

Elizabella and Benjamiah spun. Standing over them was an olive-skinned woman bedecked in black, from the bowler hat on her head to the frilly collar round her throat, from her waistcoat to her smart button-up boots. She had short silvery hair, her amber eyes lively behind a pair of pince-nez.

"Who are you two?" she demanded.

Elizabella introduced them both.

"I am Josabella Fogge, Captain of the Company of Mapmakers," she said.

"Like Mildred Fogge?" blurted Elizabella.

Seeing Benjamiah's confusion, Elizabella added, "She wrote *The Book of Barely Believable Stories*. The best book of fairy tales in Wreathenwold."

"An ancestor," said Josabella, not appearing particularly pleased about it. "What are you doing here?"

Elizabella repeated the story about a school project. Josabella studied her, not believing a word of it. Elizabella looked like butter wouldn't melt in her mouth.

"You have poor timing," said Josabella. "Our archives

are in disarray, otherwise you'd be very welcome to explore them. And for any reason you wish, I should add. The rest of Wreathenwold might consider curiosity a sin, but here we celebrate it."

The disarray was evident. Mapmakers leafed through towers of paper, rooting through drawers and cabinets, shouting and bickering and clattering into one another. It was bedlam.

"What's going on?" said Elizabella.

"We've lost something," said Josabella, looking weary. "Something we hope has been misplaced rather than stolen. I'm sorry not to be more useful. Come back another time when things are a little less chaotic."

"Maybe we could speak to one of your archivists?" said Elizabella. "They might be able to help us."

"Help you with what?" said Josabella.

"Something we're curious about," said Elizabella.

Josabella liked that. A smile appeared like a crack in stone. She called out, "Silas!"

A boy slouched over, perhaps a year older than Benjamiah. Silas was a sorry sight, an adventuring, pioneering spirit with his wings clipped, like a bird of paradise in a shabby aviary, mournful and browbeaten. He was thickset, with dark brown skin, short, cropped hair, and colorless eyes. Everything about him was downbeat, bruised, sorrowful. His belt was kitted out for the adventures life was denying him—a spyglass, a compass, a timepiece, his blue and white poppet, even a cutlass.

"Captain?" he said sulkily.

"Take these children to Vee," said Josabella. "They need some help."

Silas examined Elizabella and Benjamiah with a bewildered, helpless look.

"Captain, with respect, we have bigger problems right now, don't you think?" he said.

"Curiosity is our greatest concern," said Josabella. "Always has been, always will be. Take them to Vee."

Silas pouted, shook his head, but did as he was told. He beckoned the children on and, shoulders slouched, led them through the House of Mapmakers. Carnage dominated every room, hall, stairwell, and corridor. Nuisance the nightjar fluttered overhead, chirping, perching on shaky columns of books and drawings. Benjamiah hissed at him to behave, but it was useless.

As they meandered through the chaos, Silas barked out randomly at anybody not working, accosting people not searching fast enough, demanding that every gap, corner, and pocket be examined.

"I found her!" screamed a red-haired girl, holding up an inanimate length of string.

Silas dashed over, as did a dozen other excitable Mapmakers.

"That's a bootlace," said Silas, his hopes snuffed.

"Oh," said the girl, crestfallen.

While Silas was berating a confused-looking boy, Benjamiah leaned toward Elizabella.

"They're looking for Ariadne!"

"Oh, *really*?" said Elizabella, rolling her eyes.

Silas led them into a huge, vaulted room. Rows of bonewood shelves climbed to the ceiling, set on tracks with huge levers that could be turned to move or rotate the shelves. Like elsewhere, the archive was pandemonium. The contents of the shelves had been emptied so they could be searched, arranged in great teetering piles, crews of exhausted and thoroughly unhappy Mapmakers leafing through parchment, books, sketches.

Vee was the oldest woman Benjamiah had ever seen, so old it seemed her face had folded in on itself, all wrinkles and jowls. They found her behind a desk, itself swamped with archives evacuated from their shelves and cabinets.

She fixed Silas with a look of desperation.

"Our little thread has gone, Master Weaver," she said. "We need to give this up. Do you know how long it will take to get everything back in its place?"

"Never," said Silas. "Never. We have nothing without Ariadne. *Nothing*. Without her, the Company of Mapmakers might as well disband. We give up on everything we stand for. These archives will mean nothing. Just a big bonfire to be had. Ariadne will *never* be lost to those who need her."

"She's been stolen, I tell you," said Vee, shaking her head.

"Impossible!" declared Silas. "Out of the question. Absolutely ridiculous. Anyway, these two want to ask you something. Tell them whatever they want to hear, then sling them out. We have more important things to worry about."

He stalked off, berating and swearing, scuffing his boots gloomily. Vee looked at Elizabella and Benjamiah with milky eyes. Nuisance was making a nuisance of himself, now a capuchin, harassing the exhausted Mapmakers. Benjamiah was helpless to make him stop.

"Need some help, is it?" said Vee. "We *are* a little busy, right enough."

"I'm sorry," said Elizabella. "We won't take up much of your time. We're looking for a raven."

"A raven?" said Vee, cocking an ear.

"A dangerous raven," said Elizabella. "Or it could be a place, or perhaps a person. Whatever the case, it's somewhere people wouldn't want to go. Somewhere dangerous. I know it sounds a little strange, but . . ."

Vee waved a gnarled, liver-spotted hand.

"You think I haven't heard stranger?" she said. "Every day is stranger than the last. Can't wait for tomorrow. Not sure about a person, but I remember something about a monstrous raven. Hundreds of years ago now, mind. Could that be it? What do you want with it?"

Elizabella sealed her lips, and Vee nodded.

"Like that, is it?" she said, grunting. "Wilhem?"

A bleary-eyed boy wandered over.

"Fetch me the diaries of Archscholar Thromwell."

"Where are they?" said Wilhem.

"How should I know?" said Vee. "But these two need them. Hop to it."

Wilhem shot Elizabella and Benjamiah a rueful glance, then scuttled off.

"Might have been Thromwell," said Vee. "Memory's not what it used to be, though. Could have been Threshwell. Or Thrompson. And might not have been a raven, come to think of it. Might have been the Shemurgh. Or the Rok. Sure you aren't looking for an eagle?"

Elizabella shook her head. Wilhem had enlisted the help of other young Mapmakers in the pursuit of Thromwell's diaries. Their annoyance was palpable, even more so when Nuisance knocked over a great column of parchment. Vee only laughed. Silas returned occasionally, demanding they forget about Thromwell and resume the search for Ariadne. The young Mapmakers would do as they were told until Silas left, at which point Vee would have them resume the search for Thromwell's diaries.

They were eventually located. Vee drew upon her ency-clopedic memory and homed in on a particular passage within the great ream of parchment.

She sighed. "The Shemurgh, as I thought. Wilhem? Let's try the accounts of Captain Threshwell."

Benjamiah mouthed *sorry*, but it was no good. The moody shadow of Wilhem came and went, and Nuisance was out of control. Vee found him hilarious, Elizabella embarrassing, and Benjamiah mortifying. It took an age for the accounts of Captain Threshwell to be found, only for Vee to again disappoint.

"Let's look at Thrompson," she said.

Wilhem was furious. Silas despaired, raking his fingers through his hair.

Benjamiah felt an elbow in his ribs. It was Elizabella, who looked aghast. In her hand was Ariadne's box. It was empty.

She had escaped.

Which would be problematic enough were it not for the fact that surrounding them was an army turning the House of Mapmakers upside down in search of her. Benjamiah's stomach plunged, his limbs growing slow and cold like in a nightmare. If they found her, he would never get home!

Elizabella saw her first, eyes widening. Ariadne was snaking up a pillar of sepia manuscripts. A young woman was going through them, mechanically retrieving the topmost and sifting each page in turn.

"Create a distraction," whispered Benjamiah.

"What kind of distraction?"

"Something *distracting*," he hissed.

Careful to avoid any attention, he shuffled off in pursuit of Ariadne. He cast Elizabella an urgent look. She improvised.

"Oh!" she shouted. "Oh, a troop of monkeys-of-the-inkpot!"

It was a terrible attempt, but Elizabella was noisy and ridiculous enough to momentarily consume the archive's attention. Benjamiah reached up and snatched at Ariadne. But the thread looped away, onto the collar of a passing Mapmaker. While Elizabella feigned distress, Benjamiah gave chase. Before he could reach him, Ariadne had crossed onto the sleeve of a man rushing in the other direction.

Benjamiah was less than an inch away when Ariadne moved again. She latched on to a spyglass hanging from a belt. It belonged to Silas Weaver.

He had his back to Benjamiah, berating one of the young Mapmakers for not searching quickly enough. Benjamiah cast a helpless glance at Elizabella, whose distraction had run its course. She urged him on with a stern look.

Benjamiah turned back to Silas. Quick as a flash, he plucked Ariadne from Silas's belt. Pulling her free lifted the spyglass, which slapped into Silas as Ariadne was loosened. Silas swiveled round.

Benjamiah had no choice. He popped Ariadne in his mouth.

"What are you doing?" demanded Silas.

If he spoke, the game would be up. Ariadne was exploring the inside of his mouth, tickling his tongue and gums. Benjamiah shrugged, trying not to gag.

"Why aren't you saying anything?" said Silas, cocking a suspicious eye at him.

Benjamiah had no choice. He shrugged again, which only incensed Silas.

"Are you simple?" he demanded. "Speak!"

Elizabella appeared at Benjamiah's side.

"Forgive my brother," she said. "He's not much of a talker. And he loves spyglasses."

This only seemed to increase Silas's suspicion.

"How did you two find your way here?" he asked.

"We live two streets over," replied Elizabella.

"In which direction?"

Elizabella pointed one way and Benjamiah the other. Silas opened his mouth to demand further explanation, but was interrupted by a triumphant shout.

"Found it!" declared Vee.

Elizabella and Benjamiah rushed over, Silas watching them carefully. Ariadne squirmed in Benjamiah's mouth.

"Knew it was Thrompson," said Vee, a monstrous sheaf of parchment spread on her desk. "Like I said, though, it was hundreds of years ago. This is dated 689 SD. And it isn't a happy story. . . ."

Vee looked up, and Elizabella smiled encouragingly.

"Right you are," she mumbled. "Let's see . . . *The baker's boy tonight, not yet eight years of age, plucked right off the street . . . What madness or enchantment compels these children to persist with their nightly excursions when the dreadful creature rules the skies? . . .* Let's see. More children taken, another here . . . Here! *Another sighting of the wicked child-eater, this time from a Mrs. W—, who confirms it has the likeness of a monstrous raven, with features so abominable I dare not press for further details. The beast, it would seem, also has an appetite for shiny trinkets, which it hoards in its roost. . . .* But where, Mr. Thrompson? Where? Ah! Here. *Triumph of a kind, though no return of the taken children has been possible, nor vengeance for their fate. We have sealed off the wretched raven in the Sunken Wood that it must never leave, nor must anybody enter. . . .*"

Benjamiah was suddenly glad he couldn't speak. *Child-eater . . . ?*

"The Sunken Wood?" said Elizabella.

"That's what it says here," said Vee. "But as for where that is, Thrompson gives us nothing. And for good reason, right enough."

"Thank you very much," said Elizabella. Then, turning to Benjamiah, she said, "Let's go."

"Is that it?" demanded Silas, stalking over. "You wasted all our time to hear *that*?"

"Oh, leave them be," said Vee.

Silas ignored her. "Why do you care about this raven?" he said. "What use is the information?"

"No use at all," said Elizabella, giving her most dazzling smile. "Just curiosity."

"Tell me again how you found your way here," said Silas.

"I found her!" came a scream.

Silas dashed over to a triumphant Wilhem, who was holding a long string aloft.

"Darning wool," said Silas, despairing once again.

Elizabella and Benjamiah were on their way already, weaving a path out of the archives, negotiating the chaotic corridors and stairwells, returning to the entrance hall. Josabella Fogge, overseeing the search here, saluted them as they left.

Only when they were back on the street did Benjamiah open his mouth, pitching a slimy, indignant Ariadne into the palm of his hand. Elizabella regarded her with distaste. Then she erupted into laughter, so joyous that Benjamiah couldn't help joining in.

FIFTEEN

WITH THE RAVEN

In their desperation to protect the natural world from the dollcasters, the Root Folk turned to creating monsters. From ordinary wildlife—tigers, snakes, birds—they crafted extraordinary creatures to fight back against the dollcasters. Though relations between the Root Folk and the doll-casters are now peaceful, many of these monsters still lurk in Wreathenwold today.

—*A Brief History of Wreathenwold*,
Archscholar Collum Wolfsdaughter

THEY RODE HANSOM CABS to the Sunken Wood. The drivers would typically only take them the length of a street or two, for fear of getting lost—which meant frequent changes. Still, despite the cost, it was safer than walking. Though their money was dwindling, the wanted posters had multiplied. Every shop, tavern, and street lamp bore their roguish resemblances. Elizabella had Emba

244 • JORDAN LEES

rip some down, but there were too many—their journey became more perilous at every moment.

Night drew in. Rain splattered against the carriage, making faces on the windows. Pulling it were two clockwork horses—hooves clattering on the cobbles, the snorting and whinnying unerringly lifelike. Benjamiah felt faintly sick, Vee's words resounding in his head. *Dreadful creature . . . Child-eater . . . Monstrous raven . . .*

"What's your home like?" said Elizabella.

She had become increasingly pensive as the day wore on, camped within herself, pretending to read a Jamima Cleaves with glazed eyes.

"Very different. No magic. No dolls."

"Sounds boring," said Elizabella.

"Oh no, not at all . . . ," said Benjamiah.

And he told Elizabella about all the things he found wonderful about home, from satellites to submarines, from black holes to electrons, from chess to Einstein to loco-motives. When he'd finished explaining how a light bulb worked, Elizabella looked bewildered.

"Sounds like sorcery to me," she said. "Do you have any brothers or sisters?"

Benjamiah shook his head. "It's just me, Mum, Dad, and Grandma."

"Almost as small as my family," said Elizabella.

"Is it just the three of you?"

Elizabella stiffened, then eventually nodded. She added, "Hansel has an older brother, but we've never met him. He and Hansel don't speak."

A few moments passed in silence.

"What are your mum and dad like?" said Elizabella.

How to say it? Mum, Dad, the falling apart of the world as he knew it? Wreathenwold was nothing compared to how strange and impossible that vision was. All along, he'd feared saying it aloud, afraid it would somehow make it real.

"I'm not sure they want to be married anymore," he finally said.

Elizabella had the good grace to pause.

"Don't worry, you don't need to say anything," said Benjamiah.

"Why don't they want to be married anymore?" she asked.

"I don't know. And I don't care. They just need to fix it."

"Not everything can be fixed, though," said Elizabella gently.

"Yes, it can," said Benjamiah. "Every problem has a solution. Just like with Edwid. Somebody has taken him, and we're going to find him. Mum and Dad just aren't trying hard enough."

"I'm sure they are . . . ," said Elizabella.

"How would you know?" snapped Benjamiah.

Elizabella paused, then said, "I don't know anything about your world. It sounds different and mad and boring. But not everything can be fixed, Benjamiah. I know that for sure."

Benjamiah lapsed into stubborn silence. What would she know? She lived in a ludicrous, magical world without logic or reason.

Elizabella's face was unreadable, patched with shadow and the flare of streetlights. Rain played on the window.

"Why do you think Hansel helped you?" said Elizabella.

"Because he's kind."

"Maybe," she said. "But the city is full of lost children. He never brought any home until now. Why you?"

Benjamiah had no explanation. He'd wondered about it himself. In the breast pocket of his waistcoat was the coin Hansel had given him, a promise that no harm would come to Benjamiah, a vow to help him get home. The coin hadn't broken yet.

"I left him a promise," said Benjamiah.

"You did?"

Benjamiah nodded. "A coin. And a note," he said. "To bring you and Edwid home safe and well."

Something very unexpected happened. Elizabella's eyes filled with sudden tears, and she choked back a sob. Benjamiah was shocked. Elizabella sniffed, wiped her eyes, quickly recovering her composure.

"That wasn't a promise you could make," she said, her voice a little thick.

"I can try," replied Benjamiah.

Elizabella lapsed into a deep silence, staring out the window. Benjamiah didn't know what to say, what to think. And that meant his thoughts strayed again to terrible visions of the monstrous, bloodthirsty raven they were heading toward.

"Tell me more about Edwid," said Benjamiah. "I need a distraction."

Elizabella immediately brightened up. "The best brother in the world," she said.

Benjamiah had never seen her so alive, so animated. Edwid wasn't just her twin brother—he was her best friend, too. She talked, as the hansom shook and shuddered onward, of a brother who would do anything for her, defend her, make her laugh, and for whom she would go to the ends of the earth to bring home. And, seeing the raw and total love Elizabella had for her brother, Benjamiah knew he would go with her.

By the following day, they were drawing ever closer to the Sunken Wood. The streets grew quieter, eerie, the weather mostly drab and miserable no matter how many times they changed street. Here the city was gray and dilapidated, completely without color. Moss and ivy ran wild.

Ariadne led them down a desolate street, another that had fallen foul of the Widow. What buildings had survived her fury were ruined husks. Windows were boarded up or smashed, roofs collapsed. The weather was brighter at least, a clear sky and a pale sun. They passed a small well from where Benjamiah was sure he heard a high-pitched giggle.

"Did you hear that?" he whispered, peering into the dark depths. "Something laughed. . . ."

"I doubt that," said Elizabella, rolling her eyes.

The street ended in a passageway sealed off with stone. There was an uneven fissure between two slabs of rock, just wide enough for a child to slip through. Through it was nothing but darkness.

"Is this it?" said Elizabella.

Ariadne, dangling from the tip of a bonewood branch, nodded.

Elizabella unhooked Emba and clenched her fist round the doll. Emba ignited, a ball of flame engulfing Elizabella's hand, cool to her touch, but burning hot to any other.

"Wait here if you like," said Elizabella. "I can do this alone."

Benjamiah shook his head. Elizabella narrowed her eyes, staring at him hard, and then led the way.

They slipped into the dark, narrow gap, led by Elizabella's fiery hand. It was a tight squeeze, stone crowding them on either side. Finally they emerged in the Sunken Wood, joined by Nuisance the dormouse and a trembling Ariadne.

Fog—the thickest Benjamiah had ever seen—hid everything. They could see no farther than a few yards ahead. Beneath their feet was moist soil scattered with dead leaves and twigs, sloping downward into a cradle of pooled, cottony mist. It was deathly silent, the air damp and cold. No twittering birds, no sighing leaves.

"This is crazy," said Benjamiah. "We can't see a thing. We'll never see it coming. . . ."

"It's probably long dead," said Elizabella. "You heard Vee. Thrompson's account was from nearly four hundred years ago. Birds don't live that long."

"Maybe eating children keeps you young," said Benjamiah grumpily.

Elizabella led the way into the fog, Emba now extinguished. Benjamiah, as ever, followed.

Down and down the Sunken Wood sloped. Forms rose out of the fog on either side, boulders covered in moss, fallen trees doused in lichen, monstrous bonewood trees spearing into the sky and out of sight, their trunks as wide as town houses. Above them were the waxy arms of other bonewoods, branches strong and wide enough to walk upon.

"Elizabella . . . ," whispered Benjamiah.

She stopped and turned. Benjamiah gestured to

something on the ground. It was a small bone, smoothed and white among the leaves.

"Probably an animal," she said.

"Or a child."

"More likely an animal," said Elizabella, before striding off again.

There were gorges and ravines layered with moss and lichen. There were walls of bramble, branches like pythons, and thorns like fangs. Bonewoods grew at long, slanting angles, forming ghostly paths up into the foggy heights. Benjamiah was having difficulty swallowing. Absolutely nothing moved or stirred. Their every step rang like a siren.

Suddenly a voice echoed through the fog.

"Help me!" it cried. "Help, please . . ."

Elizabella and Benjamiah froze. It sounded like a young boy.

"Help, please!" he shouted again.

"This way!" said Benjamiah.

And it was he who ran first, chasing down the voice, Elizabella blundering in his wake. They weaved, ducking low branches, swerving the snatching brambles. Benjamiah's chest was a knot, every breath a struggle. Blood thundered through his body.

"Help . . . Please, I need help!" wailed the boy.

They were closer. Benjamiah still led the way, Elizabella just behind. The fog revealed nothing. They stopped, panting, twisting one way and the other, waiting for the boy to call again. A child's scream split the silent wood. They sensed something rushing toward them.

But it wasn't a child's shape that broke through the mist.

The monstrous raven fell like a meteor, the din of a hundred screaming children accompanying it. All they saw was a tremendous black shape punching out of the murk, a flurry of foul-smelling feathers and murderous talons and an enormous snapping beak. The children dived. There was a detonation of mud, wood, and shrubbery as the raven tore into the ground where they'd stood.

The evil bird screamed with the voices of all the children it had eaten, flapping upward. It was huge and terrible, the beat of its wings throwing gouts of air upon the scrambling children. Jet-black feathers hung limp and oily, its vast wings full of holes as though rotted. It was bony, half-dead, some skin fallen away around its breast and skull. Above the beak—hooked and bladed and snapping—it had no eyes. A rancid smell, like decay, accompanied the raven.

It was Elizabella that the raven went for, screaming, snapping. She scrambled backward and threw herself into a fallen tree. The monstrous raven ripped at it with its talons, stabbing the brittle wood with its beak and tearing it to ribbons. Benjamiah was utterly helpless. The raven, insatiable, peeled the remains of the tree away, revealing

Elizabella. It craned its head back, ready to pluck her into its mouth.

A shape rushed up. It was Emba, cast as an eagle. Emba crashed into the raven's face, pecking at its monstrous skull, slashing with her talons. The raven flailed, screeching, then did its best to grab Emba with its beak. The eagle escaped, shooting upward into the fog. The raven took off in pursuit.

Benjamiah ran over to Elizabella, lying pale and wild-eyed in the wreckage of the tree. He hoisted her up. Their hands shook in each other's palms.

"Come on," said Benjamiah.

They ran. Benjamiah thought his legs might buckle beneath him. They ducked inside the hollow of a bonewood.

"What about Emba?" he said.

Silence fell. Benjamiah knew what would happen if Emba were killed—Elizabella would drop dead beside him, like a puppet with cut strings. There was a rustle above them. Both flinched. Climbing down the hollow was a squirrel, a bluish tinge to her fur, smoky marbles for eyes. Emba.

They huddled together, catching their breath. The Sunken Wood had fallen deathly silent once more. Elizabella had cuts on her face from the shards of splintered wood. Her hands trembled in her lap. Benjamiah noticed that Emba—back in doll form—had a little tear in the fabric of her arm.

"Nothing a dollmender can't fix," said Elizabella.

They waited. Nothing moved.

"That's how she used to trick children," whispered Elizabella. "Thrompson wondered how she kept luring them out at night. She uses false cries for help from other children. Don't let her trick us again. The children aren't real."

"How can you be sure?" said Benjamiah.

"Why would there be any children here?"

Benjamiah thought it was poor logic. He and Elizabella were here, after all.

"And I know where the whisperwick is," added Elizabella.

"Where?" said Benjamiah, fearing the answer.

"Remember what Vee said?" said Elizabella. "*An appetite for shiny trinkets, which it hoards in its roost.* That must be where Edwid hid the whisperwick. It's *perfect.*"

"Oh, sure," said Benjamiah. "Completely perfect. The roost of a giant, child-eating raven. What a *perfect* place to keep something. How absolutely *perfect!*"

Elizabella hushed him with a wave of the hand. Why did she suddenly look so excited? Benjamiah felt nothing but dim, disorienting terror.

"We have to go up," said Elizabella. "Its roost will be in the trees."

"We don't."

"We do."

"We can't."

"We *are*. It has no eyes, does it? It must rely on hearing. We just have to be quiet."

Benjamiah shook his head. "It saw us. It went for us. And Emba, too. Plus, why would it hoard shiny things if it can't see them?"

"Maybe it can see a little," conceded Elizabella. "Think about it. That would make its attraction to shiny things *more* likely. It didn't attack us until you went blundering through the trees. It wanted us to make a noise."

Benjamiah watched Elizabella stand, dust herself down, take a deep breath through her nose, and stride out into the mist.

He had no choice—he followed.

They were back in the open in the damp, dense air and the silence that seemed to span the world. Benjamiah had never felt so exposed in his life.

Elizabella put a finger to her lips and continued walking.

The tension was unbearable. Benjamiah's heart was lodged in his throat, beating at the back of his mouth. Each of their steps—so slow and careful—rustled through the silence. The fear was dizzying.

"Help . . . ," called a girl's voice.

"Help us . . . ," said a boy from the same direction.

Benjamiah looked at Elizabella. She shook her head and mouthed, *Trap*. They crossed a scattering of mossy boulders in the bed of a dried-out creek, bones tangled among the weeds.

"Elizabella!" shouted the girl's voice from somewhere in the fog.

Elizabella and Benjamiah froze. How could it know her name?

"Benjamiah, please . . . ," said the boy.

Benjamiah thought he was going to faint. This didn't seem like a trap. Elizabella shook her head again, convinced the raven was playing games.

"It's us," called the girl. "Clora and Odgar . . . ,"

"Please help!" shouted the boy.

It sounded exactly like Clora and Odgar, which made it unbearable. But Elizabella was surely right—it had to be a trick. She crept on, with Benjamiah close behind. They came to one of the monumental bonewood trees thrusting out of the Sunken Wood at such an angle the children could walk up its trunk. Together they climbed the wooden path. The bonewood was slippery from the damp air. Once or twice, Benjamiah wobbled, teetering over the foggy depths. Elizabella grabbed him each time, looking annoyed at his clumsiness.

The bonewood twisted, turned one way and another, presented forks where the trunk split into boughs, each another pathway. They were climbing higher and higher, the ground out of sight. The shouts from the phantom

Clora and Odgar had stopped. Nuisance was a dormouse, shivering in Benjamiah's breast pocket. Benjamiah patted him. Emba hung from her noose.

The rush of enormous wings shattered the silence. A dark shape blew through the fog nearby, then vanished. The raven had passed without seeing them. Maybe Elizabella had been right, after all: its eyesight was poor. The children waited for a moment, then continued. They had passed into another world, a labyrinth in the sky, a warren of boughs and branches.

"Look," whispered Elizabella, stopping.

In the distance, engulfed in fog, something shone.

Her roost, mouthed Elizabella. *Come on.*

They heard the beat of unseen wings again. Branches creaked and shook, as though the raven had perched nearby. Benjamiah put his hand in the crook of Elizabella's elbow.

"Wait," he whispered. "Just think. If Edwid's whisperwick is there, don't you think the raven will notice it being carried away? We need a plan."

Elizabella grinned. She mouthed, *I have an idea.*

Elizabella having a plan never failed to worry Benjamiah.

Before he could say a word, she edged forward. The roost glittered faintly ahead. The branches of the bonewoods were getting steeper and more slippery. A fall now would be deadly. They climbed up, hopping between branches, all the while maintaining absolute silence.

From a knot between two boughs, they had a good view of the roost. It was a vast nest of dead branches, sticks, and bracken, built on the intersection of three huge bone-wood branches. It smelled as rancid as the giant raven. Within the roost was a great mound of random shiny objects. Benjamiah saw a telescope, a gold pendulum from a grandfather clock, a sword, jewelry, precious stones, and silver goblets.

"It must be in there," said Elizabella quietly. "And here's how I think we can get it. . . ."

She whispered her plan to Benjamiah. Afterward he told her it was a truly terrible idea.

"Do you have a better one?"

Benjamiah nodded. "Yes, I do. We get out of here and never come back."

"Are you going to help me or not?" hissed Elizabella.

She always did that. What was he supposed to say? She would risk everything for the whisperwick regardless. Finally he gave a tiny nod.

"Okay, wait for my signal," said Elizabella.

She moved away, hopping onto a bough running parallel to where Benjamiah sat. He watched her until the fog had almost completely erased her. He could just about make her out, blurred by the dense vapor. She fell completely still.

It all happened very quickly. Benjamiah saw Emba ignite

in Elizabella's hand, a ball of terrific flame. The screaming returned immediately. From above came a creaking sound as the monstrous raven detached itself from the trees. They heard the beat of wings among the chorus of screams. Then it plunged out of the fog, diving straight at Elizabella.

Elizabella fled, hopping between branches. This was Benjamiah's chance. He heard the raven screeching, trees being torn, as it chased Elizabella. Benjamiah ran, clambering up the bonewood boughs and dropping into the roost. The smell was truly revolting. Littering the bed were bones, droppings, rags.

Benjamiah attacked the mountain of sparkling objects. Half-blind with panic, he threw aside clocks and buckets, rings and coins and spectacles tumbling. In the distance, he could hear the raven screaming, smashing through wood, the beating of its enormous wings. Now Benjamiah was also making a racket as he crashed through the hoard in desperation, scrabbling for Edwid's lantern.

And there it was, hidden behind a golden chest encrusted with rubies. Benjamiah grabbed it and bolted, scrambling out of the roost. Only when he'd heaved himself out did he realize that quiet had fallen. No screaming, no sounds of chasing. Had the raven eaten Elizabella? He peered through the fog, the beat of his heart shaking his entire body.

Then the chorus of screams resumed as the raven burst

out of the foggy air, talons stabbing toward Benjamiah. He threw himself sideways, cradling the lantern, and ran for his life. The rabid bird chased him, smashing through branch and bough, talons and razor-edged beak raining down devastating blows. Benjamiah leaped into a hollow of the tree. The raven was too big to follow, but it tore at the wood with its beak, splinters flying everywhere.

Behind the raven, Benjamiah saw Elizabella. She was on another bonewood branch, a few yards of foggy air between them. Elizabella screamed for the bird's attention, waving her flaming poppet, whistling. But the raven had Benjamiah trapped, and it wasn't going to let him out. The hollow was disintegrating beneath the raven's fury. A few more blows of the beak and it would have him.

He had no choice but to run. When the raven cranked back, Benjamiah squirmed out. He leaped, scrambled, ran. He heard the terrible bird rise behind him with a *whump* of enormous wings. In the panic, he lost his footing. He pitched forward, losing his grip on the whisperwick. It cartwheeled briefly upward, then plunged down.

The raven was upon Benjamiah.

Elizabella would send Emba to save the whisperwick from smashing on the ground below. And, in doing so, the raven would pluck up Benjamiah, ferry him back to its roost, and devour him. He scrunched his eyes closed as it shaped its talons to snatch him. He thought of Grandma, and Mum and Dad, and wished he could give them all one last hug and say sorry for being so difficult.

Then the raven shrieked. Benjamiah risked a glance. Emba the eagle was pecking and scratching at its skull.

"Run, Benjamiah!" screamed Elizabella.

He could barely process what had happened—Elizabella had let the whisperwick fall to save him.

A vision overcame Benjamiah. The image of the whisperwick hurtling toward the forest floor. Benjamiah saw it as if he himself were flying behind it, chasing downward to stop the lantern from shattering. Impulses in the dark reaches of his mind were straining and pulling. As though a part of his mind were flying, spearing downward, right behind the whisperwick . . . Benjamiah shook the image away.

With Emba fighting off the raven, Benjamiah hauled himself up and ran. The children raced along parallel branches, away from the screeching monster, running and clambering and hopping. They hurried downward, back toward the ground, finally reaching the floor of the Sunken Wood.

They hid, wide-eyed and trembling. They gasped for breath. Elizabella was still alive, so Emba must have escaped the raven. Benjamiah couldn't look at her.

"I'm sorry . . . ," he said softly. "I'm so sorry. It just slipped. . . ."

Elizabella said nothing. She was cut and bruised, as was Benjamiah. Neither could stop shaking.

"Emba . . . ," said Benjamiah.

"She's coming," said Elizabella. "Let's go."

They crept away, crossing mossy boulders and gullies of murky water. Emba joined them shortly after, now a fox. She was wounded along her side and back. Out of the wounds smoked a fine, trembling substance, like warm air rising from a heater. When Elizabella pulled her back into doll form, there were more tears in the fabric.

"I'm sorry, Elizabella," said Benjamiah.

"It's okay," she said. "A dollmender can fix her."

That wasn't why he'd apologized. The whisperwick . . . They walked in silence. The trip to the Sunken Wood had been an abject failure. Edwid's lantern had slipped out of Benjamiah's grip and surely smashed. Elizabella was empty-eyed as she consulted Ariadne on the way out. The thread led them up the slopes and back toward the sealed tunnel through which they'd entered. It was at this point that Benjamiah noticed something was missing.

"Nuisance . . . ," he whispered.

Elizabella turned.

"He was here in my pocket," said Benjamiah. "He was there when . . ."

Then, out of the mist, Benjamiah heard a familiar thrum of wings. They saw a dark speck at first, moving awkwardly, his flight restrained and lopsided. As he drew closer, they understood why.

Dangling from his tiny claws was Edwid's lantern, safe and sound.

Elizabella and Benjamiah erupted with relief, rushing forward. Nuisance delivered the lantern into Elizabella's hands. Benjamiah cupped the exhausted nightjar in his hands and smiled the biggest smile of his life. Elizabella leaned down and kissed the bird—Nuisance looked embarrassed.

"Amazing," whispered Elizabella. "Clever poppet."

But Benjamiah thought differently. He recalled the vision of the falling lantern, the sensation of chasing it downward, the tensing and flexing of mysterious muscles in his mind.

It had been Benjamiah controlling Nuisance.

In the distant fog, they heard the raven's cacophony of screams rise again.

"Let's get out of here," said Elizabella.

"That's the best idea you've had in a long time," said Benjamiah.

Together they left the Sunken Wood.

SIXTEEN

WITH THE WELL-LURKER

A doll that suffers damage during battle must be taken to a specialist dollmender. Every moment that a poppet carries an open tear, more of its aether will be lost. If too much aether is lost, the result will be fatal to the dollcaster, whose life is bound to that of their poppet. Needless to say, tears and rips should not be mended at home with a sewing kit.

—*A Brief History of Wreathenwold*,
Archscholar Collum Wolfsdaughter

SAFELY OUT of the Sunken Wood, they perched on the ledge of the little well and caught their breath. Despite various scrapes and bumps, neither Elizabella nor Benjamiah were seriously hurt. Nuisance and Ariadne were also unharmed. It was Emba who had absorbed most of the damage. The doll lay in Elizabella's lap, torn all over. Rippling air escaped from the wounds.

"We need to find a dollmender," said Benjamiah.

Elizabella nodded. She returned Emba to her noose.

"What is that coming out of Emba's cuts?" asked Benjamiah.

"It's aether," said Elizabella. "If she loses too much, she'll die. And I'll die with her."

"We have to hurry, then!" said Benjamiah.

"In a minute," said Elizabella.

She set Edwid's whisperwick on the stone ledge, crouched, and inserted the key. In scrabbled the root. Out came the familiar click. Elizabella stiffened, took a deep breath, and opened the door:

> *A place where sunlight cannot reach,*
> *A depth no breathing thing can breach.*

Then the candle went out. Benjamiah wrote the words down in his notebook, beneath the other couplets. He had to admit it wasn't making any more sense, and they had now found three out of four. Frustration dominated Elizabella's face.

"This will *never* make sense," she moaned.

"We need all four," said Benjamiah. "It has to mean something altogether. Why would Edwid risk all this for nothing?"

They sat for a while longer, drinking milk punch and eating opples.

"You saved me," said Benjamiah.

Elizabella was silent.

"You had a choice between saving me or saving Edwid's lantern," said Benjamiah.

Still, Elizabella was silent.

"And you chose to save me."

"Are you going to keep going on about it?" she snapped.

"Thank you." Benjamiah blushed.

Elizabella fidgeted, her face stiff. "You're welcome," she said eventually. "Luckily, Nuisance saved the day. All by himself, apparently."

Benjamiah held Nuisance tightly. Elizabella stared at Benjamiah, eyes narrowed suspiciously.

She knows, he thought. *She knows it was me.*

An awkward silence formed. It was almost a relief when, from the depths of the well behind them, there came a giggle.

Elizabella and Benjamiah leaped up and peered in. All they saw was a throat of darkness plunging deep into the earth with no sign of water.

"Did you hear that?" whispered Elizabella.

Benjamiah nodded. "It was a laugh. Just like earlier. I told you I heard something."

"Who's there?" shouted Elizabella.

Her words echoed down the well. Nobody replied. Benjamiah stared, trying to unpick some sign of life from the blackness.

"We must have imagined it," she said.

"Both of us? At the same time?"

"Let's go," said Elizabella, shrugging.

They turned to leave. Then came the longest and loudest giggle yet. There was no doubt this time. Somebody—or something—was hiding in the shadows of the well.

Elizabella's eyes widened, and she looked suddenly excited.

"It must be a well-lurker!" she whispered. "I've never come across one before. . . ."

"A well-lurker?" said Benjamiah.

"Old spirits who live in wells," she explained. "According to *The Book of Barely Believable Stories*, they're the souls of children or travelers who fell down wells and couldn't get out. Now they haunt them, playing tricks and speaking in riddles. Trying to make the rest of us as miserable as them."

"What a terribly low opinion you have of me," came a voice from the well. "You would break my heart if I still had one."

Both children jumped. It was a low, strange voice, all shadow and water. Slowly they leaned over the lip of the well. Still they saw only darkness.

"Be careful," whispered Elizabella. "It probably wants us to fall in."

"I want no such thing," said the well-lurker. "There isn't room for either of you down here, thank you very much. I only wanted to help."

"Help?" said Elizabella, the word bouncing down into the shadows.

"We people of the wells know all manner of things," said the well-lurker. "All the truths, secrets, and mysteries of this world flow in its waters. I have little else to do but gather them up."

"So you know secret things?" said Elizabella. "And you'll tell us the truth?"

"Cross my heart and hope to die," said the well-lurker.

"You said you don't have a heart," called Benjamiah.

"No need to remind me," replied the well-lurker, sounding hurt.

"Why would we trust what you say?" said Elizabella.

"Ask me anything," said the well-lurker, "and see for yourself."

Elizabella's face knotted, thinking what to ask. So Benjamiah stepped in.

"What are our names?" he called.

"Too easy, Benjamiah Creek," replied the well-lurker. "You should have let Elizabella Cotton choose instead."

The children stared at each other, open-mouthed.

"That one was free," said the well-lurker. "The next, I'm afraid, will cost you."

"Here we go . . . ," said Elizabella, rolling her eyes. "What do you want?"

"Only a small payment per question," said the well-lurker. "A piece or two. We all have to make a living, after all."

"What does a spirit living in a well want with money?" said Benjamiah.

"I really can't see how that's any of your business," said the well-lurker. "Make your choice, children. You are both positively bursting with unanswered questions. I can feel it."

"Well, let's give it a try," said Elizabella.

She took out her playing cards, then sent the two of clubs fluttering down the well.

"Why does Benjamiah smell so bad?" she said.

"He needs to wash more," replied the well-lurker.

"Hey!" shouted Benjamiah, while Elizabella laughed.

"Well, there you go!" she declared. "It *does* tell the truth, after all."

In response, Benjamiah threw down a card of his own.

"Why is Elizabella so rude?" he asked.

"She's scared of people not liking the *real* Elizabella," said the well-lurker.

A hint of pink rose in Elizabella's cheeks. Now it was Benjamiah's turn to laugh.

"Why is Benjamiah so annoying?" asked Elizabella, throwing down a card.

"I'm afraid nothing can be done to help it," said the well-lurker.

"Why is Elizabella so annoying?" Benjamiah asked in return.

"I find her rather charming," said the well-lurker.

"Not fair," said Benjamiah sulkily, as Elizabella laughed.

"I remember your face," said the well-lurker suddenly.

Elizabella froze. Slowly she and Benjamiah leaned back over the well.

"What do you mean?" she said quietly.

"You look just like him."

"You mean . . . Edwid?"

"He came this way too," said the well-lurker. "We had a rather fascinating conversation."

"Tell me everything," Elizabella said, fingers gripping the stone.

The well-lurker giggled, then gave a little *ahem*. A reminder of payment. With trembling fingers, Elizabella loosened a two of diamonds and dropped it into the darkness.

"Very generous of you," said the well-lurker. "Ask your questions."

"Where is Edwid?" said Elizabella.

"Who can say?" replied the well-lurker.

"That's not fair!" shouted Benjamiah, as Elizabella paled beside him. "You said you would answer."

"I can only answer questions that have an answer," said the well-lurker mysteriously. "Try another."

Benjamiah was beginning to feel the well-lurker was a trickster, after all. He wanted to warn Elizabella, persuade her to leave, but it was hopeless—the prospect of learning anything about Edwid intoxicated her.

"You're lying," said Elizabella. "Why would Edwid tell you anything?"

"You wound me," moaned the well-lurker, exaggerating offense. "I got the impression your brother was glad to unburden himself. He'd come a long way, and been through much, with nobody to talk to."

Beside him, Benjamiah saw how this hurt Elizabella—Edwid used to tell *her* everything, until something changed.

"What did he tell you?" she said.

"Three things," said the well-lurker. "First that he was sorry, second that he was a fool, third that he was in terrible danger."

"That means nothing!" said Elizabella furiously.

The well-lurker gave another *ahem*. Against his better instincts, Benjamiah cast down a five of hearts.

"That's five whole bits," he said. "More than you've probably had in half your life. Now answer the questions properly."

Elizabella smiled gratefully at Benjamiah. He smiled back.

"Right you are," said the well-lurker. "First why he was sorry. He ran away from home to visit the Company of Mapmakers, and he wished he'd told you about it, before and after. Your brother always dreamed of being a Mapmaker, did he not?"

Elizabella nodded, looking as though something were lodged in her throat. Benjamiah recalled the sketches of Mapmakers all over Edwid's bedroom wall.

"But how did he find his way there?" he asked.

"There is no way to navigate this world of ours," said the well-lurker, "unless you are from a time before the labyrinth. Which is to say unless you are a Hanged Man. Edwid paid a Hanged Man to take him to the Company of Mapmakers. He did this by handing over the colors of his eyes."

Elizabella seemed to wobble. It must have been an awful lot for her to absorb. As far as Benjamiah could tell, the story made sense. Hansel had told Benjamiah that the Hanged Men could navigate Wreathenwold. And, after his mysterious adventure, Edwid had indeed returned to Follynook with gray, colorless eyes.

"Then what happened?" said Elizabella, her voice tiny.

"Your brother enjoyed the House of Mapmakers," said the well-lurker. "But when it came time to return, the Hanged Man was gone. Though they had agreed he would bring your brother home, he abandoned him there. Edwid was stuck. While at the House of Mapmakers, he heard whispers of some secret device of navigation. I understand that he stole it in order to return home."

So Edwid did steal Ariadne from the Mapmakers, as they'd suspected.

"Edwid ran away a second time," said Elizabella, "before he fell ill. Where did he go?"

"Somewhere foolish," said the well-lurker. "He was tricked, you see. By the crack in his bedroom wall."

"What?" said Elizabella despairingly. "That doesn't make any sense!"

Benjamiah had seen the crack. He remembered how it gave him the shivers, for no obvious reason. And hadn't both Hansel and Elizabella said that Edwid had been rambling about the crack in the wall?

"It came to him," said the well-lurker. "To him specifically, precisely because your brother had this means of navigating Wreathenwold, which he stole from the Mapmakers. It tricked him, pretending it was something other than it was. It sent Edwid to the home of Olfred Wicker, the children's author, to recover something of enormous and grave importance."

"Olfred Wicker . . . ," repeated Elizabella. "The man who wrote Jamima Cleaves?"

"The very same," said the well-lurker.

"What was the thing it wanted?" asked Benjamiah.

"Your brother did not say," said the well-lurker, "and that is a mystery even I have not unraveled. But your brother found it, took it, and escaped, rather than hand it over to the crack in the wall."

"But what *is* the crack in the wall?" said Elizabella.

"Darkness," said the well-lurker softly. "A darkness now released upon Wreathenwold, of which we should all be most terribly afraid. The magi were terrible people, children. Too much power and not nearly enough feeling. But imagine a magus so terrible that even the other magi felt compelled to imprison him. . . ."

It took Benjamiah a few moments to fully process what the well-lurker had said.

"You mean . . . ," he began, while Elizabella struggled in silence, "that the crack in the wall was a magus? Imprisoned there?"

"I do," said the well-lurker.

"And Edwid found something the magus wanted," continued Benjamiah. "And it escaped to get it from him?"

"So Edwid said," answered the well-lurker. "Which is the third thing he told me: of terrible danger. Not only for himself, but for us all. I am only glad I live down here, out of its way. . . ."

When it was clear the well-lurker could tell them nothing more, Ariadne led them to a dollmender's. Elizabella barely said a word along the way, and Benjamiah didn't blame her. Even he was reeling from the information. The well-lurker's story made sense of many things: where Edwid went both times he ran away, what happened to his eye colors, how he came to be in possession of Ariadne.

But other things seemed even more confusing now. What had Edwid been tricked into finding at Olfred Wicker's house? Why did Olfred Wicker have it in the first place? Was it the magus who had kidnapped Edwid? And what did it all have to do with the whisperwicks?

Ariadne led them to a quaint cottage called Jaundyce & Littlebrook's Dollmending. It was Lora Jaundyce who received them, an effervescent old woman with a limp and a glass eye and one of the biggest smiles Benjamiah had ever seen. A floppy, wide-brimmed hat sat on her head, wispy white hair curling out from beneath it. The shop itself was charming if incredibly messy, with books and spools of thread and boxes everywhere.

Lora examined Emba with scarred, stubby hands, muttering as she investigated the various tears in the fabric.

"What have you been up to, then?" she said, with a mischievous smile.

Elizabella and Benjamiah stared, lips buttoned.

Lora gave a tremendous, "Ha!" and winked her glass eye.

"I know that look," she said. "Don't worry, I was your age once. Absolutely nothing to see here, am I correct? Just normal, run-of-the-mill wear and tear . . ."

After another laugh and wink, Lora told them it would take an hour and would cost eleven bits and eight pieces.

Elizabella had spent the last of her money on the well-lurker, so Benjamiah paid. He handed over a nine of hearts, a jack of spades, and an eight of clubs, receiving an ace of spades in change.

"Are you okay?" he said to Elizabella.

They cleared a space on a sagging sofa that pulled them down like a quagmire.

"What do you mean?" she said.

"About everything the well-lurker said."

Elizabella gave a *mhm* and nothing more. Lora Jaundyce disappeared into the back of the shop. Through the door, they heard chatting, thrumming, clattering. Benjamiah read while Elizabella sat in deep silence, betraying nothing of what she was feeling.

Clearly, Edwid wished he'd told Elizabella about the journey to the Mapmakers. When he returned, he'd kept it secret from her. Maybe he felt guilty. In any case, it had created a distance between the twins that had never existed before. Which explained why, when the crack in the wall visited Edwid, he hadn't shared it with his sister.

Finally Lora emerged with Emba. The tears had been closed with exceptionally intricate stitching, barely noticeable.

"The stitches will vanish completely in a couple of days," she said. "Until then, no more of whatever you've been up to. Anything too stressful and the thread will snap. Do you understand?"

Elizabella nodded. Benjamiah wasn't convinced she'd really listened. After a quick thank-you, Elizabella dashed off, and Benjamiah followed.

"Where now?" he said, fearing the answer.

"Where else? The last whisperwick."

Elizabella pulled out Edwid's notebook and rifled through it, landing on the final sketch. Though disguised as a labyrinth of roads and rivers, the overall resemblance was clear. It was the Minotaur—the monster at the center of the world.

"Could it be something else?" said Benjamiah, feeling faint.

"Like what?" snapped Elizabella.

She looked sorry about it, but didn't say so. When Benjamiah had no alternative suggestions, she put the notebook back in her bag and turned her attention to Ariadne.

"Ariadne? Take us to the Shrouded Palace."

They traveled the entire day, spending their dwindling money on hansom cabs. Elizabella was as quiet as Benjamiah had known her. When he tried to draw her into conversation, whether about the well-lurker's story or something distracting like Jamima Cleaves, she replied in grunts. When they couldn't take cabs, Elizabella dragged them along at a brisk, punishing pace. Benjamiah had to plead to stop for food and drink, as much for Elizabella's sake as his own.

Night fell and they were dead on their feet. Elizabella wanted to journey through the night, but when Ariadne fell asleep in Benjamiah's palm, Elizabella relented. They got rooms for the night at a run-down inn owned by a mistrustful-looking man named Mr. Berd.

Benjamiah was alone in his room, reading *A Brief History of Wreathenwold* by the log fire, when there came a knock on the door.

It was Elizabella, a chessboard tucked beneath her arm.

"Would you like to play?" she asked.

The two children sat cross-legged on the bed, the board between them. The pieces were carved from bonewood, smoothed and warped with age. Firelight threw trembling shadows over the bedsheets. Beside the board were their final sweets from Miss Bliss's Confections, a selection of wyrm's eggs and smokeberry melts.

The prospect of playing chess filled Benjamiah with excitement. His entire time in Wreathenwold had been full of not knowing or understanding anything. Here, finally, he would have the upper hand over Elizabella. He even let her play white.

For a while, they played in silence but for the fire crackling, making moves and eating sweets. Nuisance and Emba tumbled about together, while Ariadne slept coiled in her box. To Benjamiah's dismay, it turned out Elizabella was very good at chess. In fact, after fifteen or so moves, she was clearly winning. Benjamiah was mortified.

"Edwid and I used to play," she said, her voice very small. "He was always a tiny bit better, like with most things."

Benjamiah, while trying to see a way out of the various traps Elizabella's pieces were threatening, said, "Do you believe what the well-lurker said?"

"Yes," said Elizabella. "I do. It all makes sense. Trust Edwid to get mixed up with a mad magus trapped in the wall."

Benjamiah laughed, and Elizabella joined in.

"It'll be all right, Elizabella," said Benjamiah. "We'll find him."

She started to say something else, but stopped short. Instead, she drove another of her pawns forward, a move Benjamiah hadn't even thought about. The game was going very poorly for him.

"Who do you play chess with?" said Elizabella.

"Mostly on my own," said Benjamiah. "Mum is pretty busy. Dad's terrible, but he tries. Grandma prefers checkers, but she plays with me sometimes."

"What about friends?" asked Elizabella.

As usual, any mention of the friends Benjamiah didn't have caused a squirm in his stomach. He tried his best to get himself out of the mess on the chessboard, hoping Elizabella would drop the subject.

"Well, they're missing out," said Elizabella, smiling.

Benjamiah could have sworn she actually meant it.

"Nobody much likes me," said Benjamiah. "I always thought being clever and knowing everything was the most important thing. But being stuck in Wreathenwold, completely lost, with a girl determined to get me killed—"

"Not exactly *determined* . . . ," interjected Elizabella.

"—has shown me differently," continued Benjamiah. "It isn't nice feeling lost."

"Glad I could help," said Elizabella. "Oh, and checkmate."

It was indeed. Benjamiah sulked for a while, until Elizabella offered him the last smokeberry melt and set up the board for another game. This time, Benjamiah refused to talk, fixating on the pieces. They played three more games, of which Elizabella won two and Benjamiah one.

After that, they said good night. Benjamiah fell into bed, exhausted but pleased he'd at least beaten Elizabella once. Nuisance was in doll form on the bedside cabinet. Benjamiah stared at him. Given everything he'd read and experienced about Wreathenwold so far, Nuisance was impossible. Dolls were made for dollcasters as babies and died alongside them. There were no orphaned or nomadic poppets roaming Wreathenwold, much less crossing into another world to bring people here. So what was Nuisance, and why had he attached himself to Benjamiah?

Reluctant excitement fluttered in his breast. It felt like Nuisance could be *his*, really his. Isn't that what had happened in the Sunken Wood? Maybe he could cast Nuisance the way Elizabella cast Emba. They could have that connection, that kinship, that magic. How had Elizabella described it? Like a muscle, she'd said. Like a set of muscles in the mind, to be flexed and contracted. Benjamiah knew now how they felt—they'd come to life in the Sunken Wood. In the dark, staring at Nuisance, he felt their presence.

Benjamiah found he was trembling. It was like waking up one morning with an extra limb, after living his entire life with the regular four. Actively encouraging the connection, as Honeysuckle had said he must, was a frightening thought. It felt like rejecting all the science and reason he'd loved his entire life. It felt like rejecting Mum, who would always say that magic was the name uncivilized people gave to things they couldn't explain.

Should he do it? Should he flex those muscles and make Nuisance spring up from the bedside cabinet? Though he had read a little about animal anatomy, he didn't know the details the way Elizabella did. She'd said you needed to know everything about them, inside and out. But he could source spellbooks in secret, practice, become a dollcaster himself . . . ?

It was too much. He closed his eyes, rolled over, and

chased sleep, eventually succumbing after what felt like hours.

It was still dark when he was woken by a knock at the door. Benjamiah staggered out of a deep, confused rest. It couldn't be morning already. Disoriented, he opened the door, expecting Elizabella. But it wasn't her standing there.

It was a Hanged Man.

SEVENTEEN

WITH THE HALF-FELL BRIDGE

Only the Hanged Men can navigate the city, being no longer technically living and having been here before Wreathenwold became a labyrinth. It is said the Hanged Men draw upon secret doorways, stairwells, and bridges that allow them to cross vast swathes of the city in mere moments.
—*A Brief History of Wreathenwold*,
Archscholar Collum Wolfsdaughter

THE HANGED MAN grabbed Benjamiah by the collar before he could fully process what he was seeing. Standing behind him were two more Hanged Men. One had Elizabella by the scruff of the neck, her eyes dark and sunken. The other held Emba in one hand, incapacitated by the paralyzing prickles of his glove, and Elizabella's bag in the other.

A fourth Hanged Man strode into Benjamiah's room.

He plucked Nuisance up from the bedside table and grabbed Benjamiah's things.

"Let's go," he said.

"Why?" said Benjamiah. "We haven't done anything!"

"Tell it to the Viper."

They were led down the narrow hallway, the Hanged Men looming as high as the ceiling. Other guests peered out from their rooms, only to quickly vanish upon seeing the Hanged Men.

They were led through the reception of the inn, where the innkeeper—Mr. Berd—looked smug in a nightgown and nightcap as a Hanged Man handed over a stack of playing cards. The innkeeper had recognized and betrayed them.

Elizabella and Benjamiah were ushered into the cold, shadowy morning. Waiting on the street were more Hanged Men, armed with batons. Most of their poppets hung at their hips, but two were cast as fearsome gray tigers, sphinxlike on either side of a black carriage.

"Bind their hands," said a voice. "They're slippery little creatures."

Emerging from behind the carriage was a tall, bony man dressed in the dark blue attire of the Hanged Men. This was another Inspector, but nothing like Inspector Halfpenny. There was none of her charm, her roguish untidiness, her gentleness. Inspector Cromwell was all bones and brutal angles, elongated and thin and spidery in his movements, his skin pale as though powdered and his lips thin and blood-red.

"We want to see Inspector Halfpenny," said Benjamiah.

Inspector Cromwell ignored him.

"You should be ashamed of yourself," said Benjamiah. "We're only trying to find Edwid Cotton. A missing boy that none of *you* seem to be looking for."

Inspector Cromwell descended on Benjamiah, lowering his horrid face until it was level with his. Bones squirmed beneath the papery skin.

"Quiet now," he said, his voice steady, "or the tigers will have you. She can still pluck out your eye colors afterward."

She? Did he mean . . . ?

And, with that, Elizabella's and Benjamiah's hands were bound with rope. Then they waited where they stood, trembling, half-dressed, in the punishing cold.

Benjamiah's stomach had knotted, thoughts flocking to the punishment they'd been promised. The serum dripped into his eyes, the colors sucked out and added to Gertrid's dress . . . It was abhorrent. What would Grandma, Mum, and Dad say when he returned home with empty, colorless eyes? If he ever made it home. He was beginning to fear he never would.

Benjamiah looked around. Three new figures were striding to meet them.

Two were Hanged Men. The other was Odith Murdstone, the Viper.

Cromwell dashed over. "I have them for you, ma'am," he said, bowing, his entire body quivering with excitement. "I have apprehended the beasts for you, just as you asked."

Odith waved a gloved hand, clearing the obsequious Cromwell from her path. Cromwell bowed his head and scuttled aside, now hurrying in her wake. The Viper approached Elizabella and Benjamiah—tall and muscular, she was wrapped in reddish furs and wearing long snakeskin gloves. Her smile was a dangerous curve of purple venom.

Terror spread through Benjamiah. Elizabella was perfectly still, staring at her feet.

"Look at me, girl," whispered the Viper.

Elizabella refused. Benjamiah thought his legs might give way.

"I said *look at me.*"

Still, Elizabella refused. The Viper's hand flashed forward and pincered Elizabella's ear. Though a gasp of pain escaped her, Elizabella still would not look.

"Were you taught no manners in whatever filthy hovel you were raised, girl?" demanded the Viper, shaking Elizabella by the ear.

"Leave her alone!" shouted Benjamiah.

The Viper turned, licking her lips.

"How *sweet*," she said, at which Cromwell tittered. "I

never knew rats were capable of such affection. The boy first. The girl can listen to his screams before her own turn. Into the carriage."

Finally Elizabella reacted, yelling, "No! Take mine and leave Benjamiah alone. Please! I'm the one responsible. . . ."

But it only provided amusement for the Viper. A struggling Benjamiah was dragged inside the carriage by two Hanged Men. They forced him onto the leather bench and sat either side, holding him in place.

In climbed the Viper, flooding the carriage with musky perfume. She perched on the seat opposite Benjamiah and unbuttoned a snakeskin bag. A lump formed in his throat as the Viper lifted out the spectractor. She squeezed the handles several times, making it snap like crocodile jaws. Outside, Elizabella screamed and ranted for Benjamiah to be spared, until a tiger roared and silence fell.

"What pretty eyes you have," said the Viper. "You must know they're too pretty for you. Better I make something fabulous with them than you sell them at market for bread and plumpkins."

"We didn't do anything!" said Benjamiah.

The Viper ignored him, now withdrawing a vial of clear, viscous serum. She plucked out the stopper. Benjamiah smelled it immediately—a hot, eye-watering, chemical smell.

"I understand, you know," said the Viper, lowering

a syringe into the serum. "Why should you accept such poverty when others have so much? Why not try to improve your situation by whatever means you can? But there are *consequences*, my child."

"We didn't steal anything!" protested Benjamiah.

The vile serum began filling the syringe.

"You assaulted my beautiful, good-hearted, gentle daughter," said the Viper. "In her own home. You terrified her and could have killed her. She has barely slept a night since. She's fragile. That cannot be tolerated. You must make it up to her. Hold open his eye."

Gloved hands fell upon Benjamiah, prying his eyelid open. He flailed but it was useless. The Viper rose from her seat, syringe in one hand, spectractor in the other. She trembled with excitement, tongue playing over her lips.

"Such a pretty color," she whispered. "Take comfort in knowing that poverty is not an injustice. Poverty is a punishment for weak morals. Poverty is present wherever there is indecent character. The poor are inferior people."

The Viper licked her lips again. The tip of the syringe hovered above Benjamiah's left eye, a droplet of serum gathered there.

"This will hurt a lot. But you deserve it, sweetie. Be sure of it."

She squeezed. The drop fell toward Benjamiah's eye.

It never landed. Instead, between the dropper and

Benjamiah's eye, the fat bubble of serum stopped in midair, in defiance of all gravitational laws. Everybody froze. Baffled, Odith's lips parted. Everything was still, including the drop hovering a fraction of an inch above the surface of Benjamiah's eye.

"What . . . ," began the Viper.

She extended a gloved fingertip toward the hovering droplet. Before she could touch it, the next impossible thing happened.

The first Benjamiah knew of it was a gasp from the Viper and the sound of tearing metal. In her other hand, the spectractor had come alive and begun to twist and arrange itself into a new shape. As the Viper dropped it and the Hanged Men looked on, dumbfounded, Benjamiah glimpsed how the suddenly animated spectractor rippled with dark, wavy air.

Now it was a hand, fashioned from steel and rubber and glass, flexing and unflexing its fingers. Then, quick as a flash, the impossible hand balled, bared its knuckles, and delivered blows to both Hanged Men, knocking them out cold.

The Viper was too stunned to move. The metal hand spidered up Benjamiah's chest and held up three steely fingers. Then it began counting down. Three, two, one . . .

A tremendous force exploded outward, charged with such spectacular violence that the windows smashed and the carriage chassis was ripped to ribbons. It was a deafening din, a blinding chaos, filled with the Viper's piercing scream. Benjamiah, thrown sideways in the carnage, shielded his face. He scrambled out of the devastated carriage, falling onto the cobblestones, finally looking up and trying to make sense of what he saw.

Living, shadowy shapes had formed out of the materials of the carriage, fastened together by that same hot, rippling air. Some were spindly and humanlike, while others had assumed the shapes of tigers. Some Hanged Men had been quick enough to cast them, but it was all in vain. The spindly figures relieved the Hanged Men of their batons and clobbered them across their heads, while their poppets were soundly overcome, slashed, bitten, and wrestled into submission.

The battle was concluded with brutal efficiency. Hanged Men lay spread-eagled on the cobbles, their dolls in matching poses. Elizabella had sprung forward and grabbed Emba and their bags. Nuisance had returned to life and landed on Benjamiah's shoulder as a nightjar. Benjamiah was paralyzed, captivated by the figures made from the ruined carriage.

"Benjamiah, we have to go!" said Elizabella.

She hauled him up. His legs were frail. He couldn't tear his eyes from the sorcerous shapes. From what remained of the carriage could be heard a groaning. The Viper was trapped, calling for help.

Cromwell rushed over, scrabbling to free her from the wreckage.

"My poor lady!" he wailed, starting to dig her out. Then, seeing the children, he shrieked: "Stay where you are, you devils! You will hang for this sorcery."

The Viper wailed again, caged within the wrecked carriage.

"We have to go," whispered Elizabella.

"I don't . . . ," began Benjamiah. "What are they?"

"Come *on*!"

A final desperate tug and Benjamiah was persuaded. They ran. The sky was lightening. They saw faces at windows and on doorsteps—people who had witnessed the violence, the manifestation of the sorcerous army. Benjamiah saw his own confusion mirrored on their faces. Whatever had just happened, it was something even Wreathenwolders couldn't comprehend.

The hazy air. The tremendous power that made hairs stand on end. It could only have been one thing—the aether. Only a magus could manipulate the aether in that way. But where was he? Had he been there with them? And why had he done it?

They bolted as fast as their trembling legs could carry them, following the dips and crests of the lane, ducking down tunnels and up stairwells and through archways, streaking along a misty morning until they had put two streets between them and the scene, and then three, and then four.

Finally they stopped. It was a freezing cold street, the cobbles dusted with snow, icicles stabbing from the undersides of bonewood boughs. In an alleyway, they caught their breath, bent double.

"Do we still have Ariadne?" asked Benjamiah.

Elizabella flipped open her box. Ariadne coiled upward, swinging from Elizabella's straw hat into Benjamiah's hand.

"They found her," said Elizabella. "But Ariadne played dead. Thought she was nothing but an old piece of string in a box. Good job, Ariadne."

Ariadne gave a modest wave of the tail.

A dark shape appeared suddenly in the mouth of the alleyway. Benjamiah froze. Elizabella snatched Emba from her noose.

"A friend," said Manfred Tarr, holding up both hands. "Only a friend."

Elizabella kept her fingers clenched round Emba. Manfred looked out of breath, waxy, wild-eyed. His poppet hung at his side, yellow with white button eyes.

"How did you find us?" said Elizabella.

"*Again . . . ,*" Benjamiah pointed out, under his breath.

"Word of your arrest traveled quickly," said Manfred. "I was on my way to try something a little less . . . ah . . . *dramatic*. I arrived just before . . . Well, I can't explain quite what I saw. I hoped you could."

"What were you going to do?" said Elizabella.

"I confess I hadn't thought that far ahead," said Manfred. "Most likely I would have been arrested myself. But I had to try."

"Why?" said Elizabella. "Why do you care?"

Manfred seemed to consider the question carefully.

"I know what it's like to lose a brother," he said. "I would have given anything for a little help from a stranger, if it meant bringing him home."

It was certainly said with enough feeling.

"What happened back there?" said Manfred.

Benjamiah and Elizabella traded a dark glance.

"I don't know," said Elizabella.

"It was aether," said Benjamiah. "I saw it."

"Aether?" repeated Manfred, looking grave. "But that's impossible. That would mean . . ."

"The magus," said Elizabella.

Benjamiah nodded. Manfred massaged his jaw, cane tucked beneath his arm.

"That is troubling indeed," he said. "Why would the magus rescue you?"

It was a question that concerned Benjamiah, too. Nobody had an answer.

"We think the magus has something to do with Edwid's disappearance," said Elizabella.

"In what way?" said Manfred.

Elizabella gave an abridged version of the story the well-lurker had told. Benjamiah added in Honeysuckle's dire warning about a darkness surrounding Edwid's whisperwicks, which he was now sure meant the magus. Silence gathered when they finished. Manfred looked deeply troubled.

"We have to go," said Elizabella.

Her voice shook, her fists balled at her sides. Benjamiah knew where she meant. The final whisperwick . . . Manfred looked quizzical.

"The Half-Fell Bridge," said Elizabella.

Now Manfred was aghast. "You . . . What can you mean?" he said.

"The Minotaur."

"But . . . ," said Manfred, fumbling for words. "You can't think your brother is *there*?"

"No, but something else is," said Elizabella. "We have to go. Come on, Benjamiah."

"You can't really mean to go there?" said Manfred, as Elizabella and Benjamiah made to leave.

"We have to," replied Elizabella.

"The warnings about the Minotaur are not to be ignored," said Manfred, looking severe. "He smells the lost. He feasts on them. He will hunt you down, beginning the moment you cross the Half-Fell Bridge. It's too dangerous."

"It's okay," said Elizabella. "We aren't lost."

This reply caught Manfred by surprise. His eyes narrowed, confused. Then, apparently against his better judgment, he smiled.

"No, it would seem you aren't," he said. "You are a remarkable pair. And you have a secret. That much is clear. I won't press you for it. But you must be careful, nonetheless. The Minotaur is more dangerous than anything in this city. Nobody will help you there. Nor can you expect to rely on whatever—or whomever—saved you from the Hanged Men. You'll be alone."

There was nothing more to be said. Manfred gave them each a squeeze of the shoulder, followed by a nod of encouragement. Then he left, cane tapping on the icy cobbles.

"Ariadne?" said Elizabella.

The thread stood to attention in Benjamiah's palm. Elizabella took a deep, steadying breath.

"Take us to the Half-Fell Bridge."

The journey was fraught with tension and near misses. Word of the children's arrest—and their subsequent sorcerous escape—had set the streets of Wreathenwold crawling with Hanged Men. It meant progress was slow, time wasted loitering in alleyways, beneath arches, behind statues or fountains, waiting for the coast to clear. Benjamiah was in no rush, sick with worry about the Minotaur. Elizabella huffed, and hissed, and cursed just about everybody, Benjamiah included.

Benjamiah, as much to distract himself from the tension balled in his chest as anything else, had a lot of questions.

"How does Manfred Tarr keep finding us?" he said.

"No idea," replied Elizabella dismissively.

"Why would the magus save us?" said Benjamiah.

"Not sure," said Elizabella, not really listening.

"Was the magus there with us?" said Benjamiah.

"Don't know."

"How big is the Minotaur?"

"Who knows?"

"Did the magus kidnap Edwid?"

"*I don't know!*" snapped Elizabella. "And I don't *care*. I don't care about the magus, or the whisperwicks, or Manfred or the Minotaur. I care about finding Edwid. Now be quiet and *focus*."

A hundred more questions welled at the back of Benjamiah's throat, threatening to spill out. There was an awful lot that didn't add up. What did Edwid steal from Olfred Wicker? Why had he been kidnapped? Worries nagged and gnawed at him as he traveled in Elizabella's slipstream.

On they went, creeping and dodging and edging. They burned through most of the day, exhausting the final reserves of their money on hansoms, straying into streets that grew steadily shorter, narrower, and more twisty. An element of claustrophobia settled on Benjamiah—the houses, many of them ruined and uninhabited, formed increasingly tight boundaries on either side, reducing the visible sky to a murky streak. What people they saw were dark-eyed and gaunt, suspicious of the children.

Ariadne led them out of a snaking alleyway as night drew in, delivering them to the banks of a river. It had to be the Smeath, the only river in the city according to *A Brief History of Wreathenwold*. Unlike rivers back home, the Smeath didn't flow from a known source to a known mouth. Instead, it followed a medley of courses throughout Wreathenwold, a great spiderweb of tributaries and meanders, full of confluences and forks that made it as treacherous and misleading as the city itself. Its waters rushed fierce and murky.

The bridge they came to was an ancient arch of weary stone, robed in moss, its foundations thinned by the rushing water. Hunks of stone had been ripped from the abutments at either bank, parts of the arch collapsed into the depths below. In the middle of the arch there was no stone at all— just a makeshift crossing of sodden timber panels.

"This is it," said Elizabella. "Let's go."

But Benjamiah didn't move. Elizabella turned, studying him closely. "Are you coming?"

"Do you think I'll ever get home?" he asked.

Elizabella planted her hands on her hips.

"Benjamiah," she said, "I know you're scared. But we've faced worse and made it. We can do this."

But Benjamiah stayed where he was.

"I won't force you to come," she said gently.

"I have to get home," said Benjamiah. "My family . . ."

"You will. We both will. Promise."

And then she did something very unexpected. From her pocket, she pulled a small copper coin. She took Benjamiah's hand and set it in his palm. Her promise.

Tears gathered in Benjamiah's eyes.

"So are you coming?" she said.

He looked up and saw it in Elizabella's eyes: she was as frightened as he was.

"I'm coming," he said, putting her promise in his pocket.

"Are you sure?" Elizabella narrowed her eyes.

He nodded, and relief flickered across Elizabella's face. She smiled and stood beside him. Together they would finish this journey—together they could face anything.

Side by side, they crossed the Half-Fell Bridge.

EIGHTEEN

WITH THE CENTER OF THE LABYRINTH

Technically, the Minotaur rules Wreathenwold to this day, though the city is really governed by the Captains of the ninety-eight Honorable Companies. Few have ever laid eyes on the Minotaur. It is said he is more monster than man, alone at the center of the world, eating all who stray too close.

—*A Brief History of Wreathenwold,*
Archscholar Collum Wolfsdaughter

THEY ENTERED A GHOST WORLD. Houses rose like tombstones from a bank of fog, every window empty and every doorway vacant. All life had fled or perished. Nothing breathed or shifted but them. Color had given way to grayness. The roads were slender lanes walled by gutted, hollow buildings. Here Wreathenwold truly became a labyrinth.

Creeping on, each turn brought more to frighten the children. A torn, sodden top hat in a gutter, a half-bird, half-human effigy hanging from a window, a monstrous depiction of the Minotaur—mouth gaping, eyes popping—scored into the face of a limestone wall. The sound of their every footstep seemed to carry a mile, like a siren for the beast that ruled the maze. Grotesques leered from every ledge. *A Brief History of Wreathenwold* said they'd been the Minotaur's army when he'd overthrown the Widow. Were they still alive, watching them?

The tension was sickening. Benjamiah's stomach clenched unbearably, expecting at any moment to see the grim monster storming toward them. They passed a toy shop that looked a hundred years old, its windows punched through, its front blackened by fire. Within was an array of bug-eyed dollies, jack-in-the-boxes, and toy soldiers, buried in dust and ash. They walked down a lane of abandoned bookshops, eaten by fire and half-collapsed.

Ariadne, perched on Elizabella's shoulder, seemed terrified. Nuisance was a dormouse, timidly poking his nose out of Benjamiah's breast pocket. Benjamiah stroked his fur, reassuring him.

"Ariadne?" said Elizabella.

Ariadne stood to attention, trembling from top to tail.

"The Shrouded Palace."

Ariadne quivered, bowed, and led them on.

The weather changed at every turn with disorienting frequency. Each shift was only a different kind of miserable—from sleet to drizzle, fog to biting cold, rain to fluttering snow.

The labyrinth tightened round them as they walked. Ariadne led them from the lanes of ruined buildings into streets only three feet or so wide, bordered by nothing but stone walls. Other roads were hemmed in by wild, savage hedges, snarls of thick-stemmed briars with thorns an inch long, like some nightmarish version of Hampton Court Maze. Less of the sky was visible with every turn, now a spill of black clouds from which rain speared continuously.

Panic blossomed in Benjamiah. If they lost Ariadne now, they would never find their way out. And, worse still, if the Minotaur set upon them here, there was nowhere to run and nowhere to hide. Ariadne swung left, and they found themselves creeping along streets of hedges and stone walls. Then she guided them across a mossy lawn, surrounded on either side by swells of jagged rock. It ended in a moon gate cut out of a wall of forbidding black stone. Beyond that a bridge arched over another strand of the Smeath. On the other side of the water, in full view, was the Shrouded Palace.

According to Archscholar Wolfsdaughter, it was built by the last dozen magi after weaving all the surrounding world into a labyrinth. From here, they ruled Wreathenwold, paranoid and driven mad by living too close to the aether. It was here, too, that they were murdered by the Widow, who in turn lived in the palace and devastated Wreathenwold for twenty-one dark years until she was overthrown by the Minotaur.

Now it was home to the monster at the center of the maze.

It was like Dracula's castle, all turrets and spires rendered out of pale limestone and rising far up into the smoky sky. Built on a nest of barbed rock, its towers were skinny and pointed and its windows black as bullet holes. No lights were lit. Nothing moved. The river wrapped round it like a moat, frothing upon the rocks. Grotesques occupied every available perch, their stone wings stretched and their mouths screaming.

The children edged onward, crossing the bridge. A single stairwell was hewn into the rocks, snaking up to the palace entrance. Before that was an enormous turning circle. A mighty fissure traveled its width, a great wound in the ground. Within it was a deep, hazy, hot darkness—the kind Benjamiah now associated with aether.

"What happened here?" he asked.

"I don't know," said Elizabella. "Maybe it appeared when the Widow murdered the magi. Or when the Minotaur defeated the Widow."

Benjamiah shivered. This was a dark place, haunted by

great violence. Elizabella strode forward, and Benjamiah followed, Nuisance thrumming in the air. Rain fell. Nothing moved, either around them or in the dark windows of the Shrouded Palace.

Together they began climbing the steps. Halfway up, they found a single button-up boot, no bigger than the pair Benjamiah was wearing. What had happened to the child who wore them? They picked their way up through the jagged rocks, sprayed by river water, until they reached the monumental bonewood doors, maybe twenty feet tall. They were wrecked, smashed off their hinges by some extreme force.

Benjamiah felt dizzy with fear. With a trembling hand, he gripped the two coins in his trouser pocket—the promises from Hansel and Elizabella that he would make it home safely—and in they went.

Before them was ruin and darkness. Any splendor the palace once had was long gone, descended into wreckage and shadow, the entrance hall a bird's nest of fallen timber and stone. More fissures snaked across the walls and across the floor, scars full of hot, trembling darkness. The air was stale and mildewy. Weak light fell from broken windows rising all the way to the vaulted ceiling. Whatever sculptures and elaborations had once adorned the ceiling had been lost. Rain dribbled through the cracks.

"Where would Edwid hide his whisperwick in here?" whispered Benjamiah.

"It could be anywhere," said Elizabella.

"No," replied Benjamiah. "He would have thought about it. It won't just be hidden in the rubble. The other three were hidden where they didn't look out of place. The Whispering Wood, the Viper's shrine, the raven's roost."

"Any lantern would stick out here," said Elizabella. "Look at this place."

"We need to search, but *quietly*. The Minotaur could be anywhere. . . ."

On they crept. They skirted what must have once been opulent hallways and eased through broken doors into the ruins of ballrooms, banquet halls, even a theater. The only sounds were the splattering of rain through the crumbled structure, their feet disturbing the rubble, and their anguished breathing.

"Look," said Elizabella, pointing.

Through a doorway ahead was a faint, shivering light. And, Benjamiah realized, something else.

"Is that . . . music?" he said, his stomach in knots.

It was. The tiniest fluttering of notes, gentle and serene, like a flute.

"Come on," said Elizabella.

They followed the hallway. On the walls were paintings,

except claws had slashed through the canvases. Benjamiah froze. Elizabella stared at the slashes too, trying to calm herself with long, trembling breaths.

"We can do this," she whispered.

"I can't . . . ," muttered Benjamiah.

"You *can*," said Elizabella.

It took enormous strength to continue, but continue Benjamiah did, sticking tightly to Elizabella. At the end of the hallway the door was ajar, the light filling the gap, music crackling beyond it.

"Sounds like a gramophone," whispered Benjamiah.

They looked at each other for reassurance, then eased the door open.

They had emerged on an upper level of a majestic library, shaped like a gigantic birdcage. Here the palace finally *looked* like a palace, all gold and velvet and elegance. Books rose dizzyingly high to the ribbed vaulting above, the ribs dotted with scores of lanterns. The books were beautiful, cloth-bound and embroidered and colorful. It was the most magnificent library Benjamiah had ever seen. He gazed up, momentarily forgetting himself.

A tug on his sleeve brought him back to the present. Elizabella was pointing downward.

Below was a sitting room with a roaring fire. There was a terrific bonewood desk loaded with leather-bound tomes and inkwells and parchment, the center taken up by a chessboard. By the fire was a gramophone. There was a settee on one side of the desk, and a wingback chair on the other. Occupying the wingback chair was a large, snoozing figure.

The Minotaur was nothing like any picture or painting or grotesque that Benjamiah had seen in Wreathenwold, nothing like any of the horror stories. He didn't have the monstrous upper half of a bull. Instead, he wore a gray mask, a horned bull's head hiding the upper half of his face. Below it Benjamiah could see a very human, very old mouth. The skin was bristled with silver and heavily wrinkled. He was dressed in a tortoiseshell jerkin, furs draped round his shoulders. On his feet were enormous black boots, propped on the desk. He was snoring faintly.

Benjamiah and Elizabella swapped a stunned glance. This was no monster. Just an old, snoring man in a mask.

I can't believe it, mouthed Elizabella.

Neither could Benjamiah. How could Wreathenwold be so wrong about the Minotaur? He was about to ask Elizabella, but she interrupted him.

"Look!" she hissed, jabbing a finger upward.

It took Benjamiah a moment to make it out, but hanging among the dozens of ordinary lanterns, at the highest point of the library, was Edwid's whisperwick.

"How do we get up there?" he said, dismayed.

It was a good question. There was another level above

them, but after that there seemed no obvious way to reach the highest rows of books, much less the ceiling itself.

"I'll have to climb the bookshelves," said Elizabella. "But we can't make a sound. He might not look scary, but looks can be deceiving."

Benjamiah wasn't sure. The Minotaur was snoring away, all feeble and frail. Before he could say so, Elizabella had started climbing the shelves.

"It's a puzzle," whispered Benjamiah, looking at how the pieces were arranged on the chessboard below.

He leaned forward, hands on the gleaming balustrade, craning to get a better look. It looked a fiendish puzzle with no obvious solution. Maybe if you sacrificed the rook, then . . . While leaning forward, Benjamiah inadvertently put too much pressure on the balustrade.

This proved a terrible mistake. With a tremendous splintering sound, it gave way and Benjamiah plunged clean through. He careered through the air and crashed onto the settee on the other side of the Minotaur's desk. Two of its legs buckled with ear-splitting cracks. Dust plumed. Benjamiah was dazed, his body throbbing from top to toe. He looked up, blinking through blobs of light.

The Minotaur was sitting bolt upright.

"Who the devil are you?" he whispered, in a voice as old and feeble as he looked.

Benjamiah was paralyzed and breathless. The furs had

slipped from the Minotaur's shoulders—he was so bony and frail. The mask was frightening, with large pointed horns and furiously angry eyes. But the man's lips were parting and closing as though *he* were the one terrified.

"I'm sorry, I . . . ," mumbled Benjamiah.

"You shouldn't be here," croaked the Minotaur. "It's too dangerous. It's . . ."

He moved a gnarly hand to the forehead of his mask, and then to his neck, and then rubbed his upper arms with both hands. His head turned frantically from side to side. Bizarrely, Benjamiah noticed a copy of *Jamima Cleaves and the Tortoiseshell Bullet* propped open on the Minotaur's desk, as though he'd been reading it before falling asleep.

"I don't understand," said the Minotaur. "Why on earth would you come here . . . ? *How* on earth . . . ?" He seemed deeply troubled. "Are you lost?" he asked.

Benjamiah shook his head.

"You found your way here deliberately?" said the Minotaur. "Could you find your way out again?"

Benjamiah nodded.

"How?"

Benjamiah was silent.

"What a thing . . . ," mumbled the Minotaur. "And are you alone?"

Benjamiah's eyes flicked upward. Elizabella was still climbing the bookshelves, spiderlike. She put a finger to her lips, narrowing her eyes threateningly. Benjamiah looked back at the Minotaur and nodded.

"I've never known anybody find their way here deliberately," said the Minotaur. "Let alone a little one. What in the world made you come?"

"I was just curious," said Benjamiah.

The visible part of the Minotaur's face looked sad.

"A splendid thing," he said, "but now I will have to eat you, I suppose. Do you think I want to eat you? Children don't taste very nice, I expect. But what else can I do? Would you like something to drink? I'm not sure I have anything suitable, though. Lots of rosewater, lots of poppysyrup. No milk punch or plumpkin juice, sadly. Some water?"

Benjamiah's stomach curled inward. *Eat* him? Was that a joke? If so, Benjamiah thought it was in poor taste. The Minotaur climbed out of his chair with a medley of groans and cricks and sighs, then hobbled, hunchbacked and reliant on a weathered bonewood cane, to a table by the fireplace. He poured Benjamiah a glass of water from a jug, poured himself a dose of poppysyrup, and brought the drinks back.

Benjamiah nervously gulped down the water, which was a little stale. The Minotaur sipped his smoking poppysyrup. High above, Elizabella clambered upward.

"Did you say," said Benjamiah, "that you'll have to *eat* me?"

"I suppose I will," said the Minotaur glumly. "Otherwise, before I know it, the palace will be crawling with curious children. It's unavoidable."

"But you seem nice."

"Do you think so?" said the Minotaur, sounding genuinely delighted. "That's so kind of you. Everybody has always been so frightened of me. The truth is I'm frightened of them. More frightened of them than they are of me."

"Who are you frightened of?"

"The people," said the Minotaur. "Every last one of them. Even children, who are the best of us. It's the reason I never leave the palace. One of the reasons, anyway. Even when the Captains come on city business, I'm so terribly afraid. I can't wait for them to leave."

He trailed off, taking another sip of poppysyrup.

"Aren't you too old to be frightened?" said Benjamiah.

This made the Minotaur laugh—a surprisingly deep, rich laugh that flowed throughout the library.

"You're never too old to be frightened," he replied gently. "You only have different things to be afraid of. And you get better at hiding it."

Benjamiah thought suddenly of Mum and Dad—their red eyes, their hoarse voices, pacing the house at night, unable to sleep. He'd always thought he was the only frightened one in the family. But Mum and Dad, he now realized, were as scared as he was. Maybe even more so.

"What's your name?" said the Minotaur.

"Benjamiah Creek. What's yours?"

"Mine?" said the Minotaur. "Mine? I . . . Nobody's asked me that for so long . . . Do you know, I think I've forgotten it!"

"How could you forget your own name?" said Benjamiah.

"It's been a very long time since anybody has asked, I suppose."

They sipped their drinks, a little awkward. Elizabella was still spidering upward, now just a tiny figure among the ribbed vaulting. Was the Minotaur really planning to eat him?

"Do you like *Jamima Cleaves*?" said Benjamiah, pointing to the open book—anything to distract the Minotaur from his plans to devour him.

"Oh, absolutely!" declared the Minotaur, lighting up. "My favorite books. I would even have Olfred Wicker visit sometimes. A Hanged Man would bring him. We became friends, you know. He died recently, though. Quite sudden and a bit of a mystery, it would seem. Terribly sad."

"Aren't you too old for children's books?" said Benjamiah.

"I am too old for many things," said the Minotaur. "But the day I'm too old for children's books will be a very dark day indeed."

"I like chess too," said Benjamiah, pointing to the board.

"Do you? I hate it," said the Minotaur. "It's this wretched problem. Olfred set it for me the last time he visited, and I haven't made any progress at all."

Benjamiah studied the arrangement of pieces. Gradually the solution formed in his mind.

"Do you really have to eat me?" he asked.

The Minotaur nodded, looking sad. "I suppose I do," he said with a sigh. "I'm not sure the stove is large enough, though. I might need a big pot. How small are you? Hm. I must think. There's an old cleaver somewhere. . . ."

"I won't tell anybody," said Benjamiah desperately. "About you being nice, I mean."

"Children are not very good at keeping secrets," said the Minotaur.

"They're better than grown-ups!" said Benjamiah.

The Minotaur smiled, apparently accepting the truth of Benjamiah's reply.

"I can help," said Benjamiah.

"With what?"

"The chess puzzle. I could show you the solution. In exchange for you not eating me."

The Minotaur considered this carefully. As well as wanting the puzzle solved, it seemed clear he didn't really want to eat Benjamiah.

"Very well," he said.

Benjamiah had to stand to reach the pieces. They were

incredibly heavy, carved from stone. First he sacrificed one rook with check, and then another, and finally the queen swooped in for the checkmate in the corner. The Minotaur was astonished.

"Extraordinary!" he said, massaging his jaw. "You must be a genius."

Benjamiah shook his head. "I read a lot. That's all. There's nothing special about me."

"I'm very, very old," said the Minotaur, "and I've never met a reader who wasn't special in one way or another. When you read, you connect with the world. You connect with the world as it once was, as it is, and as it one day might be. We are only dust, brief moments of aether. To read, to be curious, is the most astonishing kind of magic."

There was movement high above. Elizabella was waving. She had Edwid's whisperwick and was jabbing her finger toward the exit. She began her descent. It was time to leave.

"You don't have a doll," said Benjamiah.

He'd been in Wreathenwold long enough now to notice that anybody without a doll, either attached to their hip or cast nearby, stuck out like a sore thumb.

"No, I do not," said the Minotaur. "We magi are not so fortunate."

Benjamiah was shocked. "You mean," he said, heart thumping, "you're . . . a magus?"

"The very last," said the Minotaur.

"But didn't Osmeralda . . . She killed all the magi, didn't she?"

Mention of the Widow's name made the Minotaur flinch. Below the mask, his mouth formed a sad line.

"A name I haven't heard in some time," he said softly. "What you say is both correct and not quite correct. There were twelve *grown* magi here when Osmeralda . . . when it happened. But there was a child magus too, of whom nobody outside this palace knew. That child was me. I was here when . . . Well, I'm sure you know the story. The most awful violence. Eleven magi murdered. And throughout the Widow's dark, terrible reign she kept me here, until I was a man and found the courage to fight her."

It was a lot to absorb. A thirteenth magus, a child, kept here by the Widow until he overthrew her. But something wasn't adding up.

"There were *thirteen* magi, including you," said Benjamiah. "You said *eleven* were murdered by the Widow. That means you, but also one other. . . ."

The Minotaur froze. If mentioning Osmeralda's name had been a shock, bringing up the mysterious twelfth magus distressed him intensely.

After a long sip of poppysyrup, hand shaking, the Minotaur said, "Of the twelfth, I will not speak, my young friend."

Benjamiah's heart thudded. There had been twelve grown magi when the Widow attacked. But only eleven had died. The twelfth was surely the magus now returned to Wreathenwold. But how and why had he ended up imprisoned in the walls of Wreathenwold? What did it all mean? Something nagged at Benjamiah, something he'd read in *A Brief History of Wreathenwold*. He just couldn't bring it into focus.

He opened his mouth to ask more questions, but was met with a snore. Leaning back in his chair, boots on the table again, the Minotaur had lapsed into a drunken slumber, the bottle of poppysyrup clasped to his chest.

Above, Elizabella returned to solid ground, Edwid's whisperwick beneath her arm.

Let's go, she mouthed.

Benjamiah nodded. Before leaving, he wrapped the fallen furs round the Minotaur's frail shoulders.

NINETEEN

WITH THE TWELFTH MAGUS

Those final twelve magi were the cruelest and maddest in their long dark history. Paranoid, immensely powerful, and their minds warped by the aether, they tormented dollcasters for entertainment in the throne room of the Shrouded Palace and practiced all manner of foul witch-craft in pursuit of new, more terrible powers.

—*A Brief History of Wreathenwold*,
Archscholar Collum Wolfsdaughter

BACK ALONG the hallway Elizabella and Benjamiah scurried, navigating the rubble until they emerged at the top of a ruined staircase. It led down into a vast, domed room, where the remains of twelve thrones were set at different heights upon a rocky dais. Stained-glass windows, darkened by smoke, streaked the length of the walls. The ground was crisscrossed with cracks. It was the court itself, the epicenter of the violence that ended the magi.

The two children stopped at the foot of the dais. Elizabella was ruddy with the effort of climbing, breathing sharply, her face aglow with Edwid's whisperwick.

"I can't believe it," she said. "All these years, all the stories about the Minotaur, and he's just a harmless old man."

"Not totally harmless," said Benjamiah, recalling mention of the Minotaur's big pot. "Anyway, listen to what I found out. . . ."

As best he could, Benjamiah recounted all the Minotaur had told him about the magi, including that the Minotaur himself was a magus, and that the Widow only murdered eleven of the other twelve.

"But what does it all mean?" said Elizabella, rubbing her temples in frustration. "And what on earth does it all have to do with Edwid?"

That brought their attention back to the whisperwick. Elizabella set it down on the stone, and they knelt either side, leaning close. Elizabella withdrew the key with a shaking hand.

"This is it," she said. "The last one."

Benjamiah nodded. His belly squirmed.

In went the key. Along crept the thread. The lock clicked. Elizabella opened the door and released her brother's final couplet:

A place where nothing breathes nor creeps—
Here is where the Widow sleeps.

The candle went out.

"Did he say . . . ," said Elizabella.

Benjamiah pulled out his notebook, recording the rhyme word for word. He repeated it. Elizabella was dumbstruck.

"*Where the Widow sleeps . . .* ," she repeated. "Benjamiah, I don't understand. I just don't get it. The Widow? The Widow isn't sleeping. She's dead. Isn't she?"

"Wait," said Benjamiah.

He ripped the page out of the notebook, then tore it into four strips, one for each couplet. He shuffled them around, tutting, mumbling, until he was sure he had the correct order.

A path that goes not back nor forth,
A road that goes not south, east, west, nor north.

A place where sunlight cannot reach,
A depth no breathing thing can breach.

A door that moves not out nor in,
And guarded by our every sin.

A place where nothing breathes nor creeps—
Here is where the Widow sleeps.

The moment he'd finished reading aloud, excruciating pain sprawled throughout Benjamiah's body, starting from his chest and spearing outward in every direction like cracks in glass. He doubled over, gasping, and saw Elizabella was likewise overcome with agony. Nuisance the nightjar squalled, Emba the bear rushed to Elizabella, and Ariadne swung between them, helpless.

"What's happening . . . ?" groaned Elizabella, balled up in pain.

Benjamiah wondered if he were having a heart attack, pain flooding from the center of his chest into every corner of his body. He gasped, hitting the stone floor, struggling to breathe. Nuisance had landed on his shoulder, nuzzling him and twittering desperately.

Slowly the pain subsided enough for Benjamiah to look up. Elizabella was on her hands and knees too, gasping for air.

"What's happening?" she panted.

Though his head swam, Benjamiah suddenly recalled the book Elizabella had been reading earlier in their journey—*Jamima Cleaves and the Secret Deaths*. About a cursed secret, one that kills if ever heard, but which fights to be told, to spread . . .

"The magus tricked Edwid into stealing something from Olfred Wicker," he croaked. "We thought the whisper-wicks would reveal where it is. But we were wrong. The *thing itself* was hidden in the whisperwicks. It's a secret—a cursed secret—one nobody's supposed to know!"

Elizabella, breathlessly, said, "That's why Edwid came home so ill. Because of the secret. It was killing him. Before he came back, he split the secret up and hid it in whisperwicks so nobody would find it. He even put them in the most dangerous places he could to stop people coming across them. And now we've put them all back together . . ."

She howled as the pain returned, doubling up. Benjamiah wanted to help, but the same agony flashed through him. Nuisance crooned and Emba whined. With watery eyes, Benjamiah saw that the poem had vanished from the strips of paper—the secret lived within them now.

"What do we do?" he said.

"You said Olfred used to visit the Minotaur," said Elizabella. "He must have heard or read the secret while he was here. That's why he had it in the first place. It's the Minotaur's secret. Only he could know the Widow isn't really dead. Maybe, if we give it back to the Minotaur, it will all be over?"

Benjamiah didn't have a better idea. They helped each other up, shaking. The pain had subsided again, but Benjamiah felt violently queasy, acid bubbling at the back of his throat. His forehead was hot and clammy. There was a feverish edge to his vision. Which is why it took him a moment to process the image in front of him.

Somebody was sitting on one of the derelict thrones. He was cross-legged, cane across his lap. The red flower at his throat was the brightest thing for miles. His eyes sparkled like obsidian.

It was Manfred Tarr.

"Children," he said softly. "Whatever have you done?"

"Manfred . . . ," whispered Elizabella. "Help, please. We need to get back to the Minotaur. We found a terrible secret. It's going to kill us!"

"Oh my," said Manfred. He sounded neither surprised nor concerned, as far as Benjamiah could tell. "What kind of secret?"

"We can't say," said Elizabella. "We'd only make you ill too."

"Why do you think I'm here?" he said.

Silence followed. The children stared, unsure how to respond.

"No need to look so shocked," said Manfred, waving a spidery hand. "I knew of the secret long before you even realized what you were tracking down. Before you were even born, in fact. I know the Widow lives, but the secret reveals *where*. Give it to me. Save yourselves and be on your way."

"But it will kill you!" said Elizabella.

"It can try," said Manfred. "Nothing has killed me so far."

"You manipulated us," she said.

"How so? I only helped you along your path, and now I'm here to save your lives. Where is your gratitude, I wonder?"

"No," said Elizabella.

"*No?*" said Manfred.

"We're returning it to the Minotaur," said Elizabella. "Nobody is supposed to know this. It's too dangerous."

Manfred stood, deathly thin and long-limbed. The tip of his cane clacked on the stone, ringing through the court.

"And if I do not allow it?" he said. "If I demand that you hand it over to me rather than the dim-witted fool through there?"

"Then we'll die," said Elizabella.

"We will?" whispered Benjamiah, not sure he agreed.

Elizabella nodded, face distorted by pain and sickness.

To Benjamiah's surprise, Manfred's mouth curled into a smile.

"I expected no less," he replied. "I knew from our first meeting that this wasn't going to be as straightforward as I'd hoped. Fortunately, like any good businessman, I have some security."

"What do you mean?" said Elizabella.

"A means by which I might persuade you to trade what you have. To do so, I would need to possess something that *you* want. And I do."

Elizabella was silent, staring darkly at Manfred.

"Your brother," he said.

"Liar!" said Elizabella. "He was stolen."

"He's close," said Manfred. "A short walk. I can show you if you'd like?"

"It's a trap," whispered Benjamiah.

"A trap of what kind?" called Manfred, who apparently heard like a bat. "Do you mean that I intend to lead you to a secluded location? Can you imagine a place more lonely than this one? Follow me a short way. I will prove I'm telling the truth. We can then revisit how unwilling you really are to trade."

He cocked his head, smiling, arms spread in a conciliatory gesture. Benjamiah sensed something was terribly wrong, something even more troubling lurking beneath Manfred's trickery.

Beside him, Elizabella nodded.

"Really?" hissed Benjamiah.

"Excellent," declared Manfred. "Come. Let us have a family reunion, then."

He led the way, cane clattering, bouncing on the balls of his feet. Benjamiah wanted to tell Elizabella that none of this made any sense, but finding Edwid was all that mattered to her. Manfred led them out of the court, down the stairs, and through a series of gardens grown wild. They emerged in a copse of bonewoods in the shadow of the palace.

Rain thundered down, the sky clotted with storm clouds. And up ahead, beneath the splayed branches of an ancient bonewood tree, was a black coach. Two clockwork horses snorted at the front, dragging their synthetic hooves across the mud.

"Edwid!" blurted Elizabella.

She lurched forward, but Manfred swished his cane, planting it at her feet.

"Not so fast," he said. "We're here to discuss terms."

Nausea swam upward from Benjamiah's belly. He covered his mouth.

"Your brother is in the coach," said Manfred, "but first our deal."

"I don't understand . . . ," said Elizabella. "Who took him?"

A fissure of blue lightning opened in the sky, then vanished. Rain drummed upon Manfred's hat.

"I understand," said Benjamiah. "You took him. *You're* the magus."

Manfred tucked his cane beneath his arm, gave a formal bow, and clapped his hands together.

"Bravo," he said. "Bravo!"

"But you have a doll!" said Elizabella.

Manfred laughed. With a wrinkled nose, he lifted the yellow doll hanging from his hip between finger and thumb and threw it into a puddle.

"Decorative," he said. "I took it from that dim-witted author after breaking out of his wall. He didn't look like he'd be needing it anymore."

"You lied to us . . . ," said Elizabella.

"Simple misdirection. Don't be hard on yourselves. I have fooled greater minds than yours. I wouldn't have needed you at all if your roguish brother hadn't been so pigheaded."

"Don't talk about Edwid like that!" snapped Elizabella.

She grabbed Emba from her belt. Manfred tilted his head, looking amused.

"Careful, girl," he said. "You're only still alive because you're necessary. I could snuff you out like a candle at any moment."

Benjamiah, with a squirm of the stomach, recalled the destructive aether that had freed them from the Viper and the Hanged Men. That had been Manfred. He needed them to escape so they could track down the final whisper-wick and reassemble the secret.

Finally the thing that had been nagging at him while talking to the Minotaur came into focus. It was something he'd read in *A Brief History of Wreathenwold*, something that had seemed inconsequential at the time. *Rumors persist that one of the twelve magi betrayed his kin and helped her, perhaps himself in love with Osmeralda.*

"The Minotaur said the Widow killed *eleven* magi,"

said Benjamiah. "That's because the twelfth didn't need to be killed. The twelfth was on her side. The twelfth helped her murder the others. That was you."

"Oh, very good," said Manfred, clapping his hands. "I suspected you'd be the one to piece it together, Benjamiah. The girl is too pigheaded, like her brother."

"Why?" said Benjamiah. "Why would you murder the rest of your kind?"

"For that noblest and strangest of reasons," said Manfred, fiddling with the flower at his throat. "For love."

"But the Widow was in love with somebody else," said Benjamiah. "The one the magi refused to save. That's why she did it all."

"You were doing so well until now," said Manfred, giving a mocking pout. "No, Benjamiah, there was no other. Osmeralda was in love—that much is true—but with me. And I with her. Deeply, wonderfully in love. When we were discovered, those soulless monsters meant to execute us both. Magi should not lower themselves to love a dollcaster, they said. We were left with no choice. It was us or them. We slaughtered them all—it was not grief that made us powerful, as the legends say, but *love*. Afterward, the world was ours. For twenty-one beautiful years, Osmeralda ruled, with me behind her. And we would have ruled forever had it not been . . ."

"For the Minotaur," said Benjamiah. "He overthrew you."

Manfred nodded, looking disgusted. "It was the only point on which Osmeralda and I disagreed. I wanted to kill the little beast and be done with it. But she kept him all those years, like a pet. He betrayed us when we least expected it. Osmeralda, he hanged. Me, whom he judged more harshly for the murder of the magi, he condemned to live forever in the walls of this world. Forever in the shadows, unable to escape, sleep, die. A most barbaric punishment. But something kept me going in the darkness. A light, and that light was love. Love for Osmeralda, which neither time nor shadow nor death could extinguish."

"So the Widow is dead," said Elizabella.

"She was hanged," said Manfred, breath catching in his throat. "But while her body could be killed her soul could not. The Minotaur discovered this, imprisoning her spirit and cursing the secret. Whether out of foolishness or sorrow, the Minotaur finally slipped up. Somehow the children's author discovered the secret. I tried to coax it from Olfred Wicker, but the old fool barricaded himself in his home and meant to die with it. And then another opportunity presented itself. . . ."

A long, thin, dark smile formed on Manfred's face—like the crack in Edwid's bedroom wall. Beside Benjamiah, Elizabella shook, fists clenched.

"Everywhere I listened," said Manfred, "in walls all across Wreathenwold, searching for somebody who could help. And what should I discover? A stupid little boy had stolen from the Mapmakers their precious little thread. Now there was somebody who could find Olfred's cottage, if given the right encouragement. I was delighted it was Edwid who stole it. He was so very easy to fool."

Benjamiah grabbed Elizabella's hand to stop her charging forward. She flailed, wild and teary-eyed.

"You monster . . . ," she seethed.

"Edwid and I went to Olfred's house," said Manfred. "The old clown had locked himself away, trying to die with the secret. But secrets are so desperate to spread. With Edwid there, Olfred couldn't help but whisper it into his ear. After that, it should have been straightforward. Edwid only had to pass the secret to me and all his troubles would have gone away. But no. Your witless brother ran. Being so close to the secret gave me the strength to break free of my prison. Alas, Edwid escaped. By the time I learned of his whisperwicks, it was too late. A clever move, I have to say. Sadly, I didn't know the foolish boy well enough to locate them myself.

"But who did?" continued Manfred, smiling. "There was only one choice. His equally pigheaded twin sister. How to compel her to set off in pursuit of the mystery? There was only one option. Only one thing that would drag her from her home and her poor stupid father. I stole Edwid. Or rather I fashioned a being to steal Edwid on my behalf. Aether is a wonderful thing. And after him you came, just as I knew you would. His key led you to the whisperwicks, and your knowledge of your brother led you to each in turn. It all worked out rather well."

"You're pure evil," said Elizabella, brushing tears from her eyes.

"Oh, no need for dramatics," said Manfred, waving his hand. "Let us be civil. You have something I want, which is of no value to you. I have something you want, which is of no value to me. It's a rather straightforward affair."

"You won't let us go afterward," said Benjamiah.

"I may be many things, but a murderer of children I am not," said Manfred, in mock offense. "Now, what is your answer? This is the best offer I can make. I have other contingencies, each more unpleasant than the last. I will leave with the secret one way or another. Make it easy on yourselves."

Lightning flailed again, briefly bathing Manfred's gaunt face in unforgiving light. Elizabella and Benjamiah stared at each other. What choice did they have? Elizabella nodded.

"A wise decision," said Manfred.

He stepped forward and crouched. There was a wicked intensity in his eyes. All the bones of his face seemed harsher than before, the eyes void and flecked with ghostly silver.

"Speak it now," said Manfred. "Word for word, exactly

as you have it in your minds. Speak it together, and you'll both be free. Speak it clearly. *Now.*"

Benjamiah felt sick. Edwid had been taken because of this man. All the pain Elizabella and Hansel had suffered was because of Manfred Tarr. And now they were forced to do what Edwid never did—hand over exactly what Manfred wanted.

"*A path that goes not back nor forth . . .*," began Elizabella, with Benjamiah quickly forced to join in.

Together they recited the entire poem. With every word, Benjamiah felt the poison being drawn from his mind. It was like antiseptic, bleaching the infection from a wound. When the final word was spoken, all the pain and sickness was gone. Benjamiah felt rejuvenated, light-headed.

Manfred's eyes swam darkly as he absorbed the secret. There was no groan, no sudden yelp of pain. He screwed his eyes shut, fists clenching, mouth clamped. Then he relaxed and straightened up. There was a delirious quality to his expression as he loomed over them.

"There it is," he whispered, then, to the sky: "I am coming for you, my love."

He looked at the children—a new and intense menace on his face.

"See, that wasn't difficult, was it?" he said. "And don't you feel so much better?"

Elizabella lurched forward, setting off toward the coach.

Manfred's cane moved again, striking the ground with a *thwack*.

"Where are you rushing off to?" he said.

"We had a deal!" shouted Elizabella.

"You made a deal with a self-confessed liar," said Manfred. "If you want to be angry, be angry with yourselves."

"You said . . . You said you wouldn't hurt children," mumbled Benjamiah.

"And I shan't. But the pair of you know too much, I'm afraid. The Minotaur will enjoy you."

"The Minotaur is a harmless old man," said Benjamiah.

"Oh, that one is," replied Manfred. "A pitiful, measly degenerate, not fit to breathe the air my darling Osmeralda once breathed. His time will come when I have Osmeralda at my side again. So no, the old fool will do you no harm. But the Minotaur is an idea, a story. And stories have teeth."

Elizabella and Benjamiah stared. Manfred gave a mad, triumphant smile.

"And just to be sure," he went on, "first we must deal with your little friend. Now you'll really know how it feels to be lost."

Manfred waved his cane. A pinch of dusty metal broke from the silvery masquerade mask at its head. It cascaded to the floor, then gathered into a living shape—a hawk of dazzling, cloudy silver, fluttering up from the puddles.

Before they could react, the powdery bird grabbed Ariadne up in her beak. Ariadne writhed, struggling.

Elizabella and Benjamiah cried out together. Elizabella cast Emba as an eagle, but it was too late. Manfred's aether closed its beak and cut Ariadne in half. The two halves of thread fell to the cobbles, lifeless.

A black hole of grief opened at Benjamiah's center. He sank into it, dumbstruck, rooted to the spot, his mind a mist of fragmentary thoughts and images.

An animalistic scream tore from Elizabella's mouth. Emba the eagle gave a mournful caterwaul, then streaked toward Manfred's bird. The aether collapsed and was gone. The eagle set a course for Manfred instead. The magus swept his cane—a fountain of silvery aether briefly formed an eagle many times larger than Emba, chasing Elizabella's poppet away.

Thunder shook. Lightning lashed. Then Manfred swept and twisted and weaved his cane, his eyes gleaming malevolent and sorcerous, and a deadly smile spun upon his lips. More silvery aether cascaded from its tip, swirling and flowing. The air was hot and shivering, as though the fabric of the world were being ripped apart. Benjamiah's eyes stung with the effort of watching it. Manfred's silvery aether gathered into a cyclone of material, dragging in metal and stone and all manner of other things, gradually taking the most terrible shape.

Here was a Minotaur worthy of the horror stories. It stood ten feet tall, mighty and nightmarish, assembled from mud, metal, bone, stone, and dust. Its head was enormous, fearsome metal horns curving from its skull and its mouth a mess of teeth and drool. Its eyes were marbles of white and yellow, rheumy and rabid. It wielded hands as big as cartwheels.

The beast dropped onto all fours and gave a roar that shook Benjamiah to the bone. Spittle looped from its mouth, and its eyes bulged.

"I'm going to enjoy this," said Manfred. "This has been coming for you both since the beginning. It's been coming for you since the moment you left your little bookshop. You did well to make it this far. But now it ends. You have been lost your entire lives. Doomed to be lost. And you will die lost."

At that, Manfred smiled and walked off, leaving the children to die at the hands of his sorcery. The dreadful ethereal monster stood between them and Edwid.

"Edwid . . . ," moaned Elizabella.

There was no movement inside the coach behind the monster. Where was he? Benjamiah knew in that moment that something was terribly amiss. He had misunderstood something from the beginning. . . .

The beast gave another roar. Elizabella and Benjamiah grabbed each other, paralyzed.

The monster struck in a blur of muscle and flesh, but instinct saved the children—they just about dived out of the way. The monster smashed through the mud, then turned, scrambling up like a rabid animal. Another dreadful roar erupted from its belly. Lightning flared above. The monster lowered its head, snarling, spittle spraying from its mouth. Hot, meaty breath washed over the children. Manfred had given life to a nightmare.

It launched itself at them again, roaring, hands swinging like sledgehammers. Elizabella ran one way and Benjamiah another. Everything was chaos. The monster came after Benjamiah, chasing him through the trees. It aimed another terrific swipe at his head. When Benjamiah ducked, the hand cleaved straight through a bonewood trunk.

The monster's next blow didn't miss. Benjamiah was sideswiped, knocked off his feet as though hit by a car. His face struck the ground, mud filling his mouth. He couldn't breathe—all the wind had been knocked out of him.

The monster fell upon him, opening its stinking mouth. Its jaws plunged toward Benjamiah's throat.

A blur intercepted. It was Emba, at first an eagle, stabbing its beak at the monster's face. When the beast swatted her away, Emba landed on the mud and became a bear.

"Leave him alone!" screamed Elizabella.

She joined Emba, standing between the monster and Benjamiah.

It dwarfed them both. Emba's blows had left dents in the monster's skull. It gave a deep, guttural roar that traveled to Benjamiah's core. Then it rocked forward onto its hands and charged. The fight was hopeless. It was many times the size and strength of poor Emba. The bear fought valiantly, but was smashed aside again and again, finally left cut and broken on the ground. Elizabella was thrown aside too, squirming in the mud.

Aether flowed from Emba's wounds. Elizabella couldn't lift herself. Benjamiah could barely breathe, let alone stand. And, even if he could, what was he supposed to do?

The monster descended on Elizabella, preparing to finish her off.

Benjamiah heard a twitter from above. Nuisance the nightjar was perched on a bonewood branch. The world seemed to still and become quiet. They had been on quite a journey together. Was this where it ended? Benjamiah realized then that he had rejected magic because he had misunderstood it all along. Casting spells was just a trick of the aether. Real magic was Elizabella laughing in the sweetshop. Magic was friendship and hope and courage. Magic was Ariadne. Magic was Nuisance. Magic was kindness, never giving up, finding a way when all seems lost.

There it was in Benjamiah's mind, the muscles in the darkness. Nuisance cocked his head because Benjamiah made him do so. Benjamiah assumed control of Nuisance, just as he knew he could. Nuisance lifted from the branch, spearing toward Benjamiah's outstretched hand. Benjamiah was on his feet as the nightjar collided with his palm.

The nightjar became a doll in his hand because Benjamiah made it so. And then Benjamiah threw himself between the monster and Elizabella.

In his hand, Nuisance ignited.

He knew all about fire, how a fuel combines with oxygen to generate the reaction. He had read enough chemistry books and didn't need a Wreathenwold spellbook to summon it. A great incandescent ball of flame engulfed Benjamiah's hand. He thrust it toward the monster's face. The beast roared and scrambled back, half-blinded by the glare. It regathered its fury and charged. Benjamiah waved his fiery hand and chased the monster back again.

It was a terrific flame, blindingly bright, and the monster was suddenly circumspect. They began a dance, in which the beast circled, snapped its jaws, roared. When the monster feinted, Benjamiah lifted his flaming hand and made it retreat.

The monster lunged, its most ferocious and violent yet. Benjamiah ducked beneath its sawing arms. Then he thrust the flame up into the monster's face. A terrible howl rose as skin and fur sizzled beneath the flames, the structure of the aether giving way. Benjamiah and the beast struggled, Benjamiah doing his utmost to hold Nuisance where the flames were beginning to make its ethereal skull collapse.

The monster smashed Benjamiah sideways. It roared, lowered its metal horns, and charged, intending to gore him.

Out of nowhere sprang Emba, an eagle again, torn and wounded. She swept straight through the monster like a bullet, emerging in a spray of aether. The beast was falling apart. Benjamiah released the flaming doll, and Nuisance became a nightjar of his own accord. Controlled by Benjamiah, the bird stabbed through the very heart of the monster.

It proved the fatal blow. Finally—with an agonized roar—the spell collapsed. Manfred's dreadful beast disintegrated into a pile of mud and metal and stone.

Quiet followed, broken only by the pattering of rain. Benjamiah cast around for Manfred, but saw no sign of the magus.

Benjamiah ran to Elizabella. She was on her side, groaning and nursing her body. No doubt there were broken bones. Benjamiah was sure some of his own ribs had cracked. His head swirled, heart thumping. Elizabella stroked Emba with a trembling hand—her doll was in a bad state.

"Edwid . . . ," breathed Elizabella.

It was Benjamiah who hobbled to the coach first,

yanking the door open and peering inside. His heart sank.

He could barely bring himself to break the news. "He isn't here," he said, unable to look at Elizabella, who had limped up behind him.

"Of course he is," she said.

She climbed into the coach with some difficulty and a lot of groaning. Edwid clearly wasn't there, but Elizabella was undeterred, rooting through spaces far too small for anybody to be hiding in.

And finally Benjamiah understood, one image coming after another, steadily accumulating into the only explanation.

Edwid being ill, terribly ill, and Hansel's aghast expression as he described it. The vase containing Elizabella's mother's soulbloom on the mantelpiece, not in the center but over to one side.

Elizabella saying over and over that Edwid had been *stolen*, not *kidnapped*. And her insistence that Edwid would not be able to help Benjamiah get home.

Honeysuckle saying: *She is more lost than you know. She cannot yet say what must be said.* Benjamiah telling Elizabella about his promise to bring Edwid home safely, and her eyes bubbling suddenly with tears. The well-lurker, when asked where Edwid was, replying: *Who can say?*

The secret, the terrible secret, which—held on to for

too long—will kill the bearer. Like Olfred Wicker, who died because he kept it too long.

Elizabella emerged. Cradled to her chest was something long and thin, wrapped in silken cloth. She lovingly pulled aside one fold, and then another, until Edwid Cotton was revealed.

"Here he is," said Elizabella.

In her hands was a soulbloom, a long glassy stem ending in a big, striking, heartbreaking rose of midnight blue with a center of snowy white. The same colors as Elizabella's poppet—Edwid's, too. Like Ada's soulbloom, the colors of Edwid's were glorious and alive within the petals, flowing, darting. Benjamiah had never seen anything so beautiful and so sad.

And then Elizabella finally said what she needed to say—what she had been unable to say since the moment it happened.

"My brother died," she said. And she wept, hugging the soulbloom to her heart.

Benjamiah didn't know what to say. All the dangers they'd faced, the ferocity of Elizabella's pursuit of Edwid, and he had been dead before Manfred had even stolen him. But Benjamiah would do it all over again, right at Elizabella's side. He would do it a thousand times over. In that moment, he knew she was the bravest person he'd ever met, or ever would meet.

Benjamiah let her sob. He stood close beside her, not saying a word. He didn't need to. She knew he was there, and he would be for as long as she needed him.

Later, when Elizabella was ready, their thoughts turned to home. The coach looked like it would still drive. Together they soothed the clockwork horses, then sat side by side on the driver's bench. Edwid was in Elizabella's lap, encased in cloth, Emba and Nuisance perched as nightjars of different shades behind the two children.

"It's impossible to find our way home," said Elizabella. "You know that, don't you?"

She looked devastated. But Benjamiah thought she was wrong. Something Silas Weaver said had stuck with him: *Ariadne will* never *be lost to those who need her*. Benjamiah took the two halves of thread from the ground and knotted them together. She lay in his palm, lifeless.

And then—impossibly, wonderfully—she shivered into life. She coiled and snaked upright, joyously alive, while Nuisance and Emba crooned triumphantly and Elizabella cheered.

Benjamiah smiled. "We missed you," he said.

Ariadne gave both Elizabella and Benjamiah the best hug a length of thread could give. Elizabella asked Ariadne to take them back to Follynook, while Benjamiah picked up the leather reins of the coach.

"Do you know how to drive this?" asked Elizabella.

"I think so."

"How?"

"I read it in a book," he said.

And Elizabella laughed, and sobbed, as they set off for home.

TWENTY
WITH THE TRUTH ABOUT NUISANCE

As for myself, for all the wonders and mysteries of our world, there is nowhere I would rather be than a good bookshop. A bookshop is paradise, a bookshop is home—a bookshop is a door to thousands of worlds and more. It fills me with sadness that life is too short to explore them all.

—A Brief History of Wreathenwold,
Archscholar Collum Wolfsdaughter

ON RETURNING to Follynook, Elizabella and Benjamiah braced themselves for Hansel's fury. Elizabella even suggested slipping him a tweet-tweet so his shouting came out all high-pitched, but Benjamiah talked her out of it. In any case, Hansel only rushed forward, not believing his eyes and unseamed with pure, wild relief. He and Elizabella enjoyed the tightest and longest embrace, seeming to understand each other for the first time since

Edwid's death. They cried, and whispered, and together they cradled Edwid's soulbloom.

Benjamiah was next, clasped so tightly by Hansel that the air was squeezed from him.

"What a boy you are," he said, looking at Benjamiah with watery gray eyes. "You saved us all."

Benjamiah protested, embarrassed. Hansel was completely wrong and needed to know it. Elizabella was the hero, he blurted, and anyway he broke his promise, gesturing at Edwid's soulbloom. He hadn't brought Edwid home safely—not really.

Hansel fished something out of his back pocket. It was Benjamiah's fifty-pence piece, whole and unbroken.

"It would seem that you did," he said. "Promises are funny things, Benjamiah. The true test is whether a person does their very best to keep them. This unbroken coin says you did."

They placed Edwid's soulbloom in its vase on the mantelpiece, next to Ada's, and stood side by side before the crackling fire. Hansel had his arm round Elizabella's shoulder. There was more crying, Hansel kissing her head. Benjamiah felt a rush of incredible sadness at the thought of Edwid never rejoining his family.

The meal that night, though, was as happy as it could be. Elizabella and Benjamiah took turns recounting the story, while Hansel—rapt throughout—shifted between astonishment, bewilderment, and grave disapproval. At other times, he broke into reluctant laughter, which only made it funnier for Elizabella and Benjamiah, who were in hysterics as they described various incidents and encounters.

However, they left out the content of the secret. Though passing it on to Manfred so quickly had saved the children, telling Hansel would leave him writhing in pain and in terrible danger until he likewise passed the secret on. As far as Hansel was concerned, the children never knew the secret, and the Widow was very much dead. Neither Benjamiah nor Elizabella felt good about deceiving him, but it was for his own safety.

Benjamiah had the best sleep of his life that night. He had expected his dreams to be a menagerie of horrors— the raven, Manfred, the ethereal Minotaur—but they were nothing of the sort.

The days that followed, too, were calm and peaceful. Elizabella and Hansel were blissfully reunited. Benjamiah read, and helped around the bookshop, and finally caught sight of the mischievous monkeys-of-the-inkpot as they ransacked one of the shop's inkwells. Each was as small as a fingernail, greedily slurping at the ink before scampering away.

With every hour that passed, the question of going home grew more prominent in his mind. The time was approaching. Benjamiah wanted to see Grandma. He wanted to see Mum and Dad, too. They must all be sick with worry. Steadily he grew more anxious about finding a way back, more restless, wondering how to broach the subject with Hansel, and when the right time would be. Ariadne could lead him to Horis & Hoggish Books. But would the door be there?

He played with Nuisance, their connection not lost since the battle with Manfred's monster. The complex of impulses in his mind meant he could move Nuisance as he wished, though of course he lacked the knowledge to cast other spells. He left the forms to Nuisance, be it a dormouse, a capuchin, or a nightjar. Nuisance remained the biggest unresolved mystery. Why had he come for Benjamiah and brought him to Wreathenwold? To whom did he belong? Benjamiah suspected he would never know, and the time was fast approaching when he would leave Wreathenwold for good.

Then the Hanged Men came.

Elizabella, Hansel and Benjamiah were together in the bookshop. Hansel was organizing the shelves, Elizabella minding the counter, and Benjamiah discussing *A Brief History of Wreathenwold* with a diminutive man who claimed to have met the elusive Archscholar Wolfsdaughter in a tavern many years ago.

First through the Follynook door was Inspector Halfpenny. Benjamiah smiled, but Halfpenny's expression was grim. Two Hanged Men followed, stooping to enter. Then came Inspector Cromwell, looking meaner than ever. Two more Hanged Men followed him.

The diminutive man scuttled out of the bookshop.

"Hansel," said Halfpenny, now somewhat shamefaced.

"Inspector," replied Hansel.

He shielded Elizabella and Benjamiah from the assembled party. Inspector Cromwell shoved Halfpenny out of the way. He was all translucent skin and bones, a malevolent smile hanging from ear to ear.

"So this is where the rats keep their nest," he said.

Benjamiah felt Elizabella bristle at his side, ready to explode. But Hansel waved a hand, the calmest person in the room.

"I don't believe we've had the pleasure," he said, holding out his hand. "I'm Hansel Cotton."

Cromwell stared at the outstretched hand as though it might give him ouroboros flu. Hansel dropped his hand, apparently unoffended.

"No need for introductions," said Cromwell. "The little beasts are my only concern. They know the price to be paid for their vulgar and dangerous behavior. Let's not make things more unpleasant than they need to be."

"Casper, please . . . ," said Halfpenny. "Have some

respect. Hansel, I am sorry. Hopefully, we can sort this business out amicably. . . ."

"Enough out of *you*, Halfpenny," spat Cromwell, "or the Viper will hear of your apologetics and collusions. These are criminals. Criminals must be punished. That is the fabric of any civilized and harmonious community."

"I couldn't agree more," said Hansel, to Benjamiah's horror. "So let's sit, shall we? And we can engage in a civilized and harmonious discussion of the charges, the supporting evidence or lack thereof, as well as in good faith consider any commensurate consequences as mandated by the jurisprudence of our land?"

All were baffled. Benjamiah thought it was excellent— at least the parts he'd understood. Cromwell, probably not wanting to betray his own ignorance, gave a greasy smile. He and Hansel moved to the seating area in the bookshop. Halfpenny and the Hanged Men gathered behind Cromwell, Elizabella, and Benjamiah behind Hansel.

"The charges, please," said Hansel, smiling pleasantly.

"Theft," said Cromwell. "Trespassing. Common assault, of a child no less. Resisting arrest. Criminal damage. Witchcraft. The assault of seven law-enforcement officers, myself included."

"That isn't true!" shouted Elizabella, fists clenched. "Well, not all of it."

"Reel in your deceptive little tongue," said Cromwell, "or I shall have it out."

"Would that be according to the dictates of a civilized community?" said Hansel, smiling. "Let us begin with the theft. What was stolen?"

"That has yet to be determined," said Cromwell. "The Viper has a great many valuables in her home. For what other reason would the little beasts have been there?"

"You mean there is nothing known to be missing? Nothing found to be in the possession of Elizabella and Benjamiah that was previously known to be in Odith Murdstone's possession?"

"The children were certainly there to thieve," spat Cromwell.

"Speculation," said Hansel. "If there is no evidence, then the charge can be dismissed. Do you agree, Inspector Halfpenny?"

"I do," said Halfpenny, doing her best to hide a budding smile.

Cromwell leveled a filthy look at his colleague.

"Let's move on to trespassing, then," said Hansel. "What independent witnesses do you have?"

"Gertrid Murdstone, first and foremost," said Cromwell. "A fine, upstanding girl of excellent moral quality. Even you would draw the line at questioning her character, I imagine?"

"Oh, I wouldn't dream of it," said Hansel. "But I would note her age. Eleven, is she?"

"Her age is of no consequence."

"Is that so? Would you allow her to gamble? Would you pour her a glass of poppysyrup? Would you allow her to work as a color-trader, or trust her to raise your children? Eleven is a wonderful age, but an uncertain and confusing one."

"Get to the point," said Cromwell.

"My point is only that the charges of trespassing and common assault are contingent on the word of one child," said Hansel. "Whereas two other children—the suspects— might provide a different version of events. It's one word against another. Without independent corroboration either way, there is no substantive legal platform."

"The thieves were seen by others," said Cromwell, spittle gathering at the corners of his mouth.

"Can we review their testimonies? Can we discern for ourselves their reliability and impartiality?"

"You're being ridiculous," said Cromwell.

"Only thorough," said Hansel. "There is a difference. You have presented no evidence to support these charges save the word of a child. They must be dismissed. Do you agree, Inspector Halfpenny?"

All eyes turned to her, including the cold, withering gaze of Cromwell. She nodded, covering her mouth.

After that, Hansel serenely and masterfully unraveled the charge of resisting arrest, given there was no verifiable situation where any arrest had been attempted that Elizabella and Benjamiah defied. Cromwell looked gaunter and more ruffled by the minute.

"Now let us turn our attention to your final charges," said Hansel. "'Witchcraft,' as you put it. By which I understand you mean this business with the aether that attacked you and the Hanged Men and allowed the children to escape."

"I was there, old man," said Cromwell, "and I have the wound to prove it. I saw with my own eyes—as did half a dozen of my men—the devilry these children invoked."

"I have had the account from the children themselves," said Hansel. "I don't deny what happened. Nobody here would. I do call into question your rationality—indeed, your fitness and appropriateness for the office you hold—if you suspect these two children conjured the sorcery in question."

"I was there!" spat Cromwell.

"As were Elizabella and Benjamiah, undeniably," said Hansel. "Does being there equate to culpability? If so, you are as much a suspect as they. Or any of your men."

Cromwell floundered, a dab of color rising in his otherwise waxy face.

"I have *never* been so insulted in—"

"Then perhaps you need to get out more," said Hansel. "I'm sure many have insults they'd care to share with you. The notion that these two eleven-year-old children are capable of such sorcery is just about the most ridiculous thing I have ever heard. And I have lived a long time, Inspector Cromwell. But don't take my word for it. Let's ask your colleagues. These fine officers of law and peace. Have any of you seen or heard anything so absurd?"

Nobody spoke. Elizabella and Benjamiah exchanged a secret smile.

"Well then," said Hansel, spreading his hands, "perhaps your industry would be best served in apprehending the true culprit, a gentleman named Manfred Tarr. You will find him at the Magimmaculum when you next visit the Viper to pledge your undying devotion to her every fanatical and ludicrous request. He is masquerading as a color-trader—indeed, as a dollcaster—when he's actually a magus. Only a magus is capable of the witchcraft concerned."

"Preposterous!" cried Cromwell. "You are out of your wits."

"That's a bold accusation, Hansel," said Halfpenny.

"Visit him," said Hansel. "See for yourself. It's easily disproved. Ask him to perform a spell with the doll he stole from the corpse of Olfred Wicker."

"I will not degrade a fine gentleman with such nonsense," said Cromwell, his nose wrinkled.

"But you have no issue with coming into my home and calling my daughter a rat and a beast," said Hansel. "A thief and a fugitive. One could be forgiven for questioning what kind of man you are, Inspector Cromwell."

Cromwell erupted out of his chair, snatching his poppet from his belt. Hansel didn't even flinch. He remained where he was, smiling softly, the calmest figure for a hundred miles.

"Watch your mouth," whispered Cromwell.

"Or what? You will assault me in front of the Hanged Men and a fellow Inspector?"

Hansel stood and looked Cromwell in the eye. Cromwell was significantly taller, but didn't seem so in that moment.

"You have come here not with civility and harmony in mind," said Hansel, "but petty and criminal vengeance. I expect you brought along a pair of spectractors, and harbored ambitions of delivering these children's eye colors to the Murdstones before they'd finished their lunch. Your barbarity isn't welcome here—in my shop or in this city."

"Take them away!" hissed Cromwell.

The Hanged Men didn't move.

"I said take them away!" roared Cromwell, spit hanging from his lip.

Still, nobody moved. Halfpenny stepped forward.

"We have nothing, Casper," she said. "There are laws. We can't prove anything. Let it go."

Cromwell had transitioned from a shade of puce to sickly green. His bony fingers tensed round his poppet. Benjamiah's stomach knotted, unsure whether he could bear more violence. Finally Cromwell gave up.

"You have made your life more difficult than it needs to be," he whispered. "I will remember you well. You and these *children*. Justice will find you all. I shall make sure of it."

With that, he stalked off, storming out of the Follynook door with a volley of furious mutters. The Hanged Men followed, leaving only Halfpenny behind.

"Very nicely done," she said, with a big grin.

With Cromwell gone, Hansel quickly returned to his former frantic, nervy self. Halfpenny fetched Hansel a stiff glass of poppysyrup, and they left him to gather his composure. Elizabella and Benjamiah walked her out.

"As for you two," she said, at the door, "not being able to prove something doesn't mean I don't know it happened. Keep your noses clean. And you . . ."

She was looking at Benjamiah, eyes narrowed.

"I don't know who you are," she said. "I have a good mind to take it up with Hansel, as it's clear to me *he* knew you were somebody other than the neighbor's boy. Do you have a home to go to?"

Benjamiah nodded.

"And when are you going there?"

"Very soon."

Elizabella fidgeted beside him. Halfpenny nodded, smiled, and left.

While Elizabella tended the shop, Benjamiah sat with Hansel. He looked bewildered and shaken up.

"You were amazing," said Benjamiah.

"Never been so scared in my entire life," replied Hansel.

"It didn't show."

They sat in silence for a while, until Benjamiah couldn't hold back his question any longer.

"Why did you save me?" he asked. "From the Hanged Men."

Hansel looked up, his eyes unfocused. A gentle smile flickered into life. His eyes traveled from Benjamiah to Nuisance, who was a capuchin, playing with Ariadne among the rafters of the bookshop.

"I know that doll," said Hansel.

"You do?" Benjamiah was astonished.

"I do. I would know her anywhere, no matter how long I live."

"*Her?*" said Benjamiah.

"Absolutely," said Hansel. "Her name is Cosma. She was the doll of my best friend, Eyla. Eyla and I grew up together. Back then, my family lived in a different bookshop, far from here. Eyla was another lost child of the labyrinth, arriving at our bookshop one day with no memory of her home or family. We took her in. She loved to read, like me. We were inseparable. We'd read books together and play our favorite characters. We'd race our poppets. I was closer to Eyla than anybody else in my life, including my own brother.

"One day," continued Hansel, taking a mournful breath, "Eyla and I were reading in the cellar of the bookshop. It was . . . A fire broke out, from above. It was chaos. A brittle old wooden building, parchment, thousands of books. The whole place ignited in seconds. We ran. I thought Eyla was by my side as I raced up the cellar stairs, but she wasn't. By the time I realized she'd been left behind, my older brother was dragging me from the inferno. I screamed and struggled, but he wouldn't let me go back. Then the whole bookshop collapsed."

Hansel withdrew a handkerchief and blew his nose.

"I have lived my entire life believing Eyla died that day, along with my parents," he said. "In that cellar. But it would seem I was wrong. I now believe she found a door out of there—and out of this world, in fact."

Benjamiah was absolutely stunned. Elizabella was out of earshot, chatting away to a customer.

"What do you mean?" he whispered.

"You have her nose," said Hansel.

It took an age for Benjamiah to untangle what he meant.

"You mean *Mum*?"

"No two dolls are alike," said Hansel, smiling widely. "I knew Cosma the moment I saw her. And Cosma knew me."

As if to confirm this, Nuisance the nightjar landed on Hansel's hand and nuzzled him.

"Why didn't you say anything?" said Benjamiah.

"It was a shock," said Hansel. "I had planned to broach it with you, only you left in the middle of the night before I could."

"I don't understand," said Benjamiah. "You think Mum is . . . You think she came from Wreathenwold?"

"I do," said Hansel. "Tell me, what family does she have in your world?"

Benjamiah knew the answer, but took a while to respond. It was too much to process.

"None," he said. "She was an orphan. No family at all."

Hansel smiled. "I cannot tell you how happy it makes me to know she got out alive. I have missed her every day of my life."

"But she doesn't believe in magic!" said Benjamiah. "She's a scientist. It's impossible."

"Magic comes in many forms, Benjamiah," said Hansel. "To look at the stars and wonder, to ask questions, to explore—that's a kind of magic, is it not?"

"But why would Mum's poppet suddenly come to life and bring me to Wreathenwold?" said Benjamiah.

"Who can say?" said Hansel. "I believe Cosma brought

you here because you alone, Benjamiah Creek, had the power to save my family. Your cleverness, your goodness. The cautious counterpoint to Elizabella's—um—*spirited* approach to things. Elizabella could not have brought Edwid back without you, Benjamiah. Eyla and I promised to help each other with anything. I believe Cosma brought you here to keep that promise."

"I didn't save anybody," protested Benjamiah. "Edwid . . ."

"Edwid was beyond your power to save," said Hansel. "But you brought him home, nonetheless. You brought my daughter home. My *real* daughter. You have done more than you can ever imagine, and there's no way I shall ever be able to repay you."

Benjamiah blushed, embarrassed.

"Why didn't Elizabella tell me Edwid was . . . ," he began.

Hansel considered the question carefully. "No siblings could ever have been closer," he said. "There's no correct way to grieve. Sometimes to say something feels like giving it life. Voicing anything of which we are afraid or which causes us great pain takes a tremendous amount of courage. You didn't know Edwid had died, and I believe Elizabella saw in that an opportunity to keep her brother alive, as strange as it sounds. Until she was ready to say the words."

"I understand," said Benjamiah.

And he did, because back home he had his own fears—ones he had refused to say aloud.

"How much easier life would be without love," said Hansel, seeming to sense Benjamiah's turmoil. "Love is beautiful until it isn't. Until we lose somebody, or something. We put everything at risk for love. It's the great chance we take, and we do not always win. Think how brave it is to love a person as much as Elizabella loved Edwid, when the risk is so great. Love is the very highest form of courage. But let me tell you, Benjamiah—nobody in this world, your world, or any other would have it differently."

Hansel laid a thin hand on Benjamiah's shoulder. Benjamiah took a deep breath, thinking of Mum, Dad, Grandma, and home.

"So should I call her Cosma now?" said Benjamiah, looking at Nuisance.

"I think the choice is yours," said Hansel. "She seems to like Nuisance. There's no reason she shouldn't have a new name. Though I've never heard of such a thing, it would seem Nuisance is your poppet now, and no longer your mother's."

Benjamiah had one final question. "How do I get home?" he blurted.

"I've thought about it a lot," said Hansel, "and the answer is as elegant as it is simple. Just as Nuisance led you here, so I think—when you're ready—she'll lead you home. And will you do something for me when you get there? Tell

Eyla . . . say hello. Tell her I miss her. And tell her she has a wonderful son."

Benjamiah said he would—all but the last part. Hansel laughed.

"Will I ever come back?" asked Benjamiah. "Back to Wreathenwold, I mean."

"Who could say?" said Hansel. "Stranger things have happened. Many of them today . . ."

Benjamiah had just fallen asleep when he was awoken by a squall.

A button-eyed capuchin hung from a beam above Edwid's bed. Nuisance was smiling, jabbing her finger toward the hallway. Benjamiah got out of bed and pulled on his clothes. Not Edwid's clothes, but his own—the jumper and jeans he'd worn when he arrived. Before leaving, he fished out the coins given to him by Hansel and Elizabella and left them on Edwid's desk. Promises, neither of them broken.

It was time to go home.

He crept through the house in Nuisance's wake. Hansel was snoring faintly. Nuisance had transformed into a nightjar and fluttered through the shadowy hallway, down into the bookshop. Benjamiah took one last look around at all the wondrous books he hadn't read, would now never read. His heart beat heavy in his chest as he followed Nuisance to a side door. It led down into the cellar, where he'd surely find a doorway home.

"Are you leaving?"

Benjamiah whirled round. Elizabella was standing in her nightgown, draped in shadow. He nodded.

"Without saying anything?" said Elizabella.

"I didn't want to bother anybody."

Expecting a smart remark, he was surprised by Elizabella one last time. She smiled, gave a sigh, and walked toward him. She placed a hand on his arm.

"Silly," said Elizabella. "How could you ever be a bother, Benjamiah?"

Benjamiah blushed. Sensing his discomfort, she let go and took a step back. Was he supposed to reply to this? He had no idea what to say.

"Thank you," he said.

"For what?"

"Taking me with you," said Benjamiah. "Showing me . . . Showing me a lot of things."

"You're welcome." Elizabella flashed her crooked smile.

Silence fell. Nuisance gave an impatient chirp, a flurry of wings.

"I'm sorry about Edwid," said Benjamiah, looking down at his shoes.

Elizabella smiled awkwardly. "He would have liked you,"

she said. "He enjoyed puzzles, and books, and *learning*. Strange boys."

"I would have liked him, too," said Benjamiah.

"I have something for you," said Elizabella.

From under her arm, she withdrew a battered book. Benjamiah read the title in the soft shadow of the bookshop: *Jamima Cleaves and the Book-Eater* by Olfred Wicker. He smiled. He'd never have read a book like this before—now he couldn't wait.

"Thanks," he said.

Another silence fell. They stared at each other.

"Don't give up on your family," said Elizabella.

"I won't."

"But don't hold on too tightly to things being a certain way, either," she added. "Just say to each other that you'll always be there, one way or another."

It was what Benjamiah needed to hear—somehow Elizabella had just known. His eyes prickled with tears.

"I'd better go," he said.

Elizabella nodded. "Good luck," she said. "And thank you."

Benjamiah shrugged. "I didn't do anything."

"Oh, stop," said Elizabella. "I wasn't thanking you for those things, anyway."

"What then?"

"Thanks for being my friend."

Benjamiah smiled. Elizabella smiled back. Then, with

a final nod, he turned and followed Nuisance through the door. The staircase wound down into a cellar crammed with thousands of books, columns of fantastic tales and wondrous secrets, a whole city of marvelous stories where he could happily lose himself forever. At the back of the cellar was a door. Nuisance landed on the dusty handle, squawking and singing.

Benjamiah took a deep breath. Then he opened the door and walked through.

TWENTY-ONE

WITH HOME

Now I am an old man, sitting by the fire. As this book—and my life—nears its end, I am reminded of an old Root Folk song. It celebrates a most formidable, wonderful magic, one which protects and warms and nourishes us all. They call this magic "home."

—*A Brief History of Wreathenwold,*
Archscholar Collum Wolfsdaughter

BENJAMIAH EMERGED in the cellar of Once Upon A Time, stepping into its familiar smell of cardboard and old pages. Clutched to his chest was Nuisance, now a doll, and the Jamima Cleaves book. With a pang of sadness, he found he could no longer flex the muscles in his mind that connected him to the poppet. She flopped, without life, in his grasp. Before leaving the cellar, he saw the door to Wreathenwold had already vanished.

All was quiet in the bookshop above. How long had he been gone? It had been days and days in Wreathenwold. How angry would everybody be? Bracing himself, taking a deep breath, Benjamiah mounted the narrow staircase and slipped into the bookshop. Before doing so, he hid the Jamima Cleaves in the back pocket of his jeans—the book was more than he was ready to explain.

He was met with a scream. Before he knew it, he'd been swaddled by Grandma's many cardigans. With his face clamped to her midriff, Grandma's joyous scream went on and on, carrying for miles. The whole of Wyvern-on-the-Water must have heard it.

"He's here! He's here!" she shrieked, her voice thick with happy tears. "Zoe! Jim! It's Ben!"

"Grandma . . ."

Try as he might, Benjamiah was unable to wriggle out of her fearsome clutch. Through the weave of her cardigans, Benjamiah spied that the window—indeed the entire bookshop itself—was papered with his face. MISSING posters.

Grandma lowered her head, bringing her big, watery eyes level with Benjamiah's face. Tears rolled down from beneath the tortoiseshell glasses.

"Darling, where have you been? *Where?* We've been so *scared.* Are you okay? Are you hurt? Have you been eating? You feel thin. . . ."

Before Benjamiah could get a word in, Mum burst into the bookshop from upstairs.

Benjamiah sprang at her. Mum sobbed, gripping Benjamiah so tight, her hands closed round his frame as though she would never let go. She bombarded him with kisses, asking where he'd been, smelling wonderfully of Mum.

Grandma opened the bookshop door and screamed, to the street outside, "He's home! Ben's home!"

While Mum and Grandma hugged and kissed him, others came rushing into Once Upon A Time. First was Dad, looking like he hadn't slept in weeks. He crunched Benjamiah into a fresh hug, adding more kisses to the top of his head. Clutched in his hand was a stack of MISSING posters, which he duly threw in the air in delight. Others came in after Dad, wide-eyed and smiling like the Cheshire cat. Margie from the pottery studio, Tom and Harry from next door, even Mrs. Foxglove . . .

Slowly a hush replaced the jubilation. Mum crouched. Her nose was just like his, her face round and kind, dotted with freckles. Big coffee-colored eyes, brown hair trickling with silver.

"Where have you been, darling?" she said softly.

Silence fell. The anticipation was palpable. Benjamiah took a deep breath. "In the cellar," he said.

The room was stunned. Dad's eyes, rimmed with red,

were wide with amazement. Mrs. Foxglove muttered something unkind. Grandma lifted her glasses to dab at fresh tears.

"All this time?" said Mum.

Benjamiah nodded.

Mum pursed her lips. "Really?" she said, tilting her head to the side. That meant she was skeptical. "You've been downstairs for all this time, while we—your whole family, our whole village, the entire *country*—have been looking everywhere for you for almost two weeks?"

She was doing her best not to be cross. Benjamiah could understand that, and he nodded. "I'm sorry," he said, lowering his gaze.

Mum glanced at Grandma, at Dad. Dad looked like he wanted to laugh, cry, and shout at him all at the same time. Grandma shrugged. Finally Mum turned back to Benjamiah.

"It's okay, darling," she said. "We're just so relieved to have you back."

There followed more hugging, cheering, more questions about how Benjamiah had stayed hidden (a fort of boxes), what he'd eaten and drunk (he'd sneak upstairs at night), what he'd been doing down there (taking some time for himself). Nobody yet pressed him for an explanation. Nobody told him off.

While Dad hugged the neighbors, and Grandma called the police to let them know Benjamiah was home, Mum had fallen deathly still. She'd finally noticed the doll in Benjamiah's hands.

When their eyes met, he knew. Nuisance was no stranger to Mum—she was an old friend. She opened her mouth to say something, then thought better of it.

The rest of the day was a whirlwind. Mum and Grandma alternated in never leaving Benjamiah's side, apparently afraid he would pull another vanishing act. Dad came and went, making calls to share the happy news, buying all the neighbors flowers and chocolates, later popping out for fish and chips. He made sure Benjamiah's had extra salt and vinegar—just how he liked it.

Throughout the day, Benjamiah studied Mum and Dad, reading their interactions for clues. Was their marriage over? Was this the end of life as Benjamiah knew it? It was impossible to tell. All attention was on Benjamiah, everybody staring at him as though fearing he might suddenly dissolve. There was nothing but giddy, wild relief among his family.

After dinner and an hour watching something brainless on the television, Benjamiah began to doze. After more hugs and kisses, he traipsed off to bed. Nuisance hadn't left his side for a moment.

Lying in his dark bedroom, Benjamiah found himself wide awake. He realized he hadn't switched on his night-light.

Rolling over, he met the white button eyes of the poppet on his bedside table. He missed the nightjar, the capuchin, the dormouse.

There was a gentle tap on the bedroom door.

"Good night, sweetie," whispered Mum. "I love you."

Benjamiah sat up. "Hansel Cotton says hello."

Mum froze. After a glance down the hallway, she slipped inside Benjamiah's room and perched on the edge of his bed. Her face was cast in shadow, her lips pursed.

"Eyla," said Benjamiah.

"What did you say?" said Mum, deathly quiet.

"Eyla," said Benjamiah.

"That's not my name, Ben," she snapped.

Her tone was a shock. Benjamiah stared.

"I'm sorry," she said. "I . . . I . . ."

Rather than finish the sentence, Mum reached out and lifted Nuisance from the bedside table. Her eyes were saucerlike, glistening.

"Where have you really been, Ben?" she said, her voice a feather.

In hushed tones, Benjamiah recounted the arrival of the doll, her coming to life, the door to Wreathenwold. He described being found by the Hanged Men, then afterward being rescued by Hansel. Here he ended his story. Mum didn't need to know everything.

"I can't believe it . . . ," she said, shaking her head.

"What happened?" said Benjamiah. "The day of the fire."

Mum took a deep, shaky breath, still holding Nuisance tightly in her hands. She was trembling.

"I fell," she said. "Everything was on fire. Smoke everywhere. I was blinded, choking. I lost my way. Suddenly Hansel was gone, and there was no way out. I thought I'd die. Just before the building collapsed, I found a door. I ran through it. Too late, I realized Cosma hadn't made it through with me. I found myself in another bookshop cellar, except it was silent. No screams, no fire. And the door was gone. I'd left Wreathenwold and arrived in this world. A secondhand bookshop in Gloucestershire, of all places. Imagine how confused I was! I ended up in the care system. Foster families, orphanages. They thought something was wrong with me because I knew absolutely nothing about this world. But I taught myself as much as I could."

"And you never found a way back?" said Benjamiah.

Mum shook her head. "I was lost in the labyrinth when the Cottons took me in. I lived at an orphanage before that. Never knew my real family. I thought the Cottons had all died. Hansel, too . . ."

"Hansel made it out. And his brother. They lost their parents, though. He misses you."

Mum sniffed, then pivoted and sat cross-legged on the bed.

"How is he? Is he happy? Has he had a good life?"

Benjamiah told Mum about Follynook, the wife Hansel had lost, Elizabella and Edwid. It sounded a sad story— and it was—but Benjamiah assured Mum that Hansel was as happy as he could be, that he was witty and brave and kind. It brought a huge smile to her face.

When she ran out of questions, her gaze returned to the doll in her hands.

"Cosma came for you," said Mum.

Benjamiah nodded.

"Why?"

"Hansel says it was because of you," said Benjamiah. "Your spirit lives in Cosma. Cosma thought I could save Hansel's family."

"Save them how?" said Mum.

Images crowded him. The Viper, the raven, the Minotaur. Best to stay quiet.

"Keep your secrets, then," said Mum when he didn't answer, slapping his knee gently with the doll.

"Can I ask you something?" said Benjamiah.

"Of course."

"How can you be a scientist when you've seen all that magic?"

Mum considered the question as though she'd never thought about it before.

"It depends on what you mean by magic," she said. "Casting a doll is about knowledge and precision. It's a

triumph of *knowing*. At first, in this world, I was just happy to be safe. I was frightened by how *odd* it was. But it's no less marvelous, let me tell you. How vast this universe is, how intricate, how I can love you so incredibly much when we're both so small in the grand scheme of things . . . Don't tell me that isn't magic."

Benjamiah laughed.

"What?" said Mum, offended.

"You sound just like Dad."

Silence fell. Mum returned Nuisance to the bedside table, somewhat reluctantly. Something in her gaze tallied with what Benjamiah was feeling—grief for the lost connection.

"You need your rest," she said, standing.

"I'm sorry I left," said Benjamiah.

Leaning down, Mum kissed him on the head.

"I'm not," she replied. "I'm just so happy you're back."

"Mum?"

"Mhm?"

"What about you and Dad?"

Mum took a deep breath. "Tomorrow, darling. It's not important right now."

"I just wanted to say," said Benjamiah, "that it's okay. Whatever you and Dad decide. I know everybody's scared. And I know now that not everything can be fixed. Not everything has a clear answer."

Mum brushed a tear from her eye. "We love you, Ben," she said.

"Love you," said Benjamiah.

When Mum was gone, Benjamiah rolled over and closed his eyes. It would be okay, whatever they decided. They still had each other—there was nothing more magical than that.

As he lay in the darkness, Benjamiah's imagination soared and darted with all the things he'd seen and experienced: Nuisance the nightjar, Emba the bear; Miss Bliss's sweets and Elizabella laughing; the terror of being lost, the joy of finding a way alongside Elizabella, the best friend he'd ever had.

With no hope of sleeping, Benjamiah crept over to his desk, opened his notebook, and wrote: The Whisperwicks. The door to Wreathenwold might be gone, but there were other ways to keep it alive.

It began with the crack in the wall, wrote Benjamiah. And he wrote of his wonderful adventures until he fell asleep, right there on his desk.

ACKNOWLEDGMENTS

This book would never have happened without the kindness and support of so many people.

Thank you, firstly, to my parents, who always bought me notebooks and who have been proud and supportive no matter what. Thank you also to Adam, Becca, Jody, Callum, and all my family in both England and Scotland.

None of this would have happened without Chloe Seager, who is without doubt the best agent in town. Thank you for taking a chance on me, for your belief and support, and for being the best possible advocate for my writing. Thanks also to Georgia McVeigh for your amazing help and suggestions with the early drafts, and to everybody at Madeleine Milburn.

I'm also blessed with the most brilliant editor around. Thank you to Carmen McCullough for your belief, encouragement, insight, ideas, and expertise. It's been a joy to work with you on this book, and I'm so thankful for everything you've done.

I feel very lucky and am hugely grateful to so many brilliant people at Puffin. It has really meant the world to me. Thank you to Alice Grigg, Zosia Knopp, Maeve Banham, Susanne Evans, Beth Fennell, Clare Braganza, Magda Morris, Anda Podaru, Stella Dodwell, James McParland, Josh Benn, Katy Finch, Kat Baker, Becki Wells, Rozzie Todd, Toni Budden, Michaela Lock, Minnie Tindall, Amy Wilkerson, Memoona Zahid, Sophia Pringle, and Sarah Doyle. Thank you also to my sharp-eyed copyeditor, Jane Tait.

A huge thank-you also to my brilliant US editor, Alyza Liu, and the whole team at Simon & Schuster US: Justin Chanda, Anne Zafian, Kendra Levin, Lizzy Bromley, Amanda Brenner, Gary Sunshine, Kathleen Smith, Chava Wolin, Amaris Mang, Tara Shanahan, and Victor Iannone.

I also want to thank Vivienne To for my UK cover and Isobelle Ouzman for my US cover. They're both absolutely beautiful and never lose their magic, no matter how many times I look at them (which is a lot).

Lastly, thank you to Caroline and Violet. You are the magic in my world. Thanks for your support and patience throughout what has been a long journey. I'm sorry for all the weekends and late nights shut away writing—I hope you think this book is at least somehow worth it.

ABOUT THE AUTHOR

Jordan Lees was born in Scotland but grew up in Essex, England, where he still lives with his wife and young daughter. Having devoured stories all through childhood, Jordan then studied literature in college and has worked in publishing ever since, most recently as a literary agent. When not working, Jordan can usually be found reading whatever is lying around or losing at online chess. The Whisperwicks: *The Labyrinth of Lost and Found* is his first book.

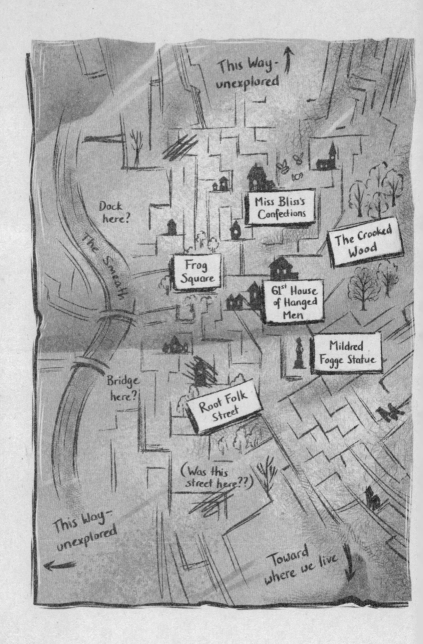